MW01503368

ESCAPING

Christmas

BECKY AVERY

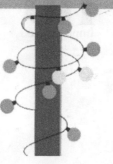

@2024 by Becky Avery

Published by hope*books
2217 Matthews Township Pkwy
Suite D302
Matthews, NC 28105
www.hopebooks.com

hope*books is a division of hope*media

Printed in the United States of America

First paperback edition.
Paperback ISBN: 979-8-89185-203-7
Hardcover ISBN: 979-8-89185-119-1
Ebook ISBN: 979-8-89185-120-7
Library of Congress Number: 2024945938

hope*books
hopebooks.com
Because the world needs your hope-filled
work is now more than ever.

To my mom, who introduced me to the magic of reading.
And my dad, who taught me about Cliff's Notes and waiting
for the movie to come out. I love and miss you both.

And to my brother, whose dedication to his dream
inspired me to chase mine. I love you.

It would also be nice if someone could show this to my brother,
because he's more of a wait-for-the-movie-to-come-out type person.

CHAPTER 1: GABBY

If someone had told Gabby Jackson a year ago that she would be living in the house she grew up in, she would have laughed and told them they were crazy. Like the rest of her family, she had set big goals for her life and had worked hard to achieve them. She graduated from college with honors. Her father had been thrilled when she agreed to come work for him, with the plan of eventually taking over the family business. Determined to make him proud, she helped expand her family's already successful insurance agency. She owned her own home. She had friends that she loved and volunteered with the women's group at church for various events throughout the year. She was happy and content with the life she had. Yet here she was...29 years old and sleeping, or at least trying to sleep, in her childhood bedroom. This room with the pink walls and soft carpet had always made her feel safe and protected until recently. Now, it felt more like a prison, but a prison she couldn't bear to leave. Across the hall, she could hear her 27-year-old brother, Jase, yelling at his virtual friends while they played video games - tonight's reason for no sleep. *"God, what am I doing here?"* thought

Gabby as she lay in bed, twisting her mother's wedding ring on her finger.

She knew full well what she was doing here, though. This is where she was needed.

More cheers came from the other room. "Way to go, Nick. Nice block."

Tucker, her parents' Brittany Spaniel, groaned and rolled on his back.

"I know, buddy, I know. This has all been a big change for you, too," she said as she rubbed his belly.

Gabby and Jase had been staying in their family home for nearly six months. Neither of them needed to be there. They each had their own home. Jase was the all-star catcher for the professional baseball team, the Detroit Defenders. He leased a luxury loft downtown near the stadium that overlooked the Detroit River. Their parents' lakefront home in Lake Harbor was only 45 minutes northeast of Detroit. Gabby had her own little house on the other side of Lake Harbor, only twenty minutes away. Yet, here they both were.

Jase had returned home in June after a torn ACL landed him on the disabled list. Being here allowed him to be close enough to the city, but with Mom and Dad to help him while he recovered from surgery. The plan had been for him to stay here for a month to get through the initial recovery and rehab, then go back to his loft. The Jackson family always had a plan. But no one had planned for what happened next.

An accident that had changed the Jackson family forever. Gabby and Jase still couldn't wrap their heads around the loss of both their parents that July night.

Their parents had gone to a charity event, so Gabby brought a pizza over to keep Jase company. Their dad jokingly told them to be good, and he loved them. Their mom kissed both their heads and said she'd see them later. Then they walked out the door. Jase joked that he wasn't sure if their parents realized their children weren't little kids anymore. Gabby and Jase knew how blessed they were, though. They had been this picture-perfect family.

When there was a knock on the door later that evening, Gabby had jumped up to answer it. Jase trailed behind her. Two cops stood on the porch with somber faces...and she held her breath and just knew what they were about to say. After that, the night was just a blur of movement and sound. Gabby had only made out pieces of what they said. "Accident...Both gone...So sorry." She had heard Jase yell at the officer, "Wrong house...Liar." Gabby felt numb like life was moving in slow motion. This was not the plan.

After that night, there was so much to do, but neither of them wanted to do it. Neither of them wanted to be there, but neither of them could make themselves leave. So, they stayed. Somehow, the rest of the world kept moving while life in their parents' house seemed frozen. The brilliant fall leaves peaked on the oak trees around their property and fell to the ground. There had even been a first frost, and the snow would come soon.

Gabby had always admired her brother. He was tall, funny, incredibly smart, and athletic. He made life look fun and easy, and people were naturally drawn to him. Now, he had become a shadow of the man he was and buried himself in his room. Gabby tried to keep her schedule booked, so she didn't have time to think about the loss they had endured. She managed to go to work every day and volunteered for every event the church had. She even tried to move back to her own home a few times, but her house felt too far away. What if Jase needed something? The anxiety was too much. She would grab a few items from her house, then make the twenty-minute drive back to her little brother. She did use the term little brother loosely. He was two years younger, but at 6'4", he was more than a foot taller than her. Still, he would always be her baby brother. He was all she had left.

"Wooo! Yeah, baby! Great shot, buddy!" Another cheer came from across the hall, momentarily distracting her thoughts.

Gabby groaned when she saw that it was 1:00 am. She had to be up in four hours. It was officially Thanksgiving, the day she had dreaded for the last month. She was going to attempt the gigantic turkey feast her parents had always prepared. It was up to her to keep traditions alive for the Jackson family.

Growing up, her only contribution to Thanksgiving dinner was waking up at 5:00 am with Dad and doing the turkey dance. It had been a tradition since she was ten. She'd woken up when her dad did that year, and she asked if she could help. He asked what she wanted to do. Somehow, he came up with the turkey dance, obviously to make it more tender.

She had grabbed the turkey under the wings, then started shaking the turkey booty, creating a song as she went. And the turkey dance tradition was born. Her dad swore that the dance made his turkey taste better. Even now, this memory made Gabby swell with pride. Gabby smiled as she thought about her dad's laughter when she made the turkey dance across the sink.

At 5:00 am, when the alarm went off, Gabby hit snooze and considered rolling over and going back to sleep. Maybe she could sleep through the whole day and pretend it didn't exist. However, when the alarm sounded again, the feeling of guilt at not having the Thanksgiving extravaganza prepared for her brother made her drag herself out of bed. *God, please help get us through this day*, she prayed silently.

Gabby threw on her robe and tucked her feet into her fuzzy slippers. She pulled her long, blond hair into a ponytail. Tucker whined at the interruption of his sleep. "So sorry to disturb you, buddy." He stretched, then jumped off the bed and trotted behind her. Gabby moved to Jase's room and cracked the door. She couldn't help a quiet chuckle at the sight before her. His strong 6'4" frame was sprawled over the giant bean bag chair. His head was leaned back while loud snores filled the room. His headphones covered his ears, and the game controller rested on the floor. Her nose crinkled at the locker room smell permeating the room. She glanced down at Tucker and whispered, "Still a man-child."

As she approached the stairs, she avoided looking down the hall that led to their parent's room...as if pretending it didn't exist would change reality.

Gabby entered the large kitchen and examined the scene confidently. She had made a list of everything she would prepare that day. It had all of the ingredients, how long each item would need to cook, and the time she would need to start each one. She had made sure that everything could be served at the same time, just as her parents would have. Everything she needed lay neatly organized on the counters. The seasonings, roasting pan, serving platter, and carving tools waited for her. She could practically smell the cooked turkey already.

With her hands on her hips. she announced to Tucker, "Time to get to work."

Tucker circled and plopped onto his kitchen dog bed to watch as Gabby opened the freezer and heaved the twenty-five pound turkey out. She hauled it over to the sink and dropped it in with a loud thud.

She wasn't sure how two people would eat a twenty-five pound turkey, not even with leftovers. But her dad had always purchased the most robust turkey he could find, so that's what she had done too. Her hands nearly froze while struggling to get the giant bird out of its wrapping. A sudden wave of sadness washed over her. She wished so much that her dad was here with her. *Breathe in, breathe out, and keep moving*, she thought to herself. She had a job to do. She didn't have time for emotions right now.

"Alright, Mr. Turkey, it's time to shake your tail feathers or, umm, shake where your tailfeather would be." She rubbed her hands together to warm them up before attempting to lift the bird. Something was off, though...way off. She didn't remember turkeys from past Thanksgivings being so cold. And why wouldn't the wings move? The wings were never frozen during the turkey dance. *What is happening here?*

She poked at the frozen mass in front of her. The skin didn't jiggle like it normally did. She knocked on the turkey, and it was rock hard. She ran some hot water over it, knocked again, and it was still rock hard. With one hand on the body of the turkey, she tried to pry a wing away with the other, but to no avail. She left the bird in the sink with hot water running over it, then wiped her hands on a towel and went for her phone. It was time to call for backup.

Holly had been her best friend since first grade, and even though it was just after 5:00 am, she knew Holly would answer. Holly was hosting her family's Thanksgiving this year, so she was probably elbow-deep into stuffing a turkey that was undoubtedly not frozen.

"Gabby?" Holly said, answering her phone. "What's wrong?"

"Hey, Holly," Gabby started, trying to sound chipper, "I'm fine, Happy Thanksgiving."

"Happy Thanksgiving to you, too," she said slowly.

"Thanks, umm, just a quick question."

"Uh oh..." Holly with a chuckle.

"So...how long does a turkey take to thaw?" Gabby sheepishly asked, hoping the answer was 30 minutes at the most.

"About three days," Holly replied. "Please tell me you are asking hypothetically and not currently trying to make a frozen turkey dance across your counter."

"What? No, no. I was just wondering, you know, just in case anyone calls me to ask."

"Someone calling you? For cooking advice?" Holly teased.

"It could happen." Gabby's voice faded.

"You tried to make a frozen turkey dance, didn't you?" Holly asked sympathetically.

"Yes," Gabby choked out but refused to cry.

"What am I going to do? I am failing my first Thanksgiving. Jase is going to be so disappointed." Gabby knew Holly would understand. It wasn't the frozen turkey. It wasn't that her brother would be disappointed. This was just the first big holiday without her parents, and it was challenging.

Holly's mother had passed away five years earlier. She had shared with Gabby that the first of everything was the most difficult. Gabby already felt like she had failed her parents in enough ways since they left. She didn't want to fail at making Thanksgiving happen.

"Gabby, it's going to be okay. You guys will get through this," Holly said gently. Gabby knew her friend didn't just mean today.

"I know." Gabby took a deep breath and fidgeted with her mother's ring.

"Want me to come over?" Holly asked.

"No, you are preparing your perfectly thawed turkey, and I don't want to get in your way."

"Do you guys want to come over for dinner?" Holly asked hopefully.

"No thanks, we'll figure something out here," Gabby replied. The mere thought of being surrounded by her friend's large family celebration made her heart ache.

"If you change your mind, just come over. And tomorrow I will pick you up at 6:00 am. We can do some shopping downtown and hopefully catch some great deals."

Shopping was not Gabby's idea of a good time, especially at 6:00 am. Still, every year, Holly managed to talk her into it. This year, she even found herself a little excited about it. Maybe it was the idea of just escaping from this house for something other than work or groceries. "Okay. That sounds good, I'll see you then."

"Great! See you then," Holly said. "Hey Gabs... Happy Thanks-giving."

Gabby felt a small smile creep across her face, "Thanks Hol, you too."

"We still have things to be thankful for, don't we, Tuck?" she said as she turned off the running water. "Let's go watch some TV since turkey apparently isn't happening today." Tucker seemed to like this idea and followed her into the family room. He hopped on the couch and nestled himself behind Gabby's legs. She covered them both with her mother's old, soft afghan that smelled like home and reached for the remote.

She stopped when she saw the framed family photo on the table by the remote. It had been their mom's favorite. They had been in Tampa, Florida, for one of Jase's last tournaments. They were all hot, tired, and ready to leave, but their mom had insisted on a family photo for the annual Christmas card. Begrudgingly, they all hiked up the stairs to the top of the stadium. Gabby and Jase were not a fan of heights, but as usual, their mom had been right about the view being the perfect background for their photo. The scene had been amazing, the bright green baseball field and the ocean sparkling blue in the sunlight beyond the stadium. Their mom set up the tripod on the top row of bleachers, angling it down towards them. She directed them to move this way and that while they nagged her to hurry up.

After their mom set the timer and rejoined them for the shot, she said, "Oh, we forgot to make Gabby taller." Unlike the rest of the family, Gabby hadn't been blessed with height. It had been a family joke about the different ways they could make her seem taller in photos. Jase took action, picking Gabby up under the arms and landing her on the next step up. Startled, she stumbled backward, crashing into Jase.

Their dad's quick reaction saved them both from tumbling backward down the cement stands. They all laughed so hard they cried. The memory still made Gabby smile.

"Sorry I failed you guys today," Gabby said, tracing her finger over her mom and dad's photo.

She missed them so much she ached. Why was it so painful? Why wasn't she stronger? *Be strong, Gabby. You have to be strong. You can't let Jase see you're upset. Be strong for him.* She took a few deep breaths and then curled deeper into the couch.

CHAPTER 2: JASE

J ase grunted as he woke up. He glanced at the clock and noticed it was nearly 11:00 am. He shifted in his oversized bean bag and removed his headphones. His back and neck were stiff. He hadn't made it to physical therapy in over a week, and his body was feeling that mistake. *I have to stop falling asleep like this*, he thought. He ran his hand through his dark, wavy hair. It was longer than he usually kept it. Rubbing his hands over the patchy beard on his face, he thought, *I need to get rid of this. I probably look homeless.* He hadn't had a haircut since the funeral, and he knew he looked ragged. He also didn't care. He didn't feel like the clean-cut all-star that people were used to seeing. Why should he pretend?

He rolled off the chair onto his hands and knees and stretched like a cat, his large frame cracking in protest. His body felt tight and sluggish. If he wanted a chance to play ball again, he was going to have to start getting back in shape. He'd been blessed with good genes. He could eat whatever he wanted and didn't gain weight.

He even gained muscle quickly when he put in a little work. But he hadn't lately.

He stood and lifted his arms above his head, then leaned side to side, trying to work out the kinks. He groaned as he took in his surroundings. Mounds of clothes covered the floor, and he wasn't sure what was clean or dirty. Plates, forks, workout gear, gaming consoles, and controllers were scattered about. And what was that smell? Jase hated living like this. He liked his place to be clean and organized, but since his injury and then the accident, he couldn't bring himself to care.

He pulled his bent leg toward his chest, and then he lost his balance when he remembered. *It's Thanksgiving.* He collapsed onto the bean bag chair. His heart felt like it had been hit with a hammer, and he considered crawling into bed. He was sure his sister was downstairs whipping around the kitchen with her timers and lists, trying to make everything perfect. Didn't she get that nothing would ever be perfect again? Mom and Dad were gone, and it sucked. The world sucked. Everything sucked. He wasn't sure there was a word that expressed just how bad everything sucked.

Jase appreciated that Gabby had moved into the house and tried to maintain a normal life. But he didn't know how she did it. She went to work every day and sat in their father's office like everything was fine. Jase could barely leave his room. He loved his sister, and he knew she missed them. He knew that people grieved in their own way, but he wished that just once, she would act like things were hard for her too. He wished she would just stop moving for one minute and sit and be miserable with him.

As he walked down the stairs, he noticed that the sounds and smells he had anticipated were absent. He surveyed the silent kitchen and saw no sign of Gabby. Had she gone out for a run with Tucker? Or gone to Thanksgiving Mass? Surely, she'd be back by now. He pulled a glass from the cupboard and turned to the sink. Then he saw it.

He had gotten his wish. There in the sink was a frozen turkey. He couldn't help but laugh as he pictured his sister's face when she realized this bird wasn't thawing anytime soon. He felt a little bad that he was happy about this when his sister was probably devastated. But he didn't feel like celebrating.

He walked down the hall into the living room, and there she was, curled up with Tucker on the couch. He felt a twinge of guilt when he noticed the tear stain on her cheek.

He gently tapped her shoulder, and she swatted his hand away. He tapped again. This time her eyes blinked open and she stared up at him with the same green eyes they had inherited from their mom. She bit her bottom lip and waited for him to say something.

"So..." Jase smirked. "There's a frozen turkey chillin' in the sink."

"Yes, there is," Gabby said, matter of factly, as she straightened up on the couch.

"I'm guessing we aren't having turkey today," he said, holding back a laugh.

"Not unless you want to gnaw on a turk-cicle." Gabby dropped her head. "I'm so sorry," She whispered. "I read the recipes, and none of them mentioned that it takes like three days to thaw a turkey!"

"Gabs, it's fine. Neither of us really likes turkey anyway." He said with a shrug. He appreciated his sister's efforts. He would just keep his mouth shut that he was secretly glad she had failed. He didn't want to do the whole big family tradition thing without the whole family.

Besides, they only ate turkey because it was tradition. They were more interested in all the sides and using the turkey for cold sandwiches over the next several days. Their dad always teased them that they ate like five-year-olds unless it was steak, lobster, or crab.

She gave him a weak smile and a small shrug, "I guess you're right."

He snatched the remote from her, plopped down on the opposite couch, and turned on the Detroit Lions football pre-game show. She didn't argue.

He noticed she kept picking up her phone, appearing uncomfortable, and glancing up at him occasionally.

"Where's your phone?" she asked him.

"I don't know," Jase replied, unsure of why she was asking.

"Keep it there," she told him.

"No problem," Jase replied. By the mixed expressions of sadness and irritation on her face, he assumed that she was getting bombarded with well-meaning texts from friends and family. He wasn't on his phone a lot, anyway. His manager, publicist, or one of their assistants helped reply to calls, messages, and social media posts. He didn't even know his social media usernames or passwords. He didn't understand why anyone cared what he was doing anyway.

"Didn't make it to Thanksgiving Mass this morning?" he asked his sister. He wasn't sure why she bothered. God obviously wasn't doing them any favors lately. But his perfect sister still went and praised God for their so-called blessings.

"Umm, no, I fell back asleep and didn't make it," Gabby mumbled, looking away from him.

"Not like it makes a difference," Jase mumbled.

"Of course it does," Gabby defended. "God is good,"

"Yeah, so good," Jase huffed. He didn't want to get into this again.

"I'm going to order Chinese. What do you think?" she asked.

"That's fine."

"The usual?"

"Of course," Jase said and turned his attention back to the TV.

Jase didn't move from the sofa until he heard his sister return from picking up dinner. He followed the smell of food to the dining room, where Gabby was pulling white paper boxes and chopsticks from a plastic bag.

He stood behind her and placed his hands on her shoulders. They both stared silently at the nearly bare table. Normally, on Thanksgiving, the table would have been covered with Mom's good holiday platters, fine china, with the fancy pumpkins, and flower decorations. Today, it held a roll of paper towels and two paper plates. He could practically hear the thoughts rushing through Gabby's head as she spread out the twelve egg rolls, white rice, wonton soup, an order of dumplings, and a dozen almond cookies. If their parents were looking down on them at this moment, they were not smiling. Well, Mom wasn't, at least. Dad probably was having a good laugh.

"Well, this is a first for the Jackson house," Jase said, squeezing Gabby's shoulders.

Gabby let out a sad laugh. "You know Dad is cracking up about how their two adult children still eat like five-year-old kids. And Mom is throwing her hands up saying, 'She could at least use the cookie cutters and form the rice into turkey-shaped mounds.'"

Jase gave a half grin as he thought about how their mom loved the holidays and never missed an opportunity to make them a little extra special. Dad had always made a big fuss over her efforts.

"This is what happens when they leave us with no adult supervision," Jase chuckled as he piled egg rolls onto his plate. His sister agreed with a soft laugh.

That's exactly what this felt like. Two kids left home alone to fend for themselves... but their parents weren't coming back this time.

CHAPTER 3: GABBY

The next morning, Gabby was waiting in the driveway before 6:00 am. At 40 degrees, it was cold enough to see a light puff of air when she breathed out. The light dusting of snow on the ground sparkled with the reflection from the street lights. *It's actually pretty*, thought Gabby as Holly pulled up. She hopped into Holly's SUV and was greeted by her friend's big smile. Her brunette shoulder-length curls bounced as she said, "Good morning!" Gabby wasn't sure how her friend could be so excited at this hour.

"I thought we'd try that new coffee shop just outside of town and then go shopping," Holly said nonchalantly. Holly owned Beans and Books, an adorable coffee shop and used bookstore she had inherited from her mom. Gabby thought it was the perfect location. Not only was it in the heart of downtown, it was also right next door to her office. Holly had been concerned for a few weeks when Loco Latte, the new coffee shop, opened up a month ago, just a couple of miles away. She had wanted to check it out but hadn't had the heart to go there yet. Gabby smiled and agreed it was time to see the competition.

As they walked in, Gabby could smell the freshly ground coffee and the sweet breakfast pastries. Gabby didn't want to admit it, but it was a cute little place. It had a trendy vibe with dark wood floors, brick walls, and funny sayings sketched onto chalkboard signs on the walls. One of them said, "You can't make everyone happy; you are not coffee." Wooden tables and chairs lined the walls. In the middle of the room, brown leather couches with colorful throw pillows invited customers to sit and relax.

The store was busier than she had expected. She noticed Holly's frown and her eyes scanning every nook and cranny of the place. Undoubtedly, Holly was counting the customers and comparing the numbers with her own shop.

"It's just a new place people want to try. There are plenty of people in town in need of a caffeine fix for two coffee shops," Gabby assured her friend, placing a hand on her shoulder.

"I hope so," Holly said as they stepped up to the wooden counter to place their order.

"Welcome to Loco Latte," said the teenage boy behind the counter. *He's a cute kid, Gabby* thought. He *will probably bring in the high school crowd.*

"Two peppermint lattes, please," Holly stated as if she was testing him.

"Umm, we don't have peppermint lattes," the kid said.

Holly and Gabby gave each other a confused glance. Directly behind the kid was a huge chalkboard drawing of a latte mug with a candy cane sticking out of it, surrounded by a pile of peppermint candies.

"Well, what's that?" Holly asked, pointing at the candy cane mug.

"That's the *candy cane* latte." The kid rolled his eyes. "See the candy cane?" he said, tracing a candy cane in the air to make sure they understood.

"Oh, of course." Gabby nodded while she and Holly held back a laugh. "We will have two candy cane lattes then."

They paid for the lattes and moved aside for the next customer in line.

"Should we let him know candy canes are made of peppermint?" Gabby asked.

"Nah. He'll catch on sooner or later." Holly grinned mischievously, obviously not willing to help the competition. "So, how was yesterday?"

"It was..." Gabby trailed off, not sure how to describe it. "It just was."

Holly put an arm around her friend. "I understand."

"I ordered Chinese," Gabby confessed.

"HA! Please tell me you ordered more than egg rolls and rice." Holly was familiar with all the times Gabby's parents insisted their children eat more than egg rolls.

"Of course, we had more than egg rolls and rice." Gabby feigned a hurt expression. "We also ordered soup, dumplings, and cookies."

"Oh good," Holly said, rolling her eyes. "But really, it was okay?"

"We survived," Gabby assured her friend. "The worst part was all the heartfelt calls and texts from people expressing how sad or how hard today must be...because hearing how sad it should be makes it better, right? Or my absolute favorite... 'You know they are up there watching, and you know they'd want you to go on celebrating life.'"

"Oh Gabs, you know they mean well." Holly squeezed her friend's shoulder before they grabbed their candy cane lattes.

"I know they mean well. It just doesn't make it any easier, you know?" Gabby said.

"I know," Holly commiserated.

"Thanksgiving was bad enough. I'm not sure how I'm going to make it through Christmas."

Gabby sighed. "Aside from trying to make it through myself, I have to shield Jase from it all. He's just having such a hard time with everything."

"I know, but you can't shield him from everything," Holly said as they walked out of Loco Latte and back to the car.

"I know I can't," Gabby said, climbing into the passenger seat. Then continued while Holly put the car in drive and turned out of the parking lot towards Main Street.

"Jase has had a rough year. First, hurting his knee. It's made him think about retiring from baseball. I think he's more worried about that decision being made for him. He moved in with Mom and Dad so they could help while he was in rehab. Then Mom and Dad..." Gabby stopped and took a deep breath. After six months, she still couldn't bring herself to say the words. "I just feel like I need to protect him, help him heal, and find a new path."

"He will." Holly smiled at her friend. "And so will you."

Gabby sat quietly while her friend parked the car in the lot behind their stores on Main Street. Grabbing her drink and her purse, she climbed out. She and Holly walked through the small alley that connected the lot to the shop's storefronts.

Gabby hesitated for a moment, not sure if she wanted to admit this out loud. "I've been thinking about what a new path looks like."

Holly glanced at Gabby with her eyebrow raised. "Really? How so?"

"I'm not sure I want to keep the agency going." Just saying those words aloud felt like Gabby was betraying her dad. But she wasn't sure she was up to living in his shadow anymore.

"What else would you do?" Holly asked.

"I don't know. Maybe open my own photography studio or an artisan store where locals can display and sell their work."

"Hmm," Holly mumbled, taking a sip of her latte. "I thought you loved having the agency."

"I do, I mean, I did," Gabby said. She wanted to explain but didn't know how to verbalize the mix of feelings she had. At least not in a way that made sense. Finally, she shrugged, "It's just different now."

"I actually do get that," Holly said, nodding her head slowly. "Why don't you think about this a little more before making any big decisions? And we'll pray about it."

Pray about it, Gabby thought. She'd been praying a lot lately, but mostly for Jase to find peace.

"Have you talked to Jase about it?" Holly asked.

"No, he has enough going on," Gabby sighed.

Holly didn't reply. She blew on her latte, causing a white puff to form against the cool air.

"What?" Gabby asked, stopping before they reached the sidewalk to face her friend.

"I just think you should talk to him about it."

"We haven't really talked about much lately," Gabby confessed. "We used to talk about everything. It just hasn't been as easy since..." Gabby paused before going on. "We talk about things like dinner and the weather. We mostly avoid talking about anything deeper than that."

"Eventually, you guys will have to talk. I mean, are you going to both live in that house together forever? And would you really want to sell the business without talking to him?"

"I know we do," Gabby snapped. "It just has never felt like the right time." Gabby felt herself getting anxious just thinking about all the things that had been left unsaid. She hated confrontation. Plus, she never knew what would upset Jase. When he got angry, he would shut down, stop speaking and walk away. Conversation over. If only there was a way to bypass the four other stages of grief and get right to acceptance.

"The longer you put it all off, the worse it will be," Holly said gently.

"I know." Gabby knew her friend was trying to be helpful, but she didn't want to feel pressured. Or even to think about this right now. She and Jase were making it work.

The Lake Harbor downtown area was bustling with shoppers. When they passed by Holly's shop, Gabby could see the relief on her friend's face that the coffee shop was packed with people. They continued down the row of stores and popped into their favorite ones. Holly picked up gifts for her family and Christmas decor for her home. Gabby mindlessly picked items up and put them back down. She didn't want to buy anything for anyone. Every trinket she picked up reminded her that she didn't have as many people to buy for this year. *Who knew shopping would bring out such emotions.* Breathing deep. she pushed her emotions into the small box inside her head labeled "to deal with later."

At the end of the row of shops was the Woods Family Christmas Tree lot. As they approached, Mr. Woods called out a jolly, "Good morning, Gabby and Holly." Mr. Woods and his family had owned the tree farm just outside of town along with this lot as long as Lake Harbor had been a town. It's where everyone bought their Christmas trees. Gabby loved that their last name was Woods; it was so perfect since they owned a tree farm. She often wondered if some great-great-great relative changed it to Woods just so it would be fitting.

"How are you ladies this morning?" he asked in his jovial voice. Just seeing him made Gabby smile. He would make a great Santa with his round belly and big white beard. As a child, she thought he was Santa, just undercover with his jeans, suspenders, red plaid, flannel shirt, and a red beanie on his head, rather than the standard red suit.

"We're good. Thank you, Mr. Woods." Gabby put on the smile everyone had come to expect from her. "How are you?"

"Fantastic! It's the most wonderful time of the year," Mr Woods sang merrily and looped his thumbs through his suspenders. "Do you need help finding trees? I have the big twelve-foot Fraser firs that your parents always liked in the back, Gabby." As soon as he said the words, he tucked in his lips like he wanted to take the words back.

"I'm so sorry, Gabby," Mr. Woods said with a sorrowful expression.

"It's okay." She forced a smile and swallowed the emotions. "I'll check them out, thank you."

Gabby hadn't even thought about getting a tree. It was a family tradition to get the tree and decorate it together. Their big white lakehouse with the wraparound porch would be decorated like a giant gingerbread house, trimmed with colorful lights and garland. The tree, adorned with all their ornaments, including the funky homemade ones, would be centered in the front window. The tree was always the centerpiece to their parents' big Christmas Eve party. Gabby swore half the town usually attended. Then, the next morning, her family would open presents in front of the tree.

When she and Jase were little, the Jackson family would drive out to the Woods Tree Farm the day after Thanksgiving and cut one down. As Gabby and Jase got older, their parents were happy just to get them to go to the lot with them. She'd go with her parents to the North Pole to pick a tree if they could just come back now.

"I just want a small one for my condo, Mr. Woods," Holly interrupted.

Mr. Woods walked them over to the smaller trees and helped Holly pick a good one. He said he would bundle it up and hold it till they were done with their shopping. Gabby promised she'd think about a tree and come back later.

"It's like little emotional grenades at every turn," Gabby said, feeling exhausted. They walked across the street to stroll up the other side. "When does that stop happening?"

"I'll let you know if it does." Holly smiled sadly, taking her friend's hand. "But I promise it does get easier."

The next few stops had more emotional bombs. People expressed sympathy and how she and Jase were in their thoughts and prayers. Gabby smiled and thanked each one graciously. She honestly appreciated the prayers. They needed them now more than ever. It was all so overwhelming, though.

When they stopped at Waterfall Jewelers, the owner, Mrs. Scotts, made a beeline for them. She wrapped Gabby in a tight, quick hug. "Gabby, I'm so glad to see you. What a coincidence that you would happen to come in today."

"Hi, Mrs. Scotts. How are you?"

"I'm fine, darling. I have something for you."

"For me?" Gabby had no idea what it could be.

Mrs. Scotts dashed off to the back room and returned with a small bag.

She spoke so quickly Gabby had a hard time understanding her. "I'm so sorry for this and for you. We just found it, and I feel awful that it was misplaced for so long. It must have fallen behind the jewelry repair counter. I immediately recognized it and felt sick about it."

She tucked the bag into Gabby's purse, urging her to open it later so as to not upset her now.

"What was that about?" Holly asked as they left the store.

"I'm not really sure," Gabby said, pulling the bag out of her purse and peering inside.

The contents inside the bag stopped Gabby in her tracks.

"What?" Holly asked, taking a peek into the bag. "No way!"

"Is that possible?"

"It's a miracle!" Holly exclaimed.

"It kind of is," Gabby said. "I'm giving it to Jase. Maybe it'll help him."

"That's a fantastic idea," Holly agreed. "Maybe wait till Christmas, make it special."

"Good idea." Gabby tucked the bag back into her purse, still thinking about Christmas looming ahead. She was dreading it.

"You know what would be great?" Gabby asked her friend.

"Winning the lottery? A house that cleaned itself?" teased Holly.

Gabby laughed. "Those would all be great! But I was thinking of an escape from Christmas."

"You want to escape from Christmas?" Holly's tone made it sound as if she were crazy to suggest such a thing. "But you love Christmas!"

"I just don't feel like celebrating. I want to hibernate till New Year."

"I'm not sure that hibernating is physically possible."

"Jase seems to make it possible," Gabby smirked.

"He does, doesn't he?" Holly agreed.

"It all just seems so pointless and overwhelming. I mean, I usually decorated my house a bit, but I realize now that my mom was the magic behind Christmas. I'm not sure how she managed to do it all. The house, the tree, the parties, the presents, the cooking, and especially cleaning it all up."

"Our moms were amazing that way. Even with my dad, three siblings, and all of their families, Christmas still isn't the same without my mom. So I completely get what you're saying."

"Maybe I can just ignore it all this year. I'm sure Jase would get on board with it. He's been ignoring life for the last few months anyway." Gabby tried to imagine what not having Christmas at the Jackson house would be like.

"If that's what you want to do, then go for it," Holly said.

"Yes, I am going to be officially cheer-free," Gabby stated. At that moment, she caught a whiff of something sweet and smiled at her friend. "Right after we get some of the roasted honey nuts."

Laughing, they headed into the Candy Corner to buy one of their favorite Christmas treats.

As they walked back to the car with their shopping bags and nutty confections, Holly turned to her friend and said, "Maybe you're right."

"Aren't I always?" Gabby said sarcastically. "But about what specifically?"

"Escaping Christmas," said Holly.

"Ha, sure. And how am I supposed to do that?" Gabby gestured around at their surroundings. The town was already decked out as if Santa's elves had come down from the North Pole and had a party.

"You and Jase could go away for Christmas," her friend said. "You could both use some time away from being in the house, surrounded by memories. You need a change of scenery. Something other than work, church, and home. And we both know Jase should get out of the house. I don't think he's left in months except for physical therapy."

Gabby knew her friend was right. It couldn't be healthy that she and her brother were living in the museum of their parents' lives. Even her office at work had been her dad's, and she hadn't changed a thing in there since she took over. They had even kept the house exactly the way their mom had kept it, with the exception of using a few more paper plates.

Moments later, they pulled into the Jackson's driveway. Gabby stared at the big house. Even though it was the home she'd always known, it felt different now. Emptier.

Getting away is a good idea, she thought. Maybe they could go far enough away that they wouldn't have to think about anything that had happened...or they could at least pretend like it hadn't.

"Where would we go?" Gabby asked. The idea of escaping was growing on her.

"I don't know," Holly said. "Someplace that doesn't feel Christmas-y?"

"Maybe someplace tropical," Gabby said. "Escape the snow and ice too."

Holly's face brightened. "I've got it!" She pulled out her phone and started typing. "Look!"

She turned her phone, and Gabby saw photos of white sandy beaches, hammocks, and underwater photos of coral and sea turtles.

"It's an all-inclusive resort in Cozumel," Holly said. "You could take photos and use that scuba certification you're always complaining you haven't used. And being a tropical island resort, I'm sure it would be less Christmas-y."

Gabby's heart felt lighter just seeing the tropical photos. "Yes, this is what we need!"

"It is," Holly said. Then, with a grin added, "And maybe you could even meet someone down there."

"Meet someone?" Gaby was confused. It was a resort. She assumed there would be lots of people, and she would indeed meet some of them.

"Yes, like a handsome someone." Holly winked at her.

Gabby rolled her eyes. Her friend was always trying to set her up or find ways for her to meet men. Gabby had been burned before. She had dated Aaron all through college. Then, just before graduation, he took her out on a date, saying that he had something "important" he wanted to talk to her about. Everyone had convinced her he was going to propose. He didn't. Just the opposite, in fact. It seems he thought life was taking them in different directions. Him in the direction of a tall, leggy brunette and her back home with a broken heart. She never saw it coming. While now she could see he really wasn't right for her, the pain of his betrayal still lingered as if it happened yesterday.

"Holly, you know I'm too busy with everything else to try to add someone to my life," Gabby said, using her standard excuse. "Besides, what use would there be meeting someone who probably lives a thousand miles away?"

"God works in mysterious ways, my friend." Holly smiled.

Her friend, the eternal optimist. This made Gabby chuckle and shake her head.

Moving her focus back to the tropical photos, her smile faded. "Do you think Jase will go for it? He's like Dad and thinks holidays should be spent at home with family. Remember that one

Thanksgiving that you and I went to Florida with some friends in college?"

"Yeah. Your dad and Jase kind of acted like it was the end of the world," remembered Holly. "But you should ask him. I think it would be good for you guys. And I can watch Tucker, so you don't have to worry about that."

"Thanks Holly, I appreciate it. Let's hope Jase goes for it," said Gabby, sounding doubtful.

"Good luck," Holly said as Gabby climbed out of the car. "See you at work on Monday!"

"Thanks, see you Monday," Gabby said, closing the door. She took a deep breath and pushed her shoulders back before heading into the house.

Tucker greeted her with his whole backside wagging excitedly as she walked through the door. "Hey buddy, where's our brother?" Tucker turned and headed up the stairs.

"Of course. It's before noon. He's probably still sleeping." Gabby walked up the stairs, gently knocked, and then opened Jase's door.

Deep breath, okay, here we go.

CHAPTER 4: JASE

J ase was lying in bed staring at the ceiling when he heard his sister knock. *What does she want?* She probably wanted him to get out of bed. He lay there quietly, thinking she might leave if he didn't respond. The door slowly creaked open, and his sister's head peeked in. *No such luck.*

"Are you awake?" Gabby asked quietly. He didn't respond.

When she opened the door a little wider, Tucker pushed past her and then jumped up on the bed.

"Hey there, Tuck." Jase welcomed him, rubbing his head between his hands.

"Hey, good morning," Gabby sat on the edge of the bed.

"What's up?" Jase scanned his sister's face. Concern immediately replaced the irritation he'd felt moments ago, and he sat up. She was twisting her ring, and she wasn't making eye contact, obvious signs that she had bad news. Or at least it was something she didn't want to tell him. *Was she sick? Dying? What was going on?*

"I wanted to talk to you about something," Gabby started.

"Is everything okay?" Jase asked.

"Oh yeah, everything's fine." Gabby smiled.

"I was shopping with Holly, and we had this idea...and I wanted to see what you thought."

Jase was still wary of what she was going to tell him. "Go on..."

"What do you think about escaping from Christmas?" Gabby blurted out.

"Escaping? From Christmas?" He gave a harsh laugh. "How exactly would we do that?"

"We can go somewhere with no decorations, no parties, no gifts, just getting away from it all. Somewhere tropical, somewhere that it seems like Christmas doesn't exist."

"I'm pretty sure Santa delivers all over the world," Jase said sarcastically.

"Well, yes, but doesn't an all-inclusive, tropical beach resort with hammocks and sea turtles sound better than being here with all the sympathetic glances and being surrounded by..." Gabby trailed off. But he knew exactly what she meant.

"All the memories," Jase finished her thought. He definitely wanted to get away from all the texts and calls from friends of their parents hugging them and crying on their shoulders about how much they missed Vincent and Jillian. He couldn't imagine going to Christmas Eve Mass, with everyone saying how they were praying for them and all that rubbish. He loved the people here, but he could use a break from all their well-meaning.

"Yeah," she said.

Jase felt a little guilt creep in. Their parents had done everything to make an amazing life for them...and now Jase and Gabby wanted to escape the memories? At the same time, he didn't want to make new memories without them.

"I like it," Jase nodded."Let's do it."

"Really?" Gabby whispered, obviously shocked by this.

"Yeah, let's go."

Gabby beamed at her brother and clapped her hands.

"Okay, how about ten days in Cozumel?" She pulled up the resort website and handed him her phone. "We can go scuba diving and snorkeling, play on the beach or in the pools, and they have all sorts of sports and activities. It even has the perfect name, Hideaway Cay."

Jase chuckled and nodded. He could barely keep up with the stream of words from her mouth while he browsed the website.

"We can fly into Cancun and take a water ferry over to Cozumel, so we don't have to do two flights." She explained. Neither of them liked flying too much, so one flight was definitely better than two.

Gabby's enthusiasm was contagious, and he could feel himself getting a little excited about it too. It had been so long since he'd felt excited about anything. Even Tucker wiggled with excitement.

"Sorry, Tuck, human kids only for this one," Gabby told him. "You'll be vacationing with Auntie Holly."

Jase scrolled through the resort amenities and looked at some excursions. Escaping Christmas was one of the best plans his sister had ever come up with. They booked a two-bedroom, oceanfront suite and two first-class tickets to Cancun that afternoon.

Mission: Escaping Christmas had begun.

CHAPTER 5: GABBY

The week before Christmas, Gabby and Jase loaded their bags into Holly's SUV.

"I can't believe you guys are really doing this," Holly said. Then she quickly added, "I wish I was coming too."

"I know. It feels weird to be leaving and not getting ready for all the parties and events around town," Gabby said, still feeling a little guilty.

"It's going to be great not having to deal with it all," Jase chimed in from the back. Tucker sat with him, enjoying the car ride.

"Thanks for driving us so early," Gabby said to Holly.

"6:00 am isn't that early. I'm more surprised to see Jase awake at this hour," Holly said, glancing in the rearview mirror back at him.

"Joke's on you, Holly," Jase smirked back at her. "I never went to bed."

"That seems more like it," Holly said to Gabby.

Holly pulled up to the departures curb. Gabby and Jase climbed out while Tucker jumped into the front seat. Jase thanked Holly for the lift and started to unload the luggage while Gabby said her farewells to Holly and Tucker.

"You sure you want to watch him?" Gabby asked. Holly reached over to give him some ear scratches, and Tucker leaned into her hand. "Oh yeah, we are going to have our own adventures. Aren't we, Tucker?" He leaned back and gave Holly a quick lick. Tucker would have a great vacation too, with lots of hiking, and if she knew Holly, too many yummy treats.

"Alright, here we go," Gabby leaned back into the car to give Tucker some last ear scratches, "Be good for Auntie Holly." He gave her a quick lick too. "Thank you, love you, and see you in ten days."

"Go relax and have some fun. Maybe even meet Mr. Right!" Holly gave her friend a big smile and a wink.

"Yeah, because I currently have so much time for Mr. Right," Gabby said with an eye roll.

"Call me when you get to the resort," Holly said.

"I will, Mom," Gabby teased. "Remember, we fly into Cancun, then a car is taking us to a ferry to go over to Cozumel, so we should be there by 6:00 pm our time. I wrote it all down on the itinerary and emergency numbers I left for you."

"Now who sounds like the mom?" Holly laughed. "Go, have a good time. I have things covered here."

"I know you do. Thank you again." Gabby waved goodbye as Holly pulled away and met up with Jase and their luggage at the curbside bag drop and check-in.

"You ready?" Gabby asked her brother.

"Heck yeah, I am. Let's blow this popsicle stand," Jase said with a grin, repeating one of their mother's favorite sayings.

Gabby had never been more grateful for having invested in the TSA Pre-Check when they saw the hour-long security line. Luckily for them, they breezed through security, even with the heavy holiday travel, and walked toward their gate. They stopped at a snack shop. Jase came out with a bulging bag of candy and snacks that looked like a ten-year-old had robbed a candy store. Gabby grabbed some Twizzlers and a couple of books.

"Didn't you pack like three books?" Jase asked, already shoving Pringles into his mouth.

"Of course I did," Gabby said, eyeing her brother and his bag of goodies. "Did you leave any food for the other travelers?"

"I think so." Jase laughed and made duck lips with two potato chips.

Gabby couldn't help but laugh. It was good to see her brother like this. He'd always been so carefree and the life of the party. He made life look easy. It had been really hard to see him so down and lost these last six months.

They found their gate and sat near the windows. Gabby glanced around at the other passengers. She noticed a teenage boy across from them who was sitting with his mom and dad. The scowl on the boy's face made it clear that he was not impressed with going on vacation. He slouched in his seat with headphones on and a hoodie pulled down far over his face. His mom was trying to talk to him, but when she spoke, he rolled his eyes and turned the other way.

To Gabby's surprise, her brother grabbed a candy bar out of his bag, rose from his seat, and walked over to the boy.

"Hey," Jase said and nudged the boy's shoe with his own. The kid let out an exasperated sigh. He briefly examined the shoes that had kicked his own. Then he looked up to meet the owner. His eyes went wide when he recognized who had nudged him. "Jase? Jase Jackson?" the boy stuttered.

"Yeah." Jase shifted his body and tugged his baseball cap a little further over his face. "Listen, be good to your mom. You only get one."

"Yes sir," the kid nodded, still awestruck and staring up at Jase.

Jase handed him the candy bar, and the mom smiled and mouthed, "Thank you." The kid asked if he could get an autograph and a photo, to which Jase complied. The kid sat down with his mom, excitedly going through the photos with her as Jase walked back over to Gabby.

Gabby sometimes forgot that outside their town, her brother was a celebrity. At home and around town, he was just Jase. When they left their little town, he was Jase Jackson, the four-time MVP and All-Star catcher for the Defenders.

Gabby smiled at her brother, so proud of him, as he reclaimed the seat next to her.

"I'm sure I was that bad too," he admitted.

"You're not wrong," she said with a smirk. ." Gabby reached her arm around her brother's shoulders.

They heard the call for first-class boarding and stood up. Gabby peered up at her brother, always amazed that he was so tall.

"All right, let's do this," Gabby said to her brother.

The lady at the gate scanned their tickets. "Happy Holidays," she said, smiling widely at them.

"We're escaping Christmas," Jase informed her flatly.

The gate agent's eyes widened, but she recovered quickly. She gave him a big smile and replied, "Well... happy escape then."

"Thank you," Gabby and Jase responded at the same time.

They walked down the jetway and into the plane, where they were escorted to their first-class seats.

"Welcome to Delta," a smiling attendant greeted them. "I'm Stacy, and I'll be here for anything you need on your flight today. Can I get you some holly-jolly hot cocoa or some festive punch?" She aimed her alarmingly white smile at Jase and batted her eyelashes.

Gabby was used to this. Ever since his junior year, when he grew to be almost six feet tall, and muscles seemed to grow overnight, girls had been throwing themselves at him. She had become Jase's sister at that point. Which was fine with her; she preferred to stay out of the limelight.

"No holly, jolly, or festive anything over here. Just a Coke, please," Gabby told the flight attendant, who seemed to just now notice her.

Stacey put her hands on her hips and said with a smile, "Okay, little grinches, Cokes for the both of you?"

"Yes, please, Stacy," Jase replied, flashing her a big smile. Stacy giggled as she strolled away.

Gabby raised an eyebrow and smirked at her brother.

"What?" he asked defensively.

"I didn't say anything!" Gabby smiled, holding her hands up.

"I'm just being friendly. Just because there's no Christmas doesn't mean I can't be friendly." He continued, "Besides, I don't have anything to offer a woman right now."

"That's not true," she said and put her hand on her brother's arm. "You are one of the most amazing guys I know." It broke her heart knowing he was so down on himself.

Stacy returned with two glasses of Coke, "Here you are. I'll be checking on you, but if you need anything, just click the call button there."

"Thank you, Stacy," Gabby replied and turned her attention back to her brother.

"So, I've been thinking about some things, like with the house and other things that we need to take care of. What next year..." Gabby was interrupted by her brother.

"Gabs, I know we have a lot to figure out and plan for and..." he stopped. "Let's just go and have a great time. We're trying to escape all the real-life stuff for a bit. So can we please just do that?"

Gabby gave him a small smile and nodded. "I guess real life will be there waiting for us when we get back."

Jase put on his headphones and started a movie. In typical Jase fashion, he was asleep before they took off. Gabby closed the plane's window so she didn't have to see how far the ground was beneath them. Then she pulled out a book and opened it. With so many thoughts rolling through her head, she never even managed to turn the page.

CHAPTER 6: JASE

Jase was jarred awake by the jolt of the wheels hitting the runway.

His nap had been surprisingly refreshing; he thought as he and Gabby deboarded the plane and entered the Cancun airport. The airport was crowded and really colorful. Gabby walked into him a few times while they walked through the airport.

"Sorry," she laughed when she did it the third time.

"It's fine," he said.

"There's just so much to look at," she said.

He agreed. He'd never seen such a colorful airport in all of his travels. There were vibrant scrolling electronic signs. Stores with brightly colored Mexican clothing, mugs, and skeleton figures everywhere.

"What's up with the skulls everywhere?" He asked.

"Dia de los Muertos," Gabby said, like he was supposed to know.

"Day of the Dead; They are sugar skulls," she continued when he just stared at her. "We have All Saints Day, and they celebrate Dia de los Muertos. It's a day they celebrate their loved ones who have passed on; it's really a beautiful tradition."

"Interesting," Jase said. He couldn't imagine celebrating death but decided not to mention that to his sister.

They followed the signs for 'Inmigración.' While many signs were in English as well as Spanish, Jase was glad he understood Spanish so well, thanks to four years of high school Spanish and having a lot of Spanish-speaking teammates.

"Here you go," Gabby said, handing him a piece of paper.

"What's this?" he asked.

"I filled out the immigration forms for us on the plane," she said.

"Thanks," he said, taking the paper from her.

Jase was impressed with how quickly they made it through immigration and got their passports stamped, even with the long lines. After they grabbed their luggage, he was happy that both their bags got the green light, meaning they didn't have to have their bags inspected. *So far, this trip is off to a good start*, he thought as they continued out of the airport.

While searching for the driver they booked to take them to the ferry, he was a little irritated with the barrage of people hounding them to take tours of their timeshares and to book other services. And relieved when he spotted a short man in a khaki pants and short-sleeved blue button-up shirt, holding a sign that read "Jackson."

"Hey, we're the Jacksons," Jase said to the man with the sign.

"Bien, welcome to Cancun. I am Alejandro," he said with a smile. "I will be taking you to the Cozumel ferry." They shook hands with him and introduced themselves. After Jase helped

Alejandro with the bags, he joined his sister in the back seat. He was grateful for the bottle of water Alejandro handed him. It was hotter and more humid than he had expected.

Jase and Gabby listened to Alejandro tell them about the local area on the hour drive to the ferry terminal that would take them over to Cozumel. Jase grunted a 'thank you' as Alejandro said "Adios y Feliz Navidad" when he left them at the terminal entrance.

"Almost there," Gabby said to him, smiling.

"Yeah," Jase said. He was beginning to regret the decision to not book a flight with a connection right into Cozumel rather than all the extra travel they needed to do now.

The ferry ride had been nice, though. The salty ocean air and the bluest water he'd ever seen was nice. Gabby called him over to the edge of the ferry to see dolphins jumping alongside. He had to admit, they were pretty cool. By the time the ferry docked, though, he was over the travel and ready to be at the resort already. It was nearly 3:00 pm, and he was ready to eat, then sit back and relax.

The last leg of the journey involved one more 20-minute ride to the resort. While Gabby and the driver chatted about what the two of them should do, see, and eat, Jase stared out the window at the water. When they finally arrived at the resort, Jase got out of the car and stretched his arms and back. Gabby was already grabbing bags out of the car and heading to the resort.

He couldn't help but smile when he saw the resort's grand entrance, surrounded by palm trees. Jase followed his sister into the main lobby. This was just what they needed. Sun, beach, and absolutely no...

"What the...?" He heard his sister gasp.

As he walked in behind her, he saw what she was gasping about. There were tall white Christmas trees decorated with starfish and brightly colored seagrass. Oversized ornaments with geometric patterns, birds, and other animals, some with flowers, all painted with bright aqua, hot pink, purple, yellow, and neon green hung from the ceiling. There were even candy cane-colored ropes leading them to the front desk. It was as if they entered Santa's Mexico workshop.

"So much for an escape from Christmas," Jase grunted.

"I'm so sorry, I didn't know," Gabby said, her eyes wide, "This wasn't on the website."

"It's fine," Jase sighed. " How would you have known?"

"Well, you'd think they'd warn people," Gabby mumbled.

"Warn them that it's Christmas?" Jase raised an eyebrow at his sister.

"Yes!" Gabby said.

"It's fine. Let's go check in." Jase shook his head and continued to the front desk.

"Bienvenidos. Welcome to the Hideaway Cay Resort." The young lady behind the desk smiled at them. She wore a satin pink Santa hat trimmed in white fur. Her name tag read Marissa.

"Hi Marissa, reservation for Jackson," Jase said.

"Si Señor Jackson, I have your reservation," Marissa said as she tapped the keys on her computer. Then looked at him and smiled. "I just need your identification and credit card, por favor."

Jase pulled out his wallet and handed them to the lady.

"Gracias," she said, handing them back. "We have a beautiful two-bedroom swim-up suite ready for you in the East wing. It's one of the best rooms at the resort. You can get into the lazy river directly from your patio and drift into the main pool."

Marissa finished typing into the computer and handed them two silicone wristbands. "Here are your wristbands for the resort.

They are your key to your room and can also be used for cashless payments in shops around the resort."

Marissa pulled out a paper map of the resort. She circled areas on the map as she informed them of all the happy holiday events happening. There was going to be a sandman-building contest on the beach. Ornament creation and cookie making in tents on the grassy area. And a special Santa story time on Christmas Day in the gardens. Activities that in previous years, Jase knew his sister would drag him to.

"What if we want to avoid festivity?" Jase asked Marissa. Her smile faded just a bit as if the idea of avoiding festivities was a strange request.

"We do have all of the regular resort activities such as tennis, golf, pools, and watersports. We offer many day excursions that you can find information about on the racks over there," she said. "We also have a concierge that can help set up excursions for you off the resort property."

They turned and noticed a large brochure rack next to a desk with a sign stating "concierge." The man sitting behind the desk smiled and gave them a wave.

They thanked Marisa, attached their wristbands, and followed the bellhop. They walked through the grand lobby, and the doors leading to the ocean opened.

They stood for a moment, gazing out at the courtyard and the ocean beyond, inhaling the fresh sea air. Jase noticed a group of five people standing near one of the palm trees. They were wearing matching blue shirts that said "Andersons' Christmas Vacation." The shirts had palm trees and what appeared to be caricatures of the whole family on them. Jase guessed they were a family vacationing together, though it seemed strange to him to see three adult children vacationing with their parents. All of them were tall and athletic. Even the parents were extremely attractive.

"Wow, look at that," Jase said to Gabby. "Not even our parents made us do that."

He was sure his sister was thinking of the coordinating outfits their parents forced them into for the annual family Christmas card photo from the time they were toddlers until nearly high school. As they grew and got more involved with their activities, the photos were usually taken on location at one of Jase's baseball tournaments. Even so, their mom had always made sure they packed coordinating outfits for a photo. He immediately disliked the family.

Gabby punched his arm. "Be nice."

They continued walking and followed the trolley with their luggage to their room. The bellhop opened the door for them and gestured for them to enter. Both of their jaws dropped when they walked through the doors.

"I think this will do," Jase said in awe.

"I think so too." Gabby smiled in agreement

The entryway led into a living room with a plush couch, coffee table, and large-screen TV. There was a small dining table and bar to the side. Floor-to-ceiling glass windows with an awesome view of the ocean. The sliding glass doors opened to a big patio with lounge chairs and a small table. Just as Marissa described, the patio had steps that led into a lazy river that flowed in front of the ground level rooms and ended in a big pool. Back inside the room, the bedrooms were located on opposite sides of the living room. He quickly scanned each of the rooms to see which one he wanted to claim, but they were basically the same. Each bedroom had a king-sized bed that had a fluffy white comforter and big pillows. Each had a private bathroom with oversized tubs and a standing shower. On the bed was a towel folded in the shape of a Christmas tree with a welcome note from the staff. Jase promptly picked the towel up by the top of the tree and flicked it until it unraveled. Other than that, the suite was Christmas-free, just as they had hoped.

CHAPTER 7: LUKE

L uke stood with his family by the palm tree their mom picked as the perfect spot for their family photo earlier that day. He had to admit his mom had chosen well. The view was something you'd see on a postcard. The palm tree trunk swooped like you could sit on it, with the nearly white sand and the bright blue ocean behind them.

While the setting was perfect, he probably could have done without the shirts his mom had made for them all. The shirts had a caricature version of each of them. His mom and sister lay in lounge chairs holding umbrella-clad drinks, Luke and his brother wore boardshorts and played football in the sand. And cartoon Dad surfed the waves. Each of them wore a red Santa hat. And in case there was any question as to who these people on the shirt were, there was a red script declaring "Anderson's Christmas Vacation" in the sand along the bottom.

His mom had bubbled over with joy when she handed the blue shirts to him, his brother, and sister.

Sophie, his sister, laughed and shook her head before putting it on.

"Thanks, Mom. These are kind of cute," Sophie told her mom with a smile.

"Thank you, sweetheart. I thought they were so fun," His mom said with a big smile.

Luke admired the graciousness of his sister. She was about 5'10, with long brown hair. Even at 29, anyone would guess her age as 21, and she was constantly asked if she was a model. He was pretty sure she had no idea how people looked at her. If she did, she didn't act like it. Sophie was the most humble and generous person he knew.

Luke's brother, Seth, thought the shirt was hilarious, putting it on immediately.

"This is great, Mom," Seth said. "I look super buff here."

"You are buff, sweetie," his mom said, patting his brother's arm.

Luke couldn't help but think how different Seth is at 25 than he had been. He had been in the Army for seven years by the time he was 25. Seth was more of a free spirit. He looked like the rest of the family. Six feet tall, with the same light brown hair and eyes. But he definitely took life less seriously than the rest of his family. In some ways, Luke envied Seth's carefree life but worried that he'd never find his true calling.

His dad put an arm around his wife and kissed her cheek. "I love it, honey. Maybe I can even learn to surf while we're here so it can be like real life. That would be fun."

"Yeah, Dad, so fun," Luke said. "Maybe then we can take a tour of the local ER while we're here."

"Haha," his dad said mockingly.

Luke liked to tease his dad about being an old man, but he had to admit that, at 61, his dad was still in good shape. So was his mom at 59. They both were active and still looked great for their ages.

"Now come on, the light is perfect, and I want to get this picture in," his mom said while directing them where to stand.

"Now, who can we get to take this," she asked. Scanning the area, spotting a woman, she headed towards her. His mom approached an unsuspecting lady who appeared to have been heading back from a jog. The jogger agreed and patiently listened as his mom explained the camera to her.

While they waited, his dad turned to them and spoke. "You guys, I get that the shirts might be a bit much, but this means a lot to your mom. She realizes you're all getting older, and our tradition of all of us going away for Christmas might not last forever."

Luke and his siblings nodded at their dad.

"We know, Dad," Sophie smiled.

"We need to make sure this year is amazing for your mom," his dad said. "We have all been so blessed, and we need to appreciate what we have while we can."

"Geez, Dad, you act like one of you is dying," Seth said.

"No, your mom and I are in perfect health and have no plans on dying anytime soon, but things happen. Not just bad things but good things too. You kids will all get married and have families of your own, and our vacations like this might come to an end."

"You're right, Dad." Luke thought about his time in the Army and the struggles he had when he came home and knew all too well that tomorrow is never promised. He made a silent vow that he would do anything he could to make sure he and his siblings go out of their way to make this trip special. Being the oldest, he also knew his dad was right. They would all have families of their own, probably sooner rather than later, and these family Christmas trips will eventually be a thing of the past.

"Mom, it's a standard camera. She's got it," Seth called to his mom. She was still explaining the camera to the jogger, who Luke was sure regretted stopping.

"I just want to make sure it's a good photo." His mom said, rejoining her family. She quickly rearranged them, tucked herself under her husband's arm, and told them all to smile. The jogger snapped a few photos, then quickly handed back the camera and jogged off.

Scrolling through the photos on the camera, she smiled and seemed satisfied.

"Thank you all for doing that," she said, almost sadly.

"We're happy to do it, Mom," Luke said. He looked at his siblings pointedly.

"Yeah Mom, this is fun," Sophie said with a smile.

"I'll pose for you anytime," Seth said. He jumped onto the low-hanging palm tree, flexing his

arms, with a huge cheesy smile. His mother snapped some photos of him and the tree. She then pointed the camera toward Luke and Sophie, who leaned into each other and smiled for their mom.

"Who's hungry?" Their dad asked, putting an arm around his mom.

They agreed they were all starving and headed towards the lobby to decide which of the many restaurants at the resort they wanted to dine in that evening.

"That jogger was cute," Sophie said to Luke as they walked back inside. "Maybe you can introduce yourself later."

"She's okay, I guess," Luke said. He wasn't interested.

"Someday, someone will catch your eye again," Sophie said.

"Maybe," he said doubtfully.

"You're too good of a catch to be alone," his sister continued.

"Thanks." He laughed. "What about you?"

"What about me?" Sophie asked with a chuckle.

"You're single too. Maybe you can find someone here."

"I'm not looking for anyone. I just need some "me" time." Sophie said, shaking her head.

"If you say so," Luke said with a chuckle.

"Speaking of couples, did you notice that couple earlier that walked out just before we took photos?"

Luke had noticed. The man was really tall, even taller than Luke, who was 6'2. The woman didn't even reach his shoulders. Neither seemed particularly happy. He felt as if he'd seen the man before, but he couldn't place where. His thoughts were interrupted by his sister.

"They didn't seem happy at all," Sophie said. "How could anyone be that upset? I mean, this is paradise."

"Maybe it was just a long trip here. Flight delays can kill anyone's spirit," Luke said, wanting to give the couple the benefit of the doubt.

"I hope so, and if that's true, I hope their vacation gets better soon." That was his sister, always hoping for good things for people. He hoped it got better for them too. No one should be that miserable in paradise, especially at Christmas.

CHAPTER 8: GABBY

"Gabby?" Holly answered the phone on the first ring.

"Hey, Holly," Gabby answered, excited to hear from her friend as she unpacked her bag.

"Hey, how was the flight and ferry? Are you at the resort?" Holly asked.

"The flight and the ferry ride were fine," Gabby said.

"Oh no, I hear a 'but' coming," said Holly.

"The resort looks like Santa is here on vacation and made himself at home." Gabby described all the tropical Christmas-themed decor to her friend.

Holly laughed. "Not much of an escape, huh?"

"Not so much. But the room and the view are amazing. I'll send you some photos," Gabby promised.

"Yes, send lots of photos. I want to live vicariously through you," Holly said.

"I will," Gabby told her friend as she discovered a wrapped box in her bag. "Hey, what's this?"

"What's what?" Holly said innocently.

"There are two wrapped presents in my suitcase addressed to Jase and me," Gabby explained as she examined the mystery gift.

"I think that's from Tucker," Holly said.

"From Tucker, huh?" Gabby chuckled.

"Yes, and he said not to open it 'till Christmas."

"There are no presents on this trip, remember?"

"Yes, but Tucker didn't understand what that meant," Holly said.

"I'm sure he didn't." Gabby laughed. She pulled out another wrapped box that she had smuggled in her suitcase and hid it in her drawer with the gifts from "Tucker."

"Now go enjoy. Make some friends."

"Yeah, I'll make friends with the festive family we saw on the way in."

"Festive family?"

"Yes, super festive. They had matching shirts and all."

"Our parents used to make us all do that when we were kids too." Holly laughed.

"These aren't little kids. They are probably close to our age. Their shirts had caricatures of each of them on it."

"That's still sweet. Just leave the festive family alone to enjoy their holiday," Holly encouraged.

"Oh, I plan on letting them be far away," Gabby confirmed. "I have to finish unpacking and jump in the shower before dinner, so I will call later this week."

"Sounds good. Talk to you later," Holly said.

"And Holly?"

"Yes?"

"Thank you. This is going to be a good trip."

Gabby finished unpacking, showered, and changed just in time to meet her brother for dinner. Gabby and Jase entered the grand lobby. They stopped at the brochure rack and grabbed all of them.

The concierge smiled, "You two are up for some big adventures on this trip." He said, making it sound more like a statement than a question.

They smiled politely and continued to the restaurant.

They chose the steakhouse at the resort. The smell of grilled steak filled the air, and they both realized they were famished after a long day of travel. After ordering appetizers, then steak and lobster tails for their main course, they turned their attention back to the brochures.

Sifting through the pile they gathered, Gabby asked, "So what do you want to do while we're here?"

"I think I might do some golf in the morning. What about you?"

"Golf?" Gabby raised an eyebrow. "In the morning?" Her brother didn't do mornings. He never had.

"Well, late morning." Jase gave a sly grin.

"I think I'm just going to take it easy tomorrow and sit by the pool and read. But I definitely want to get in some scuba or snorkeling and visit some Mayan ruins. I hope I get to see some sea turtles and maybe some sharks!" Gabby was getting more excited with each adventure. Jase seemed to be getting caught up in her enthusiasm until she mentioned sharks.

"Nope, no sharks," Jase said with obvious concern.

Gabby tried reassuring her brother. "I'm sure there won't be any sharks here."

"Yeah, I'm sure there won't be sharks...in the ocean. Where sharks live." Jase rolled his eyes. "Just be careful."

"I always am," Gabby said, giving her brother a reassuring smile.

"Oh, look," Gabby pointed, thumbing through the brochures and plucking one out. "They have parasailing."

They both cracked up, knowing full well that was never going to happen. They were both scared of heights. Their parents had tried to get them to bungee jump, parasail, and bridge walk over canyons. But the thought of plummeting to the earth kept the Jackson siblings on firm ground.

"We can probably just toss that one out," Jase said. He took the brochure and stuffed it under the plate.

They continued to browse pamphlets and enjoy their dinner. Then Jase noticed the festive family come in.

"Hey, they aren't matching this time," Jase said sarcastically, nodding his head towards the family.

"Lucky them," Gabby did her famous eye roll as she dipped her lobster in some decadent herbed garlic butter, not even glancing at the family.

"Remember when Mom and Dad used to make us wear matching outfits for the annual family Christmas card photo?" Jase asked his sister.

Gabby laughed. "Yes, I vividly remember that. I'm glad you figured out that it was easier to just submit than fight it."

"Me? What about you, little-miss fifteen-year-old-I-can't-be-caught-dead-in-this then locked yourself in your room?" Jase said, bobbing his head back and forth for added effect.

Gabby couldn't stop laughing. She had forgotten about that, "I guess I wasn't always so cooperative either."

They fell silent as they watched the festive family talking and laughing together. They seemed to be enjoying each other's company.

"Well, I won't force matching outfits on you," Gabby assured her brother.

"Thanks, I appreciate that," he said.

Gabby glanced over her shoulder at the family.

"What do you think they're doing here?"

"You mean at a vacation resort?" Jase asked sarcastically. "They're probably on vacation."

"No kidding, Captain Obvious." Gabby rolled her eyes and turned toward the family again. "I mean, the kids seem to be about the same age as us. It just makes me wonder why they are here and not at their perfect home, wherever in the world that is."

"Why don't you go ask them?" Jase shoveled a piece of steak into his mouth.

"What?" Gabby exclaimed. "No, I was just curious."

"It doesn't matter. I'm just going to stay clear of them." Jase said between bites.

Gabby took one last glance at the family that seemed so perfect. It made her wonder if people used to feel that way about her family. She found herself feeling jealous of the family, even of the stupid shirts they had worn earlier.

After dinner, Gabby decided to go sit on the beach while Jase wanted to hit up the casino.

"Don't wait up for me," Jase told her as they walked out of the restaurant.

"Oh, I won't," she said.

"And be careful," he called over his shoulder at her.

"I always am." She waved at him and watched him walk away. *He's worse than Mom and Dad.*

She took off her wedge sandals and headed to the beach, squishing the sand with her toes. The sun had set while they were at dinner. The lights of the resort sparkled/shone on the waves, illuminating them in different colors. Gabby loved the water. Every year, she was the first one to jump into the lake after the ice thawed, and she was the last one out at the end of summer. Growing up on a lake was wonderful, but she would always remember her first time seeing the ocean. She felt amazed at its size and power. The sound of crashing waves and the smell of salty air spoke to her soul.

As the waves washed over her feet, Gabby gazed up to the sky and prayed softly, "God, please let this be a good trip for us. Be with Jase and help ease his pain and anger. Help me find a way to help him while we're here. Amen."

CHAPTER 9: JASE

Jase had been enjoying playing Texas Hold'em at the casino when he caught a glimpse of the three men from the festive family entering. He quickly finished his hand and told the dealer he was cashing out.

What the...? Was God purposefully trying to remind Jase of everything that he had lost this past year? First, his knee injury that may end his career, then God ripped Jase's family from him. Two of the three people who always supported and loved him were gone in a blink. Then, when all he wanted to do was get away and forget all of that for a bit, God flaunted this perfect family in front of him as a reminder that his life wasn't perfect anymore.

Maybe it was his own fault.... Maybe he hadn't been grateful for everything he had.... But did God need to take it all away all at once? His heart felt heavy.

Jase got back to the room and hooked up his video game console to distract himself. He'd probably hear from his sister about bringing it, but it let him escape into a different world and forget about this one for a bit at least.

He felt a little bad he had told Gabby he wouldn't go snorkeling. She loved the water and was an excellent swimmer. He was pretty sure she couldn't outswim any sharks that could swallow her in one bite, though. He could at least sit on the boat and make sure she was safe. Maybe he'd go with her. He didn't know what he'd do if he lost her too. At least tomorrow she'd be safe by the pool. And he really was looking forward to some golf. He hoped his knee could handle it.

Whatever, he would think about it tomorrow. He closed the blinds of the room, plopped onto the bed, covered his ears with his headphones, and got lost in his virtual world.

CHAPTER 10: GABBY

The next morning, Gabby woke up to the sun peeking through the window shades and the wonderful sound of crashing waves. She had slept hard the whole night. Gabby smiled as she hopped out of bed and wrapped a robe around herself.

She found a teapot to heat some water and selected a lemon-flavored tea bag. As she waited for the water to boil, she tiptoed to Jase's room. Before she even cracked the door, she heard his snores. She would be shocked if he went golfing this morning. She took her tea and Bible to the patio for her morning devotional. She loved her devotional time. It always left her with a sense of peace, at least for a little bit. And being near the ocean made her feel closer to God in some way.

When she finished her reading, it was 9:00 am. A little early for the pool still, but she figured it would be less crowded at this time of day. She left a note for her brother letting him know she would be by the main pool, and he could text her when he wanted to do lunch.

She loaded her bag with sunscreen, towels, water, and a book. Then she headed to the pool. Surprised at how many people were already there, she scouted for the perfect chair in the perfect spot, right between the pool and ocean.

Selecting her lounge chair, she gently tossed her bag on the chair next to hers to save it for Jase in case he decided to join her. After she got herself situated, she leaned back and started her book. This time, she made it past the first couple of pages but not much farther before she fell asleep.

Sitting up, she realized she must have been out for at least an hour. The sun was high in the sky, and the pool was more full of other tourists. She quickly glanced around and noticed a woman a couple of chairs down from her reading a book. The woman noticed Gabby and offered a friendly smile. Gabby smiled back, embarrassed that she had fallen asleep with so many people around.

The brown-haired girl winked as if reading her mind. Then she leaned across the chair separating them and said, "Don't worry, I don't think anyone else noticed."

"Oh good," Gabby said, smiling at the stranger. Her face was familiar. The brunette wavy hair, the tall, slender build. *Oh no, she's the daughter of the festive family.* Gabby tried not to let her dismay show on her face.

"It's so relaxing here," the girl continued as she stretched her tanned, slender arms up toward the sky. "We arrived two days ago, and already I can feel the weight of the world lifting off me."

"We got here yesterday, and it has been nice," Gabby agreed.

The girl lifted her head to the sun and smiled. "I wish I could stay here forever."

Gabby thought about that for a moment. What would it be like to stay here with the beach and palm trees where no one knew her? She wouldn't have to worry about the sad-faced expressions of the people hugging her and asking if she and Jase were okay. She wouldn't have to put on a brave face and say they were fine. The reality was, she wanted to scream at them, "No, we aren't okay! Our world was flipped upside down! And last year, when we both thought we were grown adults, now it seems like a cruel joke." She and Jase felt like lost kids.

"What are you reading?" the girl asked, interrupting Gabby's thoughts.

"I'm sorry, what did you say?"

The festive family's daughter pointed at the book in her hand.

"Oh," Gabby turned her head down to the book she was holding. "*Moby Dick*, it's one of my favorites. I love classic books."

"Me too!" The girl held up her copy of *The Picture of Dorian Gray*.

"Another of my favorites!" Gabby smiled.

They fell into an easy conversation about books, comparing them to the movies made from them. Gabby enjoyed their conversation so much she forgot she had been trying to avoid talking to anyone from that family.

"My mom used to make me read the book before I could see a movie," Gabby surprised herself at being able to talk about her mom so easily.

"That's a great idea."

"It was a blessing and a curse. I usually loved the book so much the movies were always a letdown," Gabby said.

"Oh, I know."

"I read *A Walk to Remember* and sobbed through the last half of the book. I was so excited to see the movie because I liked the actors in it. But when I started watching it, all I could think was, 'Please just die already and end this horrible portrayal of the book.'"

"I know, it's always like that," the girl laughed. "I'm Sophie, by the way," she said, extending her hand to Gabby.

"Gabby," she replied, shaking Sophie's hand.

Sophie's gaze extended past Gabby, and she gave a wave. Gabby turned and saw another member of the festive family walking their way. He was tall and wore golf shorts and a polo. He had the same light brown hair as Sophie. He was tall, tan, clean-cut, with a confident stride. When she first saw the festive family, she had observed that they were an attractive family. Now, without the matching family shirts, she saw just how handsome he was. *I'd wear a caricature of him on my shirt, too,* she thought.

"Hey, nerd," the man teased Sophie as he approached. Sophie rolled her eyes at him as he sat on the lounge chair between them.

"You know you can read anywhere, right? You're missing out on paradise," he said with his arm outstretched to the crystal blue water behind them.

"Reading by the pool is my paradise," Sophie replied.

The man stared at her for a moment and said, "If you say so."

"Really, I'm good here. Besides, I'm making other book nerd friends," Sophie said, gesturing to Gabby.

The man rotated to face Gabby and said, "Hello."

"Gabby, this is my oldest brother, Luke. Luke, this is Gabby," Sophie said with a smile.

Luke smiled at her and held out his hand to shake Gabby's.

Gabby had no idea what to say. She hadn't come here to impress anyone but now had wished she'd managed to do something more than pull her blonde hair into a messy bun and throw on a Defenders visor.

Gabby could feel her face frozen in an unnaturally wide smile. "Hello," she said. She gave a soft giggle as she shook his hand. *A giggle? Really Gabby? Pull it together. You are not here for romance; you are taking time for yourself.* She gave herself a quick mental lecture. She had been around plenty of handsome men before. Her brother's entire team could have been calendar models; some of them actually were. She had never been giggly around any of them.

"Gabby and her husband just got here yesterday," Sophie continued. "How long are you two staying? Through Christmas?"

"Yes, till the day after Christmas. But..." Gabby replied.

Luke's smile faded a bit and said, "I hope you two have a nice trip."

Gabby didn't know what to say. She just sat there like a smiling sculpture while Luke turned his attention back towards his sister.

"Do you want to come golfing with us?" Luke asked Sophie.

"Yeah, no thanks," Sophie replied, shaking her head.

"It'll be fun. You and me versus Dad and Seth," he said, trying to convince her.

"Thanks, maybe next time," Sophie said.

"Fine, we'll come grab you for lunch." Luke relented.

"Sounds good," Sophie said and waved at him.

Luke stood up and glanced back at Gabby. "Nice to meet you, Gabby."

"You too." She managed a regular smile and watched him walk away.

"Brothers." Sophie chuckled.

"You don't like golfing?" Gabby tried to change the subject.

"I love it. Dad made sure we all knew how to play. He said it was an important 'business asset,'" Sophie said, using air quote fingers. "Really, he just liked playing golf, but he also liked having us around."

Gabby thought about everything her dad used to do with her, and she was hit with the pain of sadness.

Sophie continued, "We all might be a little competitive, but golf has taken on a whole new level of competition between the boys. Seth, our younger brother, actually drew blood when he hit Luke in the leg with a club the last time we all went golfing."

"Oh, ouch!" Gabby exclaimed.

"There was only a little blood, but he acted like Seth chopped his leg off. I'm waiting for the retribution. Luke is patient and will wait for just the right moment to strike. Seth is more impulsive and will just react."

"Oh," was all Gabby could say again.

"Do you have siblings?" Sophie asked.

"One brother. He's two years younger," she told Sophie.

"So you get it," Sophie said.

"I sure do." Gabby nodded.

Gabby was about to explain that it was her brother that she was here with, but the moment passed and Sophie moved on to other topics. It's not like they were all going to be hanging out, so it didn't really matter. Gross! She wasn't here for romance. She was never going to see these people again.

Chapter 11: Luke

Luke tried to walk calmly away from the pool, but his thoughts were running. *Of course, the only woman that has made me look twice in forever is married.* It wasn't just that Gabby was beautiful; there was something about her. After ten years in the military, he had gotten good at reading people. He could tell she was real. She seemed like a good person. But, of course, she was married. She was at this amazing resort over Christmas. His family was unusual, still traveling together even as adults. Most people his age were traveling with friends or significant others. Maybe he was feeling a little frustrated since he hadn't expected this year to be like this. He was supposed to have gotten married this past January. Calling it off had been the right thing to do. He didn't love her. She had only loved the idea of him. It had given him the opportunity to focus on his career and his veterans Bible study group. He just needed to stop thinking about it. Move on and enjoy being here with his family.

Every year since Luke was in elementary school, his family had gone away somewhere for Christmas. Usually, they headed north or someplace with lots of snow, and it felt like Christmas. This was the first time they'd done something tropical. He and his siblings had been skeptical, but so far, this place was great. He wasn't sure why they had been hesitant about coming when their original ski trip was canceled at the last minute, and his mom decided to book here.

He might feel a tad different come Christmas with no snow, but right now, at home, it was 30 degrees and snowing. There was no way he'd be in shorts, heading to golf right now.

Gabby was still on his mind when he remembered seeing her and her husband checking in. Sophie had mentioned they seemed disappointed in the resort, which he couldn't understand. He also wondered what kind of people wanted to be away from their families over Christmas. Sure, his family might take things to an extreme, but to not be around any family over the holidays? It seemed weird to him. Probably not the type of person he wanted in his life anyway, he told himself. Gabby didn't come across as that kind of person, though. She actually seemed a little sad. *Why was he still thinking about her?* She is married!

Maybe this was a good thing. It just meant that he was ready to meet someone new. Mentally, financially, physically, and spiritually he was in a good spot. Admittedly, he missed having someone to share life with. And it wasn't like he was going to meet the love of his life 1,000 miles from home, especially while on vacation with his family. She probably lived on the other side of the country... with her husband.

"Luke," his brother Seth called to him. "Let's go."

"I'm coming," Luke yelled back. He walked quickly over to the golf cart where Seth and his dad waited.

"No Sophie?" His dad asked.

"No. I think she was scared of Seth's backswing," Luke said, putting his leg up on the cart and rubbing his leg where the scar from their last outing was.

"Dude, your leg got in the way," Seth defended.

"Whatever," Luke said.

"So there are only three of us," his dad said, stepping between them.

"I guess so," Luke said. He put his golf bag on the cart and noticed a guy at the registration booth by himself.

"Hey man, are you playing alone?" Luke called out to the guy.

The guy glanced at Luke and then his dad and brother before replying, "Uh, yeah."

"We are missing a fourth, want to join us?" Luke asked.

The guy shrugged and hesitated, but then he said, "Sure."

The guy picked up his clubs and walked over to join them.

"I'm Luke. This is my dad, Ben, and my brother, Seth." They all shook hands.

"Nice to meet you guys. I'm Jase," he replied.

"Jase?" Seth asked with a sudden recognition, "Jase Jackson?"

Luke noticed that Jase's body tensed. He seemed uncomfortable with being recognized.

"Yeah, or at least I used to be," Jase replied.

"It's good to meet you," Seth said excitedly. "We used to watch you play at Defenders Stadium."

"Thanks, that feels like a long time ago now," Jase said, pulling at his ball cap.

"We were sorry to hear about your knee. We thought you were going to lead the Defenders to a championship win last year."

"Thanks." Jase looked away, "Me too."

"So, what are you doing now? Are you coming back next season?" Seth asked.

"Well, I um..." Jase trailed off.

Luke could recognize Jase's discomfort and raised an eyebrow at his dad.

His dad caught the meaning and interrupted Seth's questioning. "Enough shop talk, boys, let's go play some golf."

"Good idea," Jase said and loaded his bag on the cart.

CHAPTER 12: JASE

Jase sat stiffly in the golf cart. When the employee had told him he needed a partner or three-man team, he turned his frustration on God.

Thanks God. You couldn't even give me a day of golf?

Then he'd heard a man call out to him and turned to find it was the festive family yet again. *God, you've got to be kidding me*, he thought.

He had almost walked away, but then he thought about his other options or lack of other options. So he decided to tough it out. When they had recognized who he was, he really thought he'd made a mistake.

When Jase saw the lush green fairways overlooking the ocean, he was glad he had made the choice to bring his clubs and actually use them. Once they started playing, Jase relaxed and enjoyed being a normal guy again. To his amazement, he actually had a good time. He discovered he had a lot in common with the Andersons. He enjoyed their competitive spirit, and he couldn't help laughing every time Ben trash-talked to his sons, who were trailing him by five and six strokes.

"So Ben, what do you do when you're not killing them on the course?" Jase asked.

Ben laughed, "I'm actually the principal at South Bay High School."

"Right next door to Lake Harbor?" Jase was shocked. "I've played there many times. But I would not have guessed that you were a principal." Ben was not anything like the principal at Lake Harbor High, his own high school. Ben was fit and easy to be around. He had figured most principals were out of shape, middle-aged men with greasy comb-overs.

"I get that a lot," Ben said with a chuckle. "But these guys have given me a lot of practice dealing with kids. So I try to treat my students like they are my own kids."

"Lies," Seth joked. "You treat them way better than us."

"They listen better than you do," Ben said.

That had Jase cracking up. "How about you, Luke?"

"I followed in the old man's footsteps. I teach high school history and coach JV football and varsity baseball."

Seth jumped in, "Yeah, after you retired from being Captain America."

Jase turned his attention from Seth to Luke, who explained, "I was an Army ranger for eight years before I became a teacher."

Jase was impressed. "I may have to think twice before beating you in golf. I might not be seen again."

They all laughed. "I'm good with losing a fair game... Against anyone other than my family." Ben said.

"How about you, Seth?" Jase asked.

"I'm still deciding," Seth said confidently. "There are so many options. I can't seem to pick just one career."

"He'll figure it out someday," Ben said. Then, looking at his youngest, he added more firmly, "Soon."

Seth shrugged with a grin, "Someday."

Jase gave a small laugh. He could appreciate Seth's uncertainty. If baseball hadn't worked out for Jase, he wasn't sure what he'd be doing with his life.

By the seventeenth hole, Jase was leading the group by four strokes. Ben seemed happy that his sons were tied for the last two strokes behind him. Jase teed off on the last hole and hit a beautiful shot down the fairway.

"Dad, you might have to give up that golden gopher." Seth laughed.

Ben gave his youngest son the glare only dads can give.

"What's the golden gopher?" Jase asked.

"Only the most coveted prize among the Anderson clan," Ben explained, "My daughter won that gopher club cover," he said, pointing at a gopher with a gold medal around its neck.

"She won some girly golf tournament, and that was one of the prizes in her basket," Seth explained. "She kept bragging about it, so we told her we'd play her for it."

"Yeah, but Dad decided to play, too," Luke continued. "And he won."

"It's been the most sought-after prize in the Anderson family ever since," Seth said.

"There's even been blood drawn a few times." Luke pointed at a scar on his leg.

"That's true, but it's been on my club ever since." Ben rubbed the gopher's head proudly.

"How long ago was that?" Jase asked.

"Ten years ago," Ben stated proudly while his sons groaned.

"You guys haven't beaten your dad in ten years?" Jase laughed.

"Nope!" Ben smiled proudly.

"Most parents let their kids win occasionally." Seth poked at his dad with a club.

"My dad used to tell me I'd win when I earned it." Jase felt a sudden grip around his heart when he mentioned his dad.

"Did you ever beat him?" Luke asked.

"No," Jase said quietly. *And now he won't ever get the chance*, he thought.

"That's what I tell these guys, too," Ben said.

Jase gave him a half grin. He couldn't help but think that Ben knew Jase's dad was no longer with him. But how could Ben know? It was just his head playing games with him.

"The guys are right, though," Ben said. "I may lose the golden gopher today."

"Thanks, but I think it should stay in the family," Jase said. He wasn't about to take a family tradition away from someone.

"We're just glad to see someone finally beat him." Luke fake-punched his dad's arm.

"Maybe next time we can play pairs," Seth said.

Jase hesitated. Today was a pleasant surprise. He wasn't sure he could deal with more family fun, though. Yet, for some reason, he agreed. "Sounds like fun."

After they returned the carts, Luke turned and said, "Thanks for playing with us, Jase."

"Thanks for inviting me," Jase said.

"How long are you here for?" Ben asked.

"I'm here until the day after Christmas," Jase told them.

"Us too," Seth chimed in.

"Cool." Jase lifted his clubs over his shoulder. "Well, I'll see you guys around."

As he walked back to his room, Jase noticed that the lightness he had felt while he played was dissipating. By the time he made it back to his room, the dark cloud he'd been living under the past few months was back.

When he walked through the door, he saw Gabby sitting on the patio with her feet dangling in the water. She stood to greet him.

"Hey, were you golfing this whole time?" she asked.

"Yeah, I joined a couple of guys and played eighteen with them," Jase explained.

"That's fun," Gabby said, smiling. "Did you have a good time?"

"I guess," Jase muttered.

Gabby studied his face. Then asked, "Are you okay?"

"I'm fine," he snapped.

"Sounds like it," she said sarcastically.

Jase slammed his clubs into the closet, and he heard Gabby gasp. He paced the living room and rubbed his hands through his dark hair. Gabby stood as still as a statue, watching him.

Jase grabbed a bottle of water, stormed off to his room, and slammed the door behind him. He needed to calm down. He wasn't even sure where this burning anger was coming from, but he could feel it boiling inside. He took some deep breaths, but then he felt himself getting worked up again. A moment later, he burst through the door again, startling his sister, who had moved to sit on the couch.

"It's that festive family," he practically yelled as he paced the floor.

"What about them?" She asked softly.

"They just, they're just…" he stopped and plopped onto the couch next to his sister and let out a sigh. "Just that they exist."

"I get it," Gabby said softly.

"Look at us," Jase said in a mocking voice. "We have fun together with our dad. Our dad is still here to play with us. Our mom made these ridiculous matching shirts that we love showing off. We love having our faces on stupid tiny cartoon bodies doing stupid fun things together. We're just so awesome." Jase flung himself against the back of the couch, rubbing his hands on his face. He let out a loud "Arrrgh!"

This made Gabby laugh but quickly stopped when he glared at her. "Did you see them again?"

"Yes," he grunted.

"Where?" she asked.

"I played golf with them."

"You played golf with Luke and his dad?"

"Yeah, and his brother Seth…" Jase said, lifting his head off the couch. "Wait, how do you know Luke's name?"

"I met Sophie, their sister, by the pool," she explained. "Luke came to see if she wanted to play golf with them."

"I wish she had, so they wouldn't have asked me."

"Were they as awful as the shirts?"

"No, they were awesome," Jase admitted, throwing his head into his hands. "But then all I could think about was that I wish Dad were here playing with us."

He was so irritated with himself. He felt guilty about having fun, but he liked feeling normal again, even for a few moments.

"Jase, you're allowed to have fun," Gabby said, moving closer to her brother and putting an arm around him.

"It's just..." he trailed off.

"I know. Why do we still get to have fun when Mom and Dad can't?"

"Yeah."

"Mom and Dad were amazing. Do you think they'd want us to be in paradise not having fun?"

"No," Jase said.

"No, they wouldn't. They are up in Heaven having the best time ever, and we are in paradise here on Earth, and we need to try to have fun too."

He grunted in response. Leave it to his sister to sound like the people they were trying to get away from.

"I say we try having fun. Can we do that?" Gabby pleaded. "If not, and you want to go home, we can go home. I will book us on the next available flight, and we can be home tomorrow."

Jase thought for a moment about what being at home would be like right now. The whole town would be preparing for Christmas and inviting them to things. He would be sitting in their big, empty, quiet house.

"No, I want to stay." He sighed.

"You sure? I know it's more Christmas-y than we were expecting."

"It's still better than being at home right now."

"I think so too." Gabby stood up. "Why don't we get dinner? I'm starving."

Jase glanced up at his sister. Even with him sitting and her standing, she was barely taller than him.

"Okay." He stood and gave his sister a hug. "Sorry."

"For what? Having emotions? Jase, we've had the worst year ever. Emotions are going to happen. But we're here for each other... always."

"I know," he said. He couldn't understand why Gabby never let her emotions get out of control. She was always fine. *Why is she always fine? Why can't I be more like her?* he wondered.

Gabby wrapped her arms tighter around his waist and gave him a big squeeze. "Love you."

"Love you," Jase replied.

CHAPTER 13: GABBY

Gabby saw the sign for the Parilla Estrella, and the aroma of something delicious being grilled hit her about the same time. Her stomach gave a low growl when she caught the aroma of a charcoal grill. Whatever was on it smelled delicious.

"I think you'll like this place," Gabby said. "It has food stations from all over the world,"

"Does it have prime rib and potatoes?" Jase asked.

Gabby rolled her eyes. He'd never been adventurous in his choice of cuisine. She laughed and hooked her arm through his. As they approached the restaurant, she stopped. Standing at the entrance to the restaurant was the entire Anderson family. They weren't matching this time, but they could still grace the cover of a magazine with their good looks. Gabby tried to turn around, but her arm was still hooked into her brothers, causing her to slip and land with a thud on the tile floor.

Jase peered down to his sister, clearly trying to hold back a laugh. "What was that?"

"Did they see that?" she squeaked.

"Who?" Jase scanned the lobby to see who she could have seen. He laughed when he saw the cause of his sister's slip-n-fall. "The Anderson family?"

"Umm, yeah," she groaned.

The entire family walked over to them.

"Are you okay?" Luke said as he quickly stepped over to Gabby and Jase.

"Yeah, thanks." Gabby straightened her skirt.

"You sure?" Luke asked.

"Oh yeah, I fall professionally." Gabby tried to laugh it off.

"That is true," Jase said. "She's the only gymnast I know who can land flips on a four-inch beam but can't stand on her own two feet on solid ground."

"A gymnast, huh?" Luke smiled at her with a questioning eyebrow raised.

"Retired. I haven't been a gymnast since college," Gabby said. She shot Jase an annoyed scowl.

Gabby returned her attention to Luke and noticed the rest of the Anderson family standing with him. The man she assumed was their father took a step towards them.

"Jase, I was hoping we'd run into you again," the man said. "I just wasn't expecting it to be so soon."

"Hey, Ben," Jase said. "Yeah, me neither."

"This is my wife, Olivia, and daughter, Sophie," Ben said. He turned to take his wife's hand, bringing her to stand next to him. Sophie took a step forward to be next to her mom. "This is Jase, the one I was telling you about earlier."

"So nice to meet you, Jase." Olivia beamed at him.

"Nice to meet you ladies, too," he replied. Gabby noticed Jase used his charming Mr. Baseball voice.

"Hi," Gabby smiled and gave a wave to Sophie.

"Hi, Gabby," Sophie said. And explained that she'd met Gabby at the pool and gave a quick introduction to everyone else in her family.

"Would you two like to join us for dinner?" Olivia asked sweetly.

"Oh no, we wouldn't want to intrude." Gabby carefully turned to her brother and pleaded with her eyes for him to agree with her.

Olivia continued, "I'd like to hear about this golf game that should have lost my husband his prized golden gopher." She poked her husband in the ribs.

"Join us." Sophie smiled at Gabby and Jase, waiting for a response.

"Well..." Gabby hesitated. She peered up at her brother, who just shrugged.

"That's fine," Jase nodded.

"Fantastic!" Olivia smiled. Then she headed toward the hostess stand.

"Are you good with this?" Gabby whispered, taking her brother's arm again.

"It's fine. They were fun on the course," he murmured back.

"You sure?"

"Yes." He stated this as if he were trying to convince himself, as well as her. "Besides, you literally fell over yourself when you saw Luke. I think you like him."

"What?" Gabby defended. "I do not."

"Really? What was that spin move to the ground about, then?"

"The floor was slippery," Gabby insisted.

"Sure it was," Jase smirked at her. "He seems like a good guy. Just give him a chance."

"A chance for what? I'm here to relax, not...."

Gabby was interrupted by Olivia's cheerful voice saying, "Our table is ready."

They all sat down and placed drink orders. Ben led them in saying grace before they separated to explore the different food stations from around the world. Though Gabby had teased Jase about expanding his horizons, they both ended up with prime rib and crab legs. The Andersons all chose different selections from around the world. Gabby observed their plates and was scared to ask what some of the items were. Mostly, she was afraid they'd ask if she wanted to try them. Her parents had a strict rule about always trying new foods at least once. She and Jase didn't have to eat the dish again if they didn't like it, but they at least had to sample it if it was offered.

Just like earlier, Gabby and Sophie fell into an easy conversation. There was a lot of laughter as everyone rated their various food selections and shared stories of past food disasters. Gabby was delighted to see Jase enjoy himself. It was nice to laugh with him again. He even joined the fun, giving a lively rendition about their first experience eating oysters. While Jase had found a new favorite food in oysters, Gabby had a completely different reaction to the slime in the shell and spit hers out. Unfortunately, it landed on the shoulder of a man sitting near them. Gabby still felt the embarrassment of that moment.

The conversation eventually moved from food to the different places the Andersons had celebrated Christmas.

"We both come from big families," Olivia shared. "Every year, we dreaded the holidays, running from family to family or hosting everyone at our house. It felt like all the craziness took away from the meaning of Christmas. So, we started our own tradition. We escaped. We make it up to our families and friends with a huge New Year's party each year. But Christmas is ours. We go somewhere different every year and just enjoy each other as a family." She smiled lovingly at each of her children. The adoration she had for each of them brought a lump to Gabby's throat.

"That's really sweet," Gabby whispered.

"It's funny," Olivia continued, "we weren't even supposed to be here this year. We had booked a cabin at a ski resort. Then, the day after Thanksgiving, our travel agent called. She said that the people renting out the cabin had double-booked it, and we lost the reservation. Instead, she told us she had something exciting in mind that was tropical. It was a great deal, so here we are!"

How interesting, Gabby thought. Holly had shown her this resort on the same day. Her friend would say that was the hand of God. "What brings you two here?" Ben asked, interrupting her thoughts.

Gabby and Jase exchanged a knowing look and gave a nervous laugh before Gabby explained for them. "We are escaping Christmas too." She hoped that they wouldn't pry further than that. When all eyes remained on her, she added, "We wanted to escape all the holiday hustle and bustle too." There was a chorus of "Oh yeah" and "For sure" that let Gabby breathe a sigh of relief. Thankfully, no one pressed for more. She didn't want to ruin the mood or have to explain about the accident and the real reason they were escaping Christmas. Gabby knew how quickly mentioning dead parents sucked all the air out of a room. She was grateful that, at least for now, her answer had appeased everyone and let the conversation continue in the playful nature it had been all evening.

"This is so fun," Sophie told Gabby. "We should get together when we get home."

"When we get home?" Gabby asked, feeling a little confused. How would they do that? They didn't even know where they lived. It could be 500 miles away.

"My brothers said that you and Jase live in Lake Harbor," Sophie said.

"We do," Gabby replied slowly, still confused.

"We live in South Bay." Sophie squealed with delight. "We're practically neighbors."

"We are!" Gabby said excitedly. They really could get together when they get home. She thought about how well Sophie would get along with Holly.

Gabby discovered throughout dinner that Ben was the principal at South Bay High School. She had been close to having guessed their ages. Luke was 31, a history teacher, and coached at South Bay. He earned his teaching degree while serving eight years in the Army. If that wasn't impressive enough, he earned his master's in athletic administration when he got out of the military. He has a goal of being an athletic director but thought he'd miss the daily interaction with the kids. Gabby's heart melted a little listening to him talk about the satisfaction he got helping his students and players achieve their goals.

Sophie was 29 and had earned her master's in education, but chose to teach at the middle school. Olivia had been a stay-at-home mom until she got her real estate license while Seth was in high school. Now she had a thriving business, and she worked out of their home. Seth, at 24, was a free spirit. He graduated college with a business degree but hadn't figured out exactly what type of business he wanted to be in. He was happy working jobs as a lifeguard in the summer and ski instructor in the winter. Gabby admired Seth's joy for life.

This is going well, Gabby thought. Everyone around the table seemed like they were having a wonderful time until...

"So, how long have you two been married?" Sophie asked, her eyes darting back and forth between Jase and Gabby.

Gabby could feel the blood draining from her face. *Why had she not come clean at the pool?* Jase was going to kill her.

Her fear was confirmed when he nearly spit his drink out and sputtered, "What?! Who?"

The Anderson family all stopped talking and stared at Jase, then to her.

Gabby wanted to crawl under the table. *She could do that, right? She could just live there forever and never come out.*

"You and Gabby?" Sophie tilted her head, waving her finger between Gabby and Jase.

"Gabby is my sister," Jase spit out, wiping his drink off his chin and shirt.

"Sister?" Sophie and Luke asked simultaneously.

This was just getting worse, Gabby thought, still unable to form words to explain.

"What is happening here?" Jase asked, still confused at how this conversation got here.

Everyone was staring at her now. Gabby's face burned with heat as she continued twisting the ring on her finger.

"This is my mom's wedding ring." She paused, unsure how to explain without telling them about their parents.

Gabby was relieved when Olivia smiled at her, saying, "It's a beautiful ring."

"So you're not married?" Sophie asked.

Gabby gave an embarrassed laugh. "No, I'm sorry, I should have corrected you at the pool. I was caught up in the conversation, and the moment passed and I didn't think to correct it."

"Talking about books will do that," Sophie laughed

"It will," Gabby agreed softly. She moved her eyes slowly to Jase. He stared sharply at her and shook his head in disbelief. She gave him a weak smile and turned her attention back to her plate. Dinner had been going so well until that moment.

Gabby was grateful that everyone at the table had been able to laugh about the misunderstanding and resumed their conversations. Well, almost everyone. Gabby could still feel her brother's eyes boring into her.

After dinner, Gabby and Jase walked in silence back to their room. Gabby tried to stay a step ahead of her brother but could feel him staring intensely at her. Not two steps into the room, Jase started.

"You told them we were married?" Jase said quizzically.

"No," Gabby said with her hands on her hips.

Jase raised an eyebrow at her.

"I didn't say we were married... I just didn't correct Sophie when she assumed we were."

"Why not?" he scoffed.

"Sophie and I were talking, and then Luke was there and..." Gabby trailed off. She knew she didn't have any excuse that would make sense to Jase.

"Ha!" Jase laughed. "I knew you liked him."

"What? No."

"You always do this. You find a way to keep guys you like at arm's length."

"I don't even know him," Gabby said. "All I know is what I learned at dinner."

"I just know how you are. You at least think you could like him."

Gabby crossed her arms. "You are crazy. I'm not here to...."

"Yeah, yeah, yeah, you're not here to meet someone."

Gabby had no defense. Jase was right. She hasn't let a man get close in years.

"Anyway. I'm going to go to read on the patio," Gabby said.

"I told Seth I'd meet him for a drink and maybe go play pool or something."

Gabby was happy to see her brother doing something besides playing video games and found herself overly excited about it. "Good! Go have fun!"

Jase gave her a half grin. "Thanks."

"I'm going on the 8:00 am snorkeling tour tomorrow if you want to join me."

"8:00 am... yeah, no. But thanks," Jase laughed.

"Then I'll see you when I get back. We can go to the pool and get lunch or something."

"Sounds good. Night, Gabs." Jase turned and walked out of the room.

Gabby grabbed her book and went out the door to sit on the patio. She dangled her feet in the water, gently drifting by their room, and the warm breeze swept around her. It was dark out, but she could still hear the waves. She tried to enjoy the moment, but Jase's words crept back into her head. "You never let anyone close." That might be true, but she was busy. She had work, and Jase, and the house, and... well, even before the accident she didn't have time. As she thought of Luke's incredible smile, she thought maybe she was ready to make the time. Maybe...

She was still replaying the evening over in her head when she went to bed. She tossed and turned all night. When her alarm went off at 6:30 am, she decided to shake off the embarrassment from yesterday and have a good day.

She hadn't heard her brother come back last night, and she wondered if he actually had. She put on her green two-piece bathing suit, sheer, black cover-up, and her favorite sun visor. Then she filled her bag with her towel and snorkeling gear and left her room.

She wasn't surprised to see Jase snoring on the couch in the living room. While the couch was nicely cushioned, it was barely wide enough for his whole body. *What was his deal about not sleeping in a bed anyways?* Even when they were little, he would sleep on the floor, bean bag chairs, couch, or nearly anywhere but his bed.

"Jase?" she whispered and gave his shoulder a shake. No reaction.

"Jase?" She tried again and was greeted with a low grunt. Finally, his eyes cracked open.

"Good morning," she sang.

He rolled in toward the couch and murmured, "Go away." He never had been a morning person.

"You sure you don't want to go snorkeling with me?"

He responded by taking the small pillow he had curled into his arm and hitting her with it.

It was barely a tap, but it made Gabby stumble backward and trip over the table before landing on her backside again.

"Oh!" Gabby groaned.

Jase didn't move. He just grumbled, "Is there blood?"

Gabby laughed. That had been their parents' response whenever they heard things get knocked around the house. Unless there was blood, they probably weren't going to check. Not making a fuss over the little injuries toughened them up, her mother had claimed.

"No blood," she replied.

"Good, then you won't get eaten by sharks."

"So you really don't want to come?

"Go. Have fun."

"You too." Gabby picked up her bag, slipped on her flip-flops, and headed to the dock.

CHAPTER 14: LUKE

Luke was having breakfast with his parents on the patio of the Anderson family's villa. He noticed a woman walking on the path. It was Gabby. *Where is she off to so early in the morning,* he wondered. Watching her continue down the path, he caught a glimpse of a snorkel and fins peeking out of her bag. He pushed his plate away and announced, "I think I'm going to skip golf and do some snorkeling."

"Snorkeling?" His parents asked simultaneously. They followed the direction of Luke's gaze to see Gabby walking down to the docks. His dad smirked at him and said, "You enjoy snorkeling, son."

"What?" Luke asked defensively.

"I didn't say anything." His dad held his hands up in defense. "It just seems like a good day for snorkeling."

"It does," his dad nodded, still smiling. "I've just never known you to be such a big fan of deep water."

"I don't know what you're talking about," Luke said.

This was true, though. He wasn't proud to admit that he didn't care for the water. Lakes and pools were cool, but the ocean was a whole different beast. He considered jumping into the ocean the equivalent of breaching a building in the Army. He wasn't invited. The people inside didn't want him there and were probably going to fight back. The ocean was the sharks' home, and he hadn't been invited to jump in. Especially since, unlike the Army, there was no intel team monitoring the ocean letting him know the best plan. But it could be worth it to be able to get to know Gabby better, especially since she was not married to Jase.

When Luke arrived at the marina, he was directed to Dock 3. Once he found it, he stepped onto the wooden dock and saw a sign towards the end for "Cruise Cozumel" in front of a big white boat.

As he approached a man with a white linen shirt and wide brimmed straw hat leaned over the side of the boat and waved him towards him. He was a middle-aged man with a deep tan and a small beard. "Captain Rivera."

"Buenos dias," he said with a big smile and heavy Mexican accent. "Are you here for the snorkel?"

"Yes, I am," Luke said.

"Welcome." The man reached a hand out to help Luke aboard.

"Thank you," Luke replied as he boarded the ship.

The captain peered behind Luke then down the dock, then back to him and asked, "Solo Uno? Alone?"

"Si, yes, I'm here alone." Luke wondered if that seemed odd to the captain. He was almost embarrassed until the captain spoke again.

"Ah, no worries my friend. I am Captain Rivera, and I will introduce you to all the single señoritas," the captain said, doing a little samba dance.

This made Luke laugh. He liked the captain immediately and was sure he was a tourist favorite.

"You are even in luck, my friend," Captain Rivera continued. "There was a very pretty señorita that is here alone too. Go make friends."

He pointed Luke towards the front of the boat, informing him they'd leave right at 8:00 am. Luke thanked him and started scanning the boat for Gabby. He noticed her lounged at the front of the boat.

Luke stopped at the bar and picked up a couple of lemonades. Then he walked over, not sure what to say. He was standing over her awkwardly. She suddenly looked up from where she was sitting and noticed him.

"Oh!" Gabby gasped.

"I didn't think my hair was that bad in the morning," Luke joked.

Gabby shaded her eyes, and recognition crossed her face. "Oh, hi Luke."

"Good morning," he smiled at her and handed her a cup.

"What's this?" She took the cup of pink liquid with green specks.

"Strawberry mint lemonade," Luke said, taking a sip of his own glass. "Pretty good."

Gabby eyed the pink liquid then took a sip. "Thanks," Gabby said. Her gaze searched the area around him. "Is your family here too?"

"No, my parents and Sophie have a 9:00 am tee time, and as you can imagine, Seth will probably be sleeping till dinner."

She laughed. "Jase might be as well. Didn't you go out with them?"

"I went for one game of pool then left. I can't hang with the owls anymore. I've always been more of a morning person," Luke said, sitting next to her.

"Me too. 10:00 pm is late for me."

They sat in silence for a moment. Luke wasn't sure where to go from here. "So, you're going snorkeling, then?"

Really Luke? He cringed. *That's the best you can manage? Of course she's going snorkeling; it's a snorkeling excursion.*

"Snorkeling? I thought this was the whale hunting boat?" She said seriously.

"Haha, Ishmael," Luke said, referencing Moby Dick.

"Does that make you Queequeg then?"

Luke was surprised and impressed. "You've read Moby Dick?"

"Of course I have," Gabby gasped, acting offended and holding her hand over her heart.

"I didn't mean..."

"I know, but yes. Moby Dick is one of my favorites. I'm actually reading it again now," she said, pulling her copy out of her bag to show him.

"Mine too. I love the way that Melville brings all the characters to life. Even the ship took on a life of its own."

Captain Rivera called for final boarding, and the boat finally shoved off.

"I hope our sea vessel doesn't meet the same fate as the Pequod," Luke said.

"I hope not either, but I think we'll be okay," Gabby smiled at him.

The boat glided through the water toward the reef. Luke could see Gabby relaxing. The water was obviously her happy place.

Luke, on the other hand, hoped she hadn't noticed he was gripping the railing as if his life depended on it.

"You okay there, Ishmael?" Gabby asked, observing his white knuckles.

"Oh, yeah," Luke glanced nervously at the water and tightened his grip on the rail. "This is good."

"Are you not a fan of the water?"

"I am, I love it. It's not the water, it's the sea creatures that could swallow me whole if they wanted."

"I think we're safe here. This reef won't have anything that can swallow you whole."

Luke sighed, "Fantastic."

"They'll just nibble you off piece by piece," Gabby teased.

"What?" Luke's voice raised up a couple octaves.

"I'm kidding, you'll be fine. I'll protect you from the scary fishies."

"Are you mocking me?"

"A little, yes," Gabby said, offering a sweet smile. "If you don't like water..."

"It's not the water,"

"I'm sorry, if you don't like the sea creatures, why are you going snorkeling?"

Luke knew he couldn't say, *I saw you and followed you.* He was so out of practice. He didn't know what to do or say, but now he was sitting here not saying anything. Gabby probably thought he was an idiot who couldn't form words. *Say something, anything.*

"I just thought it would be a good time to start overcoming fears." That was the best answer he could come up with.

"Good for you," Gabby said. "I need to start doing more of that too."

"Oh yeah? What scares you?"

"Spiders."

"Spiders?"

"Yes, it doesn't matter what size, in my mind they are all out to kill me." Gabby shivered.

Luke laughed. "Okay, spiders. Anything else?"

Gabby stared at him a moment. He knew there was something there and wondered if she'd tell him. She opened her mouth and was about to say something when there was an announcement over the speaker.

"This is Captain Rivera; if you haven't retrieved snorkeling gear, please see Juan, and he will get you fitted. We will be arriving at the reef in five minutes."

"Do you need gear?" Luke asked.

"No, I brought my own," she said and reached into her bag, producing a mask and fins.

"Of course you did. I'll be right back." He got up, still curious about what she was going to say.

CHAPTER 15: GABBY

Gabby watched Luke walk over to get his equipment. She was surprised to find herself so relaxed around him. She couldn't remember the last time she felt so at ease with a man. She was always concerned about doing and saying the right things. Around Luke, she was just Gabby. Gabby who made corny jokes that no one usually understood.

Luke came back with his mask on and muttered through the snorkel, "Does this make me look funny?"

Gabby couldn't help but laugh, but put on a serious face and said, "Not at all. You pull it off well."

He took off the mask and pulled his shirt over his head. *Whoa,* Gabby had not expected to see such a well-defined body under his shirt and felt her face flush.

Luke asked, "You ready?"

"Yeah." Gabby was embarrassed for ogling him, so she turned away and said, "Let's do this."

After the boat was anchored, she and Luke waited while the other passengers were in the water before making their way to the entry platform. Gabby had her underwater camera strapped to her wrist, ready to dive in. Luke, she noticed, was a little hesitant.

"I'll get in first and wait for you," Gabby reassured him.

"I'll be right behind you."

Gabby lowered herself into the water and gracefully pushed away from the boat. She turned and treaded water, waiting for Luke to join her. She wasn't sure how he managed to look so goofy in the mask and fins and so handsome at the same time. Juan was explaining to Luke how to enter the water when, with a giant splash, he fell in, not so gracefully.

Gabby gasped.

Luke surfaced, coughing up water.

"Oh my gosh, are you alright?" Gabby asked, trying not to laugh.

"Great," he sputtered. He managed to get his mask and snorkel back into place and swim his way over to Gabby.

"I don't think you have to worry about the little fishies," Gabby chuckled.

"No? Why not?"

"Pretty sure your belly flop scared them all away."

"Sorry about that."

"Don't worry about it. I'm sure they have bigger things than you crash in after them," she teased.

"What?" Luke asked with a nervous laugh. Gabby remembered him not being fond of the idea that there could be giant sea creatures.

"You know..." Gabby said, trying to think quickly to reassure him that it was safe. "Boats and rafts and things."

Luke eyed her skeptically. "Yeah, boats and things."

"Ready?" Gabby asked with a big smile.

"Sure."

They put their snorkels in and started off to explore the reef. It was so beautiful, with the bright corals, seagrass, and colorful fish swimming alongside them. Gabby was excited to see that Luke seemed to be enjoying himself as he glided through the water. She dove down to take photos of some iridescent fish when a stingray floated by, and she took some shots of it. She was excited to find a couple seahorses floating in the reef. The biggest thrill for her, though, was when a huge sea turtle swam by her. On her way up, she gracefully glided around Luke, taking a few shots of him. He was cute trying to pose for her in the weightlessness of the water.

They both surfaced. His smile was so genuine she had to smile back.

"This isn't so bad, is it?" Gabby asked.

"No, it's really beautiful down there; I'm not sure what I was so nervous about."

"It's so amazing," Gabby said. She loved every moment of this.

"You are," Luke said

"What?"

"You are very at ease in the water," Luke stammered. "Even with the mask and snorkel covering your face, I can see how happy this makes you. Like you really belong here."

"It's my happy place. My parents used to joke that I was part mermaid." Her smile faded at the sudden thought of her parents. Luke must have noticed because he swam a little closer. She forced a smile and continued, "I used to think if I prayed hard enough that I would grow a fin in the water, like in the movie Splash."

Luke laughed, "I think you might be part mermaid."

"Are you ready to explore more?" Gabby was ready to return to the beauty of the sea and leave the sad memories behind.

"You bet," Luke appeared to be genuinely excited to go back down there.

Gabby and Luke searched the reefs, and Gabby snapped more photos. They took an underwater selfie with a sea turtle. Gabby even caught a couple of photos of Luke looking like he was talking with a giant grouper and, to her surprise, he didn't take off swimming for the hills. Luke seemed to find it all amazing and not at all the same guy who had been hesitant to get into the water.

Luke smiled over at Gabby, waved, and reached down for the starfish beneath him. Suddenly, he gave a bubbly scream and started kicking towards the boat at top speed. Startled by this, Gabby scanned the reef for the cause of his distress when she spotted the baby nurse shark slithering across the ocean floor. It was so cute, she snapped a few photos of it. It couldn't have been more than two feet long. But for someone who wasn't altogether comfortable with the sealife, she could see how this baby shark probably resembled Jaws.

Gabby swam back to the boat to check on Luke, who had already managed to climb into the boat and wrapped himself in a towel.

She approached him gently when she got back onboard, "You okay?"

"I'm good," he started, "For someone who was almost attacked by a shark."

She stifled a laugh, "It was just a baby nurse shark. They won't hurt you."

"That was a baby?"

"Mhm."

Luke seemed to be embarrassed by his reaction to the shark. Gabby was equal parts entertained and concerned.

He reached for Gabby's towel and put it around her shoulders. "Aside from Jaws, this was actually pretty fun."

Gabby smiled at him. "I'm glad you enjoyed yourself. I'll have to send you the photos from today."

"I'd like that, thanks," he said. "What are you doing when we get back?"

"Probably going to see if Jase is awake and if he wants lunch."

"I should probably see what my family is doing too. Maybe we could all have lunch together?"

Gabby's smile faded a bit when she thought of not having her whole family here. Her parents would have loved this. Luke must have noticed the change of expression.

"Are you okay?" Luke asked.

"I'm fine," Gabby put on a smile and hoped she sounded convincing. "Lunch all together sounds good."

"If you ever want to talk," Luke started slowly, "I've been told I'm a good listener."

"Thanks," Gabby said. It had been a long time since she'd opened up to anyone. Part of her wanted to talk, but part of her wondered if she'd ever be ready.

CHAPTER 16: GABBY

Gabby took a deep breath as the boat docked. She gathered her stuff and lined up behind the passengers waiting to disembark. Captain Rivera was handing something to each person as they left. When Gabby reached the front, the captain handed her a little starfish painted like Santa. Gabby thought about all the starfish they had just spotted while snorkeling.

Captain Rivera said, "Don't worry, señorita. These special estrellas de mar were found washed up on the beaches. They needed a new home, si?"

She smiled and gladly accepted the ornament.

"Muchas gracias, Capitan," she said, thanking the captain for a great trip.

"These are fun. My mom will love this," Luke said, observing the Santa starfish with a smile.

Gabby held her starfish, rubbing her thumb over the ridges. This was exactly the type of thing she would have loved to decorate with at home. It was something to remind her of this wonderful excursion. But they were festive-free and keeping the ornament felt like a betrayal to her brother. Quickly, she handed hers to Luke. "Here, you can have mine too."

He seemed confused. "I can't take this. Besides, it seems like something you'd really love." He put the starfish back in her hand.

"I can't," she insisted, handing the starfish back to him.

"Can't?"

"My brother and I came here to escape Christmas," she started. "And this is too festive for the Christmas-free zone."

Luke raised an eyebrow and asked, "Do you really hate Christmas?"

"No." Gabby tried to compose herself as she sat down on a bench. "I used to love Christmas. My house would be a replica of Santa's workshop. I love making decorations and gifts for people. I love baking and the lights. I loved it all."

Luke sat down next to her and waited for her to continue.

"My parents died earlier this year in a car accident. Jase and I moved into their house to take care of things and each other. Thanksgiving was miserable. All of our friends and our parents' friends were calling and texting to remind us how hard it was without our parents there." Gabby took a deep breath then gave a short laugh. "Like we didn't know how miserable or how hard it was."

Luke took her hand. He didn't say anything, just let her continue.

"My mom made a huge deal out of holidays, especially Thanksgiving and Christmas. Everything was always perfect. I tried to do it this year, but I didn't know that you had to let a turkey thaw so long before Thanksgiving day."

They both laughed over that, and she went on. "So, my best friend convinced me that getting away, out of the house and the office and the town with emotional memory bombs at every turn, was a good idea. So Jase and I decided, no Christmas this year. We showed up here, somehow thinking Christmas didn't exist in the tropics and...."

"It's still here," Luke finished her sentence.

She'd finally said it out loud. Her parents were gone. They weren't coming back. And once she said it, she could feel the tears. But refused to let them fall.

Gabby took a deep breath, giving herself a moment to re-group, then continued, "And now I'm on a dock in paradise, complaining about my life to a stranger."

Luke wrapped an arm around her shoulder. "You saved my life from a giant deadly shark; we aren't strangers anymore."

Gabby thought back to the cute baby shark. "Yes, I saved you from getting eaten alive," rolling her eyes but smiling a little. She appreciated that Luke wasn't trying to give her a pep talk about how her parents were in a better place, watching over them, or that they wouldn't want Gabby and Jase to not celebrate. That might all be true, but being on the receiving end of such thoughts didn't make anyone feel better.

Gabby sat next to Luke, grateful for his silence.

"I got it," Luke said, making her jump a little. "I can't make Christmas disappear. And I'm pretty sure the resort will call the cops and kick me out if I destroy the decorations...but there are tons of things to do here that don't involve holidays. We'll do them all."

"I can't hijack your Christmas too. You're here with your family." She didn't want her misery to infect their family Christmas. Not that she wouldn't mind spending the time with him, but still.

"It'll be fine. Besides, I always wanted to help harbor a fugitive."

"A fugitive?"

"A fugitive from Christmas," he said.

This made them both laugh.

She couldn't believe this person, who was a complete stranger, was willing to give up all the family fun to help her escape from Christmas.

"Okay, sounds like fun," Gabby agreed.

"So what are you doing now?" Luke asked.

"Lunch. I'm starving after all that shark fighting."

"Ha ha..." Luke gave a mocking laugh.

"Do you still want to go to lunch?" She asked, hopeful that he did.

"I definitely do. I'll grab my family, and you get Jase, and we'll meet at that Cantina place in about an hour, if that works for you."

"Sure, I'd like that." Gabby smiled at him. She actually felt excited about seeing him again.

"Great," Luke said as he stood up. Extending his hand to help her to her feet, he picked up her beach bag, slinging it over his shoulder. "Come on."

Gabby walked next to him along the path back to the resort area. She was grateful that his demeanor hadn't changed towards her when she told him about her parents. When they got to the point on the path they had to go different directions, he handed her the beach bag.

"So I will see you in a little bit?"

"See you in a bit," Gabby said and felt like she floated all the way back to her room.

CHAPTER 17: JASE

J ase was lounging on the couch, flipping through TV channels. He'd had a decent time last night with Luke and Seth. Hanging out with the guys made him realize that he missed his team. Playing a game of pool and kicking back with his teammates felt like a lifetime ago.

Then he remembered one of the last vacations with his family about ten years ago. It was after a tournament in Florida. His parents decided they should stay a few extra days after the tournament was over and hang out as a family. His dad said they were getting older and didn't know how many more chances they'd have to do vacations together. Jase had been irritated when they made him stay rather than fly back with his team. But he ended up having a great time. They only stayed an extra three days but had fun like they had when they were little kids. They must have played 15 rounds of putt-putt and eaten 10 pounds of crab legs in those three days. He remembered when they were leaving for the airport how he wished they could stay a few more days. His dad had been right, though. After those three days, there had only been one more family vacation. Life happened. They were all busy. Even though his parents and Gabby had still traveled to see him play ball, it wasn't the same as having time just to be a family. He wished he'd made the time to do that. He'd give anything for his parents to be here on this vacation.

His thoughts were interrupted when he heard Gabby walk in.

"Hey," he said. "What have you been up to?"

"Hey there," Gabby said quietly.

Gabby dropped her bag in a chair and sat down on the coffee table. "I went snorkeling."

"Did you have fun?"

"I did. It was beautiful. I'll have to show you the photos later." She smiled as she described exploring the reef.

Jase sat up, observing her as she talked about the fish and the turtles. She was smiling, like really smiling. He hadn't seen her like this since, well, he couldn't remember the last time she had smiled like this.

"Luke was there," he interrupted her.

"What?"

"Luke went snorkeling with you."

"I mean, he didn't come with me..."

"But he was there."

"Yes, he was there too." Gabby blushed.

"And his family?"

"No, just him."

"Hmm...." Jase smirked at his sister. "Did you have a good time with him?"

"I did." Gabby smiled. But then her eyes dropped to the floor, and she was twisting her ring.

"But...?" Jase asked, sitting up to look at her.

"Umm," Gabby hesitated. "I kind of told Luke about Mom and Dad."

"You did?" Jase was more surprised than angry.

"I did. I was just...and he was...." Gabby clearly was struggling to describe what had happened.

"Did it make things weird?" he asked curiously.

He was sure his sister knew what he was asking. A strange thing happened when you told people that someone close to you had died. Most people didn't know what to do or say, so they ended up saying the most random things, usually the wrong things.

"No, he was actually really comforting and didn't say anything. He just listened," Gabby said.

"Good. I told you he was a good guy." Jase smirked at his sister.

"I never said he wasn't."

"Whatever you say."

"I'm just not looking for..."

Jase threw his head back with a grunt. "I know, I know."

He just sat there, silent. *Why did she have to be so frustrating sometimes?* It shouldn't surprise him. She never wanted to show if she was too happy or too sad. It was like she waited for permission to have emotions.

"Anyway, do you want to grab lunch?" Gabby asked.

"That's a great idea. I'm starving," Jase said, grateful to talk about something else. He rose and headed to his room to change. Keeping the door cracked, he could hear his sister still talking to him.

"Being out all night will do that to you. What time did you guys get in?"

"I'm not sure," Jase said. Slightly irritated that she was questioning him like Mom would have. He was a grown adult and hadn't had to answer to anyone about what time he got in since high school.

"Did you have fun?"

"It was good to get out. And Luke and Seth were cool."

Jase felt surprised that he actually did have fun. He'd enjoyed their company. He wasn't just saying it to appease his sister. This is what he needed to get out of the rut he'd been in. *Maybe this trip was just what they both needed after all*, he thought. He finished getting changed and walked back into the living room. Gabby was leaning over the back of the couch facing him.

"I'm glad you had a good time with them." She gave him a small smile.

"Yeah, me too," Jase said, sliding his feet into his flip-flops.

"I kind of told them we'd join them for lunch," Gabby said, biting her lip.

"You did?" Jase wasn't sure how he felt about that. Luke and Seth were cool, but being around the whole family still made him feel a little sad and angry. On the other hand, it would distract Gabby from talking about the things they needed to talk about... the stuff he wasn't ready to talk about yet. He knew they had agreed not to, but he also knew keeping Gabby distracted would ensure those topics wouldn't be brought up.

"Are you okay with that? If not, I can call and tell them no," Gabby asked

"Yeah, that's fine," he said. He couldn't help thinking that maybe she was avoiding being alone with him too.

"Then I'm gonna shower and change too," she said. Getting up off the couch, he watched her go to her room.

He missed when things were easier between them. He remembered when they were in elementary school, they fought a lot. As punishment, their mom would put them on the couch, make them hold hands, and say nice things to each other. It made him chuckle thinking about that now. They'd become friends by middle school and rarely fought. By high school, they were best friends. He wondered if it would ever be like that again. He wondered if anything would ever feel normal again.

CHAPTER 18: LUKE

L uke hated that Gabby was in so much pain. He understood the pain of grief and hurt for her. He wished he could make it all better for her somehow, though he knew there wasn't anything he or anyone could do. It's not like he could bring her parents back. So he would do the only thing he could think of... help her escape it.

He got back to the villa around noon. He quickly changed and was sitting down on the couch as his parents and Sophie walked in from their morning golf game.

Sophie sat next to her brother and asked, "So, how was snorkeling with Gabby?"

"It was good," Luke said, trying to play it cool. He was still trying to process everything that she had told him. "I invited Gabby and Jase to have lunch with us."

"You like her," Sophie smirked.

Luke just smiled at her, not sure what to say. He did like Gabby, but he wasn't sure he was ready for something new. He also wasn't sure that Gabby was either, with all she had been through this year. He couldn't deny that there was something about her that made him want to be around her.

Sophie watched her brother. "Luke, it's been a year since you and Priscilla broke up. She's moved on, and you need to, too."

"I am," Luke defended. Just the sound of Priscilla's name made him feel guilty, though. She had been his high school sweetheart. They had dated on and off again while he was in the Army. They reconnected when he came home. He'd asked her to marry him after graduation from grad school, but they decided he'd start his career before setting the wedding date. He started teaching, and she was moving up in her marketing firm. He knew they were growing apart and becoming different people. He ended things and felt so awful about hurting her. He had made a promise to her that he had broken and he still cared about her, but he didn't want to spend the rest of his life with her.

"You didn't do anything wrong with Priscilla," Sophie said. "You both deserve to have someone you are head-over-heels for. You shouldn't get married just because you've been dating for so long."

"Yeah. You're right," Luke said with a shrug.

"Aren't I always?" his sister gloated.

"Always a pain?" Seth said, coming out of his room. Still in his pajamas, he flopped himself between Luke and Sophie.

"Ha ha," Sophie said with an eye roll.

"What's she right about, then?" Seth asked Luke.

"Nothing," Luke said, wanting to change the subject.

"About him needing to move on and ask Gabby out." Sophie told Seth, then giving Luke a 'You know I'm right' stare.

"Even if I wanted to, I don't think Gabby would right now," Luke said.

"Why do you say that?" Sophie asked.

"She and Jase have had a rough year," Luke answered, shifting on the couch.

"Because of Jase's injury?" Seth asked.

"No, their parents died earlier this year." Luke immediately regretted saying it. He felt like he'd just betrayed Gabby's trust.

"What?" Luke's siblings said in unison.

"There was a car accident, and they both died," Luke said. "But you can't say anything about it."

"Why?" Sophie asked.

"They are here trying to escape Christmas and, I guess, forget that it happened," Luke said.

"How do you forget your parents died?" Seth asked.

"You can't," Luke said, shaking his head. He understood the wanting to forget. But he also knew that it wasn't going to happen. "Look, they're just trying to make it through their first Christmas without their family."

"That's why they weren't excited about all the holiday activities here," Sophie said sadly. "It makes sense now since they came here hoping to escape Christmas."

"I can't imagine what they are going through," Seth said.

They all sat silent. Luke wasn't sure he should have told them.

"We will help them," Seth said.

"How?" Luke asked. "I just said you can't tell them, you know."

"I know, but we can be like Santa Security, protecting them from Christmas," Seth said.

"We can keep them busy with non-Christmas activities," Sophie said. "Good idea, Seth."

"Thanks." Seth smiled proudly. "Should we get shirts and badges?"

Luke laughed. "No. What are we, ten? Besides, I think that would blow our undercover status. Remember, you guys aren't supposed to know this."

Olivia and Ben came into the room, eyeing them all suspiciously.

"What are you three up to?" Olivia asked.

Luke and his siblings filled their parents in on their Santa Security plan to help the Jacksons.

Luke noticed that his parents didn't seem shocked about hearing that Gabby and Jase's parents had died. Maybe it was just him, but it didn't seem like news to them.

Olivia was laughing at her kids. "We are so proud that we raised children who grew into amazing adults."

Ben smiled at his wife and put his arm around her shoulder. "We did good."

"I love that you guys are so thoughtful and want to make this holiday special for Jase and Gabby, but let's not go overboard. Just be yourselves and be their friends. That's what they need right now."

"So, no uniforms?" Seth asked with disappointment.

Luke shot him a warning look.

"I'm kidding," Seth said with his hands in the air. "Undercover, I got it."

They all laughed then browsed through the brochures scattered across the table trying to come up with non-festive activities to do.

On their way to lunch, Luke pulled his mom aside. "Hey Mom, did you already know?"

She smiled at him. "I think it's so sweet of you all to help Gabby and Jase navigate this painful season of their lives."

"Yeah, but did..." Luke started to ask.

"God works in mysterious ways, my dear," she interrupted him.

"What do you mean?" Luke was confused.

"What are the chances that the Jacksons ended up at the same resort as us?" she asked.

"I don't know," Luke said, shaking his head.

"Maybe it's what we all needed," Olivia said, linking her arm with Luke's.

Luke was confused by what she meant. Who needed what? He was about to ask her what she meant but decided to let it rest as they walked into the restaurant.

CHAPTER 19: GABBY

When Gabby and Jase walked into the Coz Cantina for lunch, they saw the Anderson Family already sitting at a round table just inside the entrance.

Seth was the first to notice them. He stood up and said loudly, "Hey! Are you two stalking us?"

"Oh, no! We...I thought Luke said..." Gabby stuttered, feeling embarrassed. Hadn't Luke told his family she and Jase were joining them?

"Oh hush, Seth." Olivia swatted her youngest. "Luke already said you'd be joining us, and we saved seats for you."

"Thank you," Gabby said, breathing a sigh of relief.

"Hey guys," Jase said.

Gabby and Jase sat between Luke and Sophie. Everything on the menu sounded delicious. Apparently, everyone else was hungry too, because they ordered a lot of food. After ordering, Sophie recounted how she had almost beaten her dad in golf today. To Ben's delight, though, he was still the keeper of the Golden Gopher.

Olivia turned the conversation to Jase and Gabby just as the food arrived.

"So, Jase, what did you do this morning?" she asked.

"Well, until about thirty minutes ago, I was sleeping," he stated as he dug into his nachos.

"Just like Seth." Olivia chuckled, "You must have needed it."

"I did. I actually think I've slept better here the past few nights than I have since..." Jase trailed off.

Olivia smiled softly at him. Was it just Gabby's imagination, or was there sadness hidden in her smile?

Olivia turned her attention to Gabby. "I hear you had quite the adventure snorkeling."

"Yes, it was so beautiful. Luke will have to show you the photos," Gabby said.

"Luke said you basically saved his life," Olivia gushed. This made Gabby laugh until she caught Jase's wide-eyed reaction. He was horrified.

"Saved his life?" Jase said, "Was there danger?"

Gabby was about to explain the baby shark when Luke jumped in. "There was a huge shark," spreading his arms out as wide as they would go, exaggerating the size of the nurse shark.

Gabby laughed and pulled Luke's hands closer together. "Maybe more like this."

"There were sharks?" Jase growled. Gabby could hear the concern in his voice.

"I was sure I was about to get eaten," Luke exclaimed, and everyone laughed. Everyone but Jase.

"They were baby nurse sharks," Gabby tried to assure Jase. "Harmless, I've swam with them many times."

Jase's brow furrowed, and he crossed his arms tightly across his chest, obviously not amused.

"I just want you to be careful. Sharks could attack anytime," Jase said. "You're all I have left."

Sophie asked, "What do you mean she's all you have left?"

Gabby met Jase's eyes. As if he could read her thoughts, he nodded.

Gabby took a deep breath. Was she really going to be able to say the words aloud again?

"We are the only family we have left," she said softly. It was the second time in one day that she had to admit it. But this time, she was more concerned about Jase hearing it spoken out loud. Gabby peered to her right to gauge Jase's reaction. His jaw was tight, but he nodded again.

"We lost our parents in a car accident in June," she said.

To Gabby's surprise, Jase spoke up. In a low voice said, "We came here to escape Christmas, and instead, we landed right in the middle of Santa's Caribbean vacation spot."

Gabby scanned the faces around the table. Jase was staring at his plate of nachos. Everyone else was shifting their eyes back and forth between her and Jase. She noticed that no one seemed particularly surprised. Yet none of them had the dreaded look of sympathy that she and Jase normally received. When her gaze landed on Luke, he gave her a friendly smile and covered her hand in his. This simple gesture sent a tingle through her whole body. She could feel her face flush and hoped that no one noticed, especially Luke.

Everyone sat silent for a moment. Then Ben spoke up, "We're sorry that you two are going through this. We can only imagine how difficult this Christmas is. But we are happy to join you in whatever activities you want to do, if you'll let us."

Gabby and Jase shared a quick glance with each other. Jase's eyes were wide in surprise but then changed to confusion.

"We can't let you avoid Christmas. You all are like the most festive family we've met," Gabby said.

"We can't replace your family, but Christmas isn't about Santa and gifts or even where you are. It's about being with the people you love. And God put you in our path to give you some extra love," Olivia said kindly.

"Besides," Seth added, "have you seen all the cool excursions they have here?"

Gabby felt relieved when Seth and Sophie started listing all the activities they'd researched. ATV excursions, Mayan Ruins, stand up paddle boards, fishing, and the list went on.

Gabby smiled slightly at Jase and reached for his hand. The band-aid had been ripped off. They said the words out loud and survived. And instead of pity, they'd met with love and understanding. Jase still appeared uncomfortable, but as the different activities were listed, he started engaging in the conversation.

They decided on a jungle adventure the next day. Gabby hadn't heard what all was involved, but everyone seemed excited about it, so she agreed.

Gabby had stuffed herself full of the delicious Mexican food. From the comments around the table, everyone had. Luke and Seth had made an afternoon tee-time, but Jase declined the invitation. Ben and Olivia were taking a catamaran ride. Sophie invited Gabby to sit by the pool with her. Gabby agreed to meet her there later. Olivia had them all exchange phone numbers and made sure everyone agreed to meet in the lobby the following morning for their jungle tour in case they all didn't see each other the rest of the evening.

Gabby wasn't altogether shocked that Jase didn't want to golf. He probably wanted some time to himself after the conversation over lunch. Gabby and Jase walked back to their room in silence. Jase opened the door for her, still not saying anything. Gabby was just about to ask Jase how he was feeling when her phone rang.

She saw it was Holly and answered with a smile.

"Hey, Holly!"

"Hello there! How's vacation?" Holly asked in a chipper voice.

"It's really great so far," Gabby said and sat down on the couch. Great may have been an overstatement, but she didn't want her friend to worry.

"Fantastic! And how is Jase?"

Gabby put the phone on speaker. "He's right here. Say hi, Jase."

"Hi, Holly," Jase said.

"Hey there, are you having a good time?" Holly asked.

"I actually am," Jase said as he sat down next to her.

Gabby was relieved when she heard him say that. He sounded like he was sincere and she noticed he even had a slight smile.

"I'm so glad!" Holly gushed. "Are you meeting all the single ladies?"

"Ha! Funny, Holly," Jase said, rolling his eyes.

"But you two are doing good? All festive-free in paradise? Have you seen the crazy holiday family again?"

"Funny you should ask," Jase said. Looking down at Gabby with a smirk.

"We just got back from lunch with them," Gabby added.

"What?" Holly sounded surprised. "I thought they were a holiday explosion you were trying to avoid?"

"We are still festive-free," Gabby confirmed. "But they are pretty cool."

"They are," Jase agreed with a nod. "We're all going on a jungle adventure tomorrow, and Gabs had a date with Luke today."

"What?!" Holly squealed.

"I did not! Gabby protested. "I went snorkeling this morning, and he just happened to be there too."

"I see," Holly said.

"And there were sharks," Jase stated, obviously still upset about the encounter.

"Nurse sharks," Gabby explained. "They are harmless."

"I just want you to be careful; sharks could attack anytime," Jase said. "You're all I have left."

"I know, but I've snorkeled and have gone scuba diving hundreds of times. I'm always careful."

"Jase," Holly continued, "You know she's a pro at swimming and diving. And she would never put herself in danger."

"I know," Jase conceded.

"I want to hear more about this date," Holly stated.

"It wasn't a date!" Gabby protested.

"Holly, you should have seen her giggly and blushing," Jase teased.

"I was not," Gabby said, but couldn't hide her smile.

"Sure, you weren't," Jase teased. "Holly, I'm off to play my game, talk to you later."

"Alright, have fun," Holly said.

Gabby watched her brother walk to his room. She was still concerned about his reaction at lunch. That was yet another thing they would probably sweep under the rug rather than actually talk about it.

"I think this trip has been really good for him," Gabby said, lowering her voice so Jase couldn't hear her. "He's already gone golfing and even made plans to go fishing with the guys later this week."

"With your new boyfriend?" Holly cooed.

"Oh, stop it. You know I don't have time for dating. I do think this trip has been good for him. But seriously, Jase totally freaked out over the sharks at lunch. Just as I think he's getting back to the old Jase, something happens and I'm concerned about him all over again."

"We'll just have to keep praying for him. You have to give him time. You know everyone comes to terms with grief in their own time and way."

"I know. I just wish he'd want to be in the real world again and experience life and not hide in his virtual world with invisible friends. I'm not even sure he's talked to many of his teammates since he's been injured."

"He will. Just give him time. Anyway, I want to hear more about your new boyfriend."

"Oh my gosh, Holly! You are insane. I have too much going on with work and Jase and the house to worry about a man too."

"I know you have *so* much going on that you couldn't possibly take time out for fun and romance," Holly said sarcastically.

"Exactly," Gabby said with a little giggle.

"So, how did you guys end up going snorkeling together?"

"I went snorkeling. He just happened to be there too." Gabby clarified. Then she recounted the day's snorkel adventure to her friend. She told her about the fun she and Luke had and how easy it was to be with him. She admitted that he and his entire family seemed wonderful. "But I'm not sure, Holly. Jase still really needs me."

"Please, you're on vacation. What's a little fun and flirting? Where are they from, anyway?"

"Are you ready for this? They're from South Bay." Gabby gave a little laugh.

"South Bay? Like right next door, basically?"

"Yes, that South Bay."

"Interesting, sounds like God's handiwork," Holly said. Gabby could hear her smile through the phone.

Gabby laughed. "God's handiwork, huh?" *Hmm*, she thought, *maybe it was?*

What were the chances that people who lived practically next door to each other would meet a thousand miles away at a place neither of them had planned on being?

"God does work in mysterious ways," Holly said.

"He does. How's Tucker?" Gabby asked, wanting to change the subject.

"He's great," her friend assured her. "We've gone hiking on some trails, and he's been coming to work with me. I got him a bed for the cafe, and the customers absolutely love him."

"He's not going to want to come home," Gabby exclaimed.

"I might not give him back." Holly laughed.

"Give him some love from us," Gabby said.

"I will. Now, you two go have some more fun," Holly said.

"We will. Love you," Gabby said.

"Love you," Holly replied before hanging up.

Chapter 20: Jase

Jase closed his door, still feeling conflicted over the conversations that went down over lunch.

Who were these people? Why would they want to give up their Christmas vacation to spend it with two siblings who wanted nothing to do with Christmas? They seemed like the most Christmas-y people ever. How could they want to give that up?

Maybe Luke wasn't such a great guy for Gabby. She had to save him from a shark? And why was she swimming with sharks?

As he considered everything bad or that could go wrong, he could hear his sister talking with Holly. Gabby was saying how much fun she had snorkeling. Jase hadn't heard her excited about anything in so long.

Holly was right. Gabby was an excellent swimmer and had taken diving courses and had never done anything stupid in the water. He just can't help but worry that something would happen and she'd be gone. Then he'd be all alone.

He had continued to eavesdrop on his sister's conversation.

"I think this trip has been really good for him," Gabby said, lowering her voice. "He's already gone golfing and even made plans to go fishing with the guys later this week."

"With your new boyfriend?" Holly said.

"Oh, stop it. You know I don't have time for dating. I do think this trip has been good for him. But seriously, Jase totally freaked out over the sharks at lunch. Just as I think he's getting back to the old Jase, something happens, and I'm concerned about him all over again."

Right, like the old me will ever be back; how could she think he could come back, Jase thought.

"We'll just have to keep praying for him. You have to give him time. You know everyone comes to terms with grief in their own time and way," Holly said.

"I know. I just wish he'd want to be in the real world again and experience life and not hide in his virtual world with invisible friends. I'm not even sure he's talked to many of his teammates since he's been injured." Jase heard his sister say.

I like my virtual friends; they don't judge my moods and keep asking if I'm okay, he thought.

"He will. Just give him time. Anyway, I want to hear more about your new boyfriend."

"Oh my gosh, Holly! You are insane. I have too much going on with work and Jase and the house to worry about a man too." Gabby said.

When he heard that, he couldn't listen anymore. He was still grinding his teeth over her words. Give him time? Like time could fix missing his parents? Being angry that they're gone? He guessed time had let Gabby heal, but he couldn't bounce back like superwoman out there. He still didn't know how she could just go on like nothing happened...like Mom and Dad weren't gone...like life hadn't stopped in June. Even here, in this amazing little piece of paradise, he was so sad and angry. Angry about everything. And the moments that it seemed to pass, something happened and the anger returned.

Anxiety and anger had him returning to his room to pace. He was unsure of what to do when he noticed his phone light blinking. *Oh great, another missed call from Sam,* he thought. Sam had been his agent for the last ten years, and his calls were becoming more persistent. Jase was sure he was calling to give him bad news. He was probably being released or traded, and he didn't want to hear more bad news. Tossing the phone back onto the nightstand to deal with later, he flopped onto the bed, his thoughts still spiraling.

He wasn't going on a jungle adventure. He wasn't going to go fishing. He wasn't going anywhere with the Andersons. He was done with them all, and he would just camp out in his room the rest of the trip. Well... he'd have to go on the jungle adventure. There was no way he was leaving his sister in the hands of someone that needed rescuing from a baby shark.

He put his headset on, turned on his game, and turned off the world. Enough thinking for today.

CHAPTER 21: LUKE

Luke was resting in the hammock, recovering from lunch. He was constantly impressed with his family. His parents loved Christmas. Even though his family hadn't been home at Christmas for years, they still went all out on decorations and even a tree. And now his parents were all willing to forgo their normal Christmas fun for two people that they had just met. His brother and sister loved Christmas too, but they were happy doing any activities, and they had big hearts just like their parents.

While he was thinking about his amazing family, Seth plopped himself into the hammock with Luke. Seth leaned back and put his feet right by Luke's head.

"Seriously, bro?" Luke growled at his brother.

"What? It looked comfy," Seth said dramatically, wedging himself next to his brother.

Luke glared at his brother. Seth didn't even notice because his eyes were already closed.

"This is nice," Seth said, stretching a little.

"It was," Luke said, hinting that this hammock was not designed for two.

"Hey, Luke?"

"Yeah?" Luke asked, still slightly annoyed.

"What do you think would happen to us if Mom and Dad died?"

"What do you mean?" He asked, not sure where his brother was going with the question.

"When you told us earlier about the Jacksons losing their parents, I felt sad for them. But it wasn't until Gabby was telling us that I saw how devastated they both seemed. And then I thought what it would be like if we suddenly lost Mom and Dad."

"I know," Luke said. His brother and sister had never experienced loss before. It's something that can't be explained until you have gone through it firsthand. Even then, there's no explaining grief.

"You know what else I don't get?" Seth continued, "You hear about siblings fighting and not speaking after their parents pass away, but Jase and Gabby don't want to be separated from each other."

"Their family was close. Like ours is," Luke said.

"What do you mean?" Seth asked.

"We talk a lot about this in my veterans group. When people lose someone, they are angry. Then, they fight because they want someone to blame. Sadly, it can be easier to take it out on those closest to you."

"That's stupid," Seth huffed.

"It's what people do when they don't know where to place their anger and don't know how to find comfort in God," Luke explained.

"I hope when it's our time to go through that, we don't fight."

"I don't think we will," Luke said, offering his brother a grin.

Luke hoped he was right. He hoped he remained close with his siblings now, no matter what happened in life.

"So..." Seth started again. "About Gabby...."

"What about Gabby?" Luke asked suspiciously.

"I think you like her," Seth said.

"Yeah, she and Jase are cool," Luke admitted.

"They are," Seth said. "But you know that's not what I meant."

Luke laughed. His brother was more perceptive than people gave him credit for. Seth was right; Luke did like Gabby. He just wanted to be near her and get to know her better. In such a short period of time, he felt a connection with her that he couldn't explain. He knew she was going through grief that he couldn't fully understand. He didn't even want to imagine losing either of his parents, let alone both at the same time. He wanted to find a way to help her through it.

"Yeah, I do," Luke finally admitted.

"I knew it," Seth said, poking his brother's leg. "So, what are you going to do about it?"

"I don't know. She's not like other women I've met, and she certainly isn't like Priscilla."

"Dude, you need to let her go."

"I have," Luke said, defending himself.

"No, you still feel guilty for calling it off, and you shouldn't."

"I'm the one who called it off one week before the wedding."

"Yeah, and she was dating someone else three weeks later," Seth reminded him. "She's even engaged to him now."

Luke thought about that.

"She knows you did the hard work of calling the wedding off. You basically took the burden off her having to do it."

How had Luke never realized that before? Was his little brother right? It didn't even bother him that Priscilla had moved on. He actually felt good about it and hoped that the new man in her life would make her happy.

"Thanks, bro," Luke said, slapping Seth's leg. "You're not so bad."

"I am pretty awesome," Seth said with a wide grin.

"And so modest."

"That's not one of my strong suits. Why should I downplay how awesome I am?"

"Lord, help us all. Now we just need to get your life situated, and we'll be all set."

Seth sat up. "Why'd you have to go and ruin a good moment like that?" Still smiling at his brother, Seth grabbed the sides of the hammock and tipped them over to the ground. They landed on the grass with a thud.

Luke rolled to his back to see Sophie peering down at them. She was wearing a wide-brimmed hat and holding a tropical umbrella drink in her hand. "We are all adults now, right?" Sophie asked, shaking her head at them.

"I'm not sure what it is about being on vacation with Mom and Dad that makes me still feel like a kid." Seth beamed.

"You are still a kid," Luke said to his brother, grabbing him in a headlock.

"Yes, obviously Seth is the only child here," Sophie said with a smirk directed at Luke. Then she sat on a lounge chair and opened a book.

After Luke and Seth untangled themselves, they got up and joined their sister.

"I was just telling Luke he needs to ask Gabby out on a proper date," Seth stated.

"That is a great idea," Sophie agreed enthusiastically. "It's obvious how much you like each other."

"What makes you think she likes me?" Luke asked.

"I just do," Sophie shrugged at him.

"That's not an answer," Luke said.

"It's just the way you look at each other. But be careful; she has gone through a lot and is probably being torn in a lot of different ways right now. So she's delicate, emotionally speaking."

His sister's words made Luke more hesitant.

"But you should do something while we're here. What's the harm in some one-on-one time?" Sophie said.

"That's true. Maybe we'll see that we don't have that much in common."

"I doubt that." His sister gave a little laugh. "Oh, and if you want to be on her brother's good side, ask him first."

"You want me to ask Jase out on a date?" As soon as Luke asked, he realized what his sister meant.

"No, you buffoon," Sophie shook her head like he was the biggest moron on the planet. "Ask him if he's okay with you asking Gabby out on one."

"Got it, and good call."

Luke was going to ask her out. Later. He did want to talk to her. Picking up his phone, he found her number and pressed the green icon to call her.

As the phone rang, he thought about what he was going to say. *Why hadn't he thought this through more?*

"Hello?" Gabby's sweet voice came through his phone. Just hearing it made him smile.

"Hello?" Gabby repeated.

"Gabby. Hi," Luke said.

"Hi." It sounded like she was smiling.

"Hi," Luke repeated.

Silence

"Luke?"

"Sorry, hi Gabby, it's Luke."

"Hi again," he heard her laugh. He was blowing this.

"I just wanted to see if you were ready for tomorrow."

"Ready for the jungle adventure?" She asked.

"Yes," Luke said stiffly.

"I don't know what is involved, but Jase and I will be ready," she said confidently.

"It'll be fun, I promise," he assured her.

"I'm going to hold you to that," Gabby said.

"You can hold me to that," Luke said. *Why can't I think of another reason that I called?*

"Sounds good," she said.

More silence.

"Was there anything else?" Gabby asked him.

They had talked so easily all the other times. Why could he not form words now?

"No, just have a good night, and we'll see you at eight tomorrow in the lobby."

"Oh," she said, sounding confused. "Have a good night, too, and I'll see you tomorrow."

"Okay, see you tomorrow. Good night," he rushed the words out so quickly it sounded like one big long word and hung up. He was not good at this. He hadn't asked a woman out, really ever. He and Priscilla had just been together all the time, and it turned into dating. The dates he'd been on recently had either been blind dates or the woman had asked him out. He needed to pull it together. He reminded himself that he taught high school– he wasn't in high school.

"That was smooth, bro," Seth said mockingly, "'Ummmm ummm hi.' Maybe send her a note next time with checkboxes. Do you like me, yes? No? Maybe?"

Luke just shook his head, knowing his brother was right. *Tomorrow will be better*, he thought.

CHAPTER 22: GABBY

What was that about? Gabby wondered as she hung up the phone. She gave a little laugh. She took a deep breath and wanted to make sure that Jase was, in fact, good to go tomorrow. He seemed fine at lunch, but once again, she saw his mood swing some.

Nervously, she poked her head into Jase's room. He was deep in virtual war or something. He acknowledged her with a nod, and she motioned for him to take his headset off.

"Be right back guys," he said to his virtual squad. He removed one side of his headset and grunted at her. "Yeah?"

"Are you still up for a jungle adventure in the morning?"

"I guess."

"If not, it's no big deal. I'll just call them and let them know. I'm sure they'll be okay with it. "

"I said it's fine," Jase snapped. His response made Gabby jump a little. She watched him close his eyes and take a deep breath.

Then said more calmly, "I am still up for a jungle adventure to-morrow."

Okay," she responded quietly. " We're supposed to meet in the lobby at 8:00 am for the shuttle."

"Ugh, 8:00 am is really early," Jase complained.

"I guess for some of us, it is." Gabby offered him a slight grin. "I can wake you up."

"That's fine," Jase said flatly.

"Okay," she said, giving him a small smile.

"Anything else?" he said, holding his headphones, indicating that he was ready to get back to his game.

"Ummm, no." She shook her head.

"Then I'm going to get back to saving the world."

"Good luck," she said with a hesitant smile.

He put his headset back on without responding. "Jackson's back," he said to his friends. Gabby backed out of his room, clos-ing the door as she left. Jase had always had a bit of a temper and was quick to get there, making Gabby walk on eggshells when she wasn't sure of his mood, which was often lately.

She decided to shake it off and go read on the patio for a while. Before she knew it, hours had passed. The sun was setting over the ocean, and the sky was brilliant shades of pinks, purples, and blues. Jase was still in his room, and the sounds indicated that he was still playing his game. She couldn't understand how he could play for that long. But then she gazed down at the book in her hand and realized that she actually did understand. She ordered a couple sandwiches from room service. When they arrived, she knocked on Jase's door and offered him one. He gave a quick "thanks" and went back to his game.

Gabby ate her sandwich on the patio, listening to the waves. There was a gentle breeze and music drifting from somewhere in the resort. She thought about today and the Andersons' offer to help them escape from Christmas. She felt lighter having said the words that her parents were gone. She had managed to say it out loud, and the world hadn't come to a grinding halt. Not only that, but God put people on her path that were trying to make it easier. She went to bed feeling grateful and hoped that Jase would be able to feel some of that too.

The next morning, Gabby was nervous and excited about the day. She wasn't a fan of not knowing the exact plans, but she was excited to see Luke again. Last night, she had been tempted to search through every brochure they had to find details about what they would be doing today. Maybe a Jeep ride to see the wildlife? Or some ATVing through the jungle? Then she had decided maybe she needed more spontaneity and surprises, at least good surprises, in her life.

After she dressed quickly, she packed a bag for the day. Then she went to wake up Jase. To her astonishment, he was already in the living room, ready to go.

"Whoa, I thought I was going to have to drag you out of bed." Gabby hoped this was a good sign that he was in a good mood.

"Nah, I was up already," he said. Seemingly in a good mood, Gabby's hopes seemed to be confirmed.

"Is this because you were up all night and haven't gone to sleep yet?"

"That doesn't sound like something I would do." He smirked at her and picked up his backpack. "I grabbed a couple of waters and some protein bars from the gift shop for us too."

Now she was really shocked. *Who is this person?* she thought, but she just said, "Thanks."

"Ready?" Jase asked her.

"Ready for anything," she replied and smiled. Her brother's enthusiasm for the outing was shocking, but she was thrilled to see a glimmer of the outgoing man he used to be.

CHAPTER 23: JASE

O f course, Jase was up. He had been awake all night playing video games. He was tired now, but there was no way Gabby was going into the jungle without someone who could protect her.

"You hungry?" Gabby asked him.

"Not really." Jase handed her a protein bar, taking her hint.

"Thanks," Gabby said, taking the bar. "I'm surprised you're not hungry; you can always eat."

"I had one of those already," Jase explained. He didn't mention his call for room service at 6:00 and the breakfast of eggs, toast, bacon, hash browns, pancakes, fruit, and sausage. So, maybe it wasn't small, but she was right. He could always eat, and he needed to keep up his strength.

As they walked into the lobby, he saw the Andersons waiting there. Of course, they were already there. They were perfect.

"Morning, guys," Sophie greeted them each with a hug.

Neither Jase nor Gabby were big huggers, but he watched his sister have a certain glow when she hugged Luke. *What did she see in this guy?* She needed to save him from a baby shark, for the love of God. Jase had thought Luke was cool at first, but she needed someone who could be strong for her, not someone who needed saving.

"Where's Seth?" Gabby asked.

Olivia grinned, and they all followed the direction of her gaze to a chair where Seth had a leg draped over the arm and his head resting on the back. The sound of snoring made Jase chuckle.

"How long were you all waiting here?" Jase asked.

"Only about three minutes," Sophie said, rolling her eyes.

"Oh Jase, maybe Seth is your real brother," Gabby said, poking his side. "Jase can sleep anywhere and through anything."

"So can Seth," Sophie said.

"It's a talent," Jase said, defending himself.

The front doors opened, and a tall, skinny man dressed in all khaki entered the lobby. "Anderson party?" he asked.

"Yes, that's us," Olivia said.

"Buenas dias, I am Diego and will be driving you to your jungle adventure." He gestured toward the door. "We will have a thirty-minute ride to the park."

They followed Diego to load into the luxury bus.

Jase and Seth each took a seat and spread out for naps. *Thirty minutes is a perfect nap time*, Jase thought as he settled into the seat.

Before closing his eyes, he noticed that Gabby picked a seat between Luke and Sophie.

Jase must have dozed off quickly because he didn't even remember the bus moving. He was awakened to Gabby poking him.

"Wake up, sleeping beauty," Gabby said.

He groaned and stretched. "Just ten more minutes."

"Maybe you should have gotten some sleep last night. This excursion is going to be at least six hours."

"I'll be fine," Jase said, unfolding himself from the seat.

He noticed they were still trying to rouse Seth as well. Luke pulled a bottle of water out and dumped it over his brother's head.

Seth jumped. "Dude, what did you do that for?"

"You weren't waking up." Luke shrugged.

"Ugh, really?" Seth wiped his face with his shirt.

Gabby laughed. "Aren't you glad you don't have a brother?" she asked Jase.

Jase didn't answer. *Having a brother might be easier*, he thought. *I wouldn't have to worry so much about a brother. But I still wouldn't trade her in for a brother.*

They unloaded from the bus and stepped into a very humid jungle. Jase could feel little beads of sweat gathering on his back already. He put his sunglasses on and scanned the jungle around him. There was a sign for ATV rides. *That's cool*, he thought. *I could be up for this kind of adventure.*

"Hola, Buenos días." A young man greeted them. He was probably in his early twenties and looked like he was in shape. The khaki cargo shorts and blue polo with a logo led Jase to assume he was their tour guide.

"You must all be the Anderson party," he said cheerfully. "I am Ferdinand, which means brave journey. I am about to take you all on a journey, for which you will need to be very brave," he said in a serious tone.

What in the world have the Andersons gotten us into? Jase thought.

Jase looked around to see that everyone in their group appeared a little nervous. Then Ferdinand burst out laughing.

"I kid with you all. We are going to have a wonderful adventure. After a short safety message, we will fit you with helmets, and then you can choose your ATV. We are going to explore some caves. Then we will take a swim in the underworld. You may have heard of cenotes?"

"Did he say underworld?" Jase whispered to his sister.

"I think so," she replied with a nervous laugh.

"I guess not, so I will tell you." Ferdinand continued, "Cenotes are natural pools of water under the earth's surface. We only know they are there when the ground falls into them. I think you would call it a sinkhole. The Mayans consider cenotes to be an entrance to their "underworld" or "Xibalba," where their gods live, and their spirits reside after death."

Jase had to admit he was impressed with Ferdinand's storytelling already. Everyone else seemed to be, too, noticing his sister and the Andersons staring at Ferdinand with wide eyes.

"After a swim, we will return here for muy delicioso lunch, followed by more adventures."

"This will be great!" Gabby said to Jase.

Jase didn't admit it, but the excursion did sound like fun.

Jase paid close attention to the quick safety course but felt a little silly having to strap on a helmet. All the ATVs appeared to be identical, so he climbed onto one of the remaining ones after everyone else had chosen theirs.

Jase revved up his ATV and followed Ferdinand. He could feel some of the tension starting to melt away. They rode over a dirt path and through puddles. Ferdinand would make stops along the path to regale them with stories about Mayan history.

Ferdinand had everyone line up their ATVs, shut them down, and follow him on foot. They approached and then explored some of the Mayan ruins. The large stone structures were impressive.

"This is San Gervasio, one of the very few Mayan ruins that have not been destroyed," Ferdinand explained.

"There is evidence that Mayans had been here from as early as 100 B.C." Ferdinand paused. "Their world was forever changed on May three of 1518. This is when the first Spanish explorer, John de Grijalva, arrived. He had sailed from Cuba with peaceful intentions. Three days after Grijalva and his crew arrived, they held the first Holy Mass on Latin American soil. People of Cozumel are particularly proud of this, as more than 90% of the population is Catholic. In 2018, a new church was built to commemorate the 500th anniversary of that first Holy Mass. *Santa Cruz de Cuzamil* was built on the very site where that first Mass was held."

Even though Jase wasn't so sure about God right now, he did feel proud to be Catholic at the moment. He wondered what it would have been like to be at that first Mass.

Ferdinand continued, "A year after Juan de Grijalva arrived, another Spanish explorer arrived in Cozumel, Hernán Cortés. At the time, about 20,000 Mayans lived on the island. Using peaceful tactics, Cortés convinced the chief of the Mayans to submit and convert to Catholicism."

"Peaceful tactics?" Jase asked. "He came to conquer and used peaceful tactics?"

Ferdinand laughed. "Intimidating, but yes, no violence. He offered gifts to the Mayan people in exchange for loyalty to the Spanish Crown."

"You usually don't hear of the intruders taking over by bringing gifts," Luke said.

Ferdinand nodded, "This is true. But they indeed offered gifts. It is also said that the large army with advanced weapons would not leave until the Mayans submitted.

"Ah." Jase said, "Peaceful intimidations."

"What you see around you is one of the few remaining Mayan temples. Sadly, Cortés destroyed many of the temples and religious sculptures." Ferdinand continued his tales as they explored the ruins on foot.

"So everything they had known and believed growing up was just destroyed?" Jase asked. "Just gone in a blink?"

"Yes," Ferdinand said. "And that was not all that was destroyed. Sadly, a new religion and gifts were not all Cortés and his crew brought. They also brought smallpox, something that had not existed here. It spread quickly, and only a few hundred of the 20,000 Mayans survived."

Jase was humbled. He felt for these people. He surprised himself when he asked, "So, what happened after that?"

"Most of the remaining Mayans moved to the mainland after that. The island was left uninhabited for centuries."

"Centuries? Like hundreds of years with no one?" Seth asked.

"Occasionally, cruise ships would stop here for a while," Ferdinand informed him.

"There were cruise ships that came here in the 1700s?" Seth asked.

Ferdinand laughed heartily. "No, I just wanted to make sure I had all of your attention still."

The group laughed.

Ferdinand continued, "But there were ships...pirate ships. This was a very dangerous area of the Caribbean for a very long time. I keep hoping to discover buried treasure someday. So far, I have not found anything."

Everyone seemed interested at the mention of pirates. Jase didn't get the pirate fascination, but he was intrigued by Ferdinand's storytelling. It was so different when you were able to stand in the spot where the stories took place. Ferdinand had a way of taking you back to that time. Jase wondered if Gabby's books did that for her. If so, he was starting to understand her love of reading.

They left the ruins and walked back to their ATVs. After following Ferdinand for about 20 minutes, they approached the entrance of the caves. Before entering, Ferdinand stood on his ATV and continued with the stories of pirates.

"Two of the more famous pirates who came here were Henry Morgan and Jean Laffite. Morgan saw the cenotes and caves as excellent hiding places. We will now explore the caves. You never know what you might find here."

Ferdinand started his ATV and drove through the entrance to the cave. Jase was the last to enter.

The cave was larger than Jase had imagined, about 3 feet above his head. But he still felt claustrophobic in the stuffy caves. The ATVs echoed off the earthy walls. Vines hung from the ceiling, and he couldn't help wondering what could be hiding in them. He rode behind Gabby, who had given him a nervous glance before they entered the dark hole in the earth. *Just keep your eyes on Gabby and get through this,* he told himself.

By the time they exited the caves, they were all caked in mud and dirt. Riding further through the jungle, Jase could see that everyone was stopped ahead.

They dismounted the ATVs and gathered around Ferdinand.

"Most of our fresh water comes out of cenotes, so it is illegal to swim in them," Ferdinand said. "But I feel like you are an adventurous group and are willing to break a few laws. Our jails aren't that bad here if we get caught."

Jase was pretty sure everyone was thinking the same thing: that wasn't going to happen. He'd seen TV shows about jails in other countries. That was not part of his agenda for this trip.

Jase felt Gabby lean into him, "I'm not going to go to jail here."

"Me neither. I've seen *Locked Up Abroad*, and none of that seems 'not that bad,'" Jase said.

They were interrupted by Ferdinand laughing again. "I kid you again. This cenote is legal to swim in. You people are too fun."

They all laughed nervously and followed Ferdinand anyway.

Jase couldn't see any water, just a flight of old, damp, wooden steps leading up a small hill.

As they ascended, the steps creaked with every step. Jase was sure they were going to give out at any moment. Once at the top, they had to take a few steps down. Then, beneath them sat a crystal blue pool of water.

"Wow!" The word escaped his mouth as he took in the view in front of him.

"Have you ever seen anything so beautiful?" Gabby asked.

Jase shook his head. He thought of his mom and how much she would love this. She probably would never want to leave. She would tell them stories about how fairies and magic animals must live here.

Jase, Gabby, Sophie, Olivia, and Ben decided to jump off the low platform, while Seth and Luke decided to jump off the high ledge above. Seth and Luke shouted "Geronimo" and jumped effortlessly, feet first, into the blue glowing water below.

Gabby floated over next to him with a smile on her face. "This feels amazing."

"It does," Jase agreed.

"You know what this makes me think of?" Gabby asked.

"Mom and her magical stories?" Jase said.

Gabby smiled, "Were you reading my mind?"

"It's like someplace she would have described in her stories."

"Yes, and Dad would be complaining about the heat and bugs."

"For sure. In fairness, the bugs always loved to eat on him more than anyone else."

That was true. It was the family joke that the last mosquito of the season would hunt their dad out to bite him before it died.

Jase found himself relaxed and surprisingly happy as he floated in the cenote. Maybe it did have magical powers. Maybe it would just keep letting him drift away and take him to one of the magic lands. Logically, he knew that wasn't going to happen, and he wasn't sure what brought about this little feeling of joy. But he'd take it because he was sure it wouldn't last.

After the group dried off from their swim, Ferdinand led them back to the ATV center. Jase was starving, so it was perfect timing when Ferdinand informed them that they would have lunch before the next part of their adventure.

"There's more?" Jase asked.

"Oh yes! You book our full-day adventure tour," Ferdinand said, as if that explained it all.

"What more could there be?" Jase asked.

Seth grabbed Jase's shoulder. "The best part, the part that I was the most excited about, is next!"

Jase stared at him, feeling confused. Seth pointed across the road, and Jase saw it. *Oh no, how could this be happening?* He wasn't going to do this. And he knew for sure Gabby wasn't going to do it. How had he missed this when they arrived?

"Ziplining, buddy!" Seth declared.

CHAPTER 24: GABBY

"Ziplining?!" Gabby nearly shouted.

"Yes, ziplining," Jase hissed at his sister.

"Like way up in the air, way above the ground?" Gabby asked.

"Yes, that kind of ziplining," Jase confirmed.

"I can't do that. How are you going to do that?" Gabby cried.

"No way. Not a chance," Jase said. "I would lose my lunch over the jungle. And that is just the type of thing that ends up on the internet."

Gabby was shocked that her brother had even thought of something being on the internet. He never checked out his social media. How were they going to get out of doing this?

"Okay, after lunch, we are going to say that we are too full and can't do it," Jase said.

"Sounds good, we'll go with that," Gabby agreed.

Gabby and Jase joined the Andersons at the outdoor wooden table. Their lunch consisted of make-your-own tacos, as well as rice, beans, and fresh fruits and veggies. No one spoke for at least five minutes as they enjoyed the local cuisine. Seth finally broke the silence. With his mouth half full, he mumbled, "Everything is so delicious."

Everyone agreed, and the conversation resumed, as they talked about their adventure through the jungle.

"My favorite part was jumping into the cenote," Seth said enthusiastically.

"The cenote was amazing, but I loved the ruins," Luke said. "I wish I could bring my classes here so they could see this history and touch it with their own hands."

Gabby smiled. She admired how much Luke enjoyed his students and wanted to bring history to life for them. Her thoughts were interrupted by Sophie.

"My favorite was the stories that Ferdinand told. He should write them in a book."

"That's a great idea," Gabby agreed. Then she turned to Jase. "What was your favorite part, Jase?"

"I think I liked the cenote best, but really I liked everything," he said noncommittally. Then he glanced over at the zipline and back to Gabby. "Well, at least so far."

Gabby caught his meaning and gave him an understanding nod.

"What was your favorite part?" Luke asked Gabby.

"Everything," she said with a huge smile. "It was all great – the sites, the stories, swimming in a magical pool, I loved it all."

Gabby wished she had taken more photos, but she'd been too busy enjoying the sites and the stories. At least they had managed to take a good group shot of them all.

After lunch ended, Gabby and Jase trailed behind the Andersons over to the shed to get fitted for the harnesses.

"Remember, we are too full and don't want to get cramps," Gabby whispered to Jase.

Jase nodded.

While the Andersons were getting fitted, Ferdinand explained the safety features and pointed out the five towers above connecting the six sections of zipline.

"Jase?" Seth motioned for Jase to come over to him. "Come on man, time to suit up."

Jase gave Gabby an apologetic look. He glanced back over to Seth, who was still waving him over, and then back at Gabby with an expression that said he didn't know what to do. Finally, he shrugged and said, "Sorry, sis." He turned towards Seth, "I'm coming."

"What?" Gabby gasped, grabbing her brother's arm.

"I can't act like a wuss in front of them." Jase shrugged at her and trotted off to the hut to get fitted.

"Great teamwork," Gabby told him. What was she supposed to do now?

Luke walked up to her, smiling. *That smile could melt ice,* she thought.

"Hey, you ready?" he asked her.

"Well, um..." she stammered, not sure what to say. "I'm good down here. Safe. On the ground."

"Come on, this is safe." Luke pointed to a sign that read 502 days accident-free.

"So that means they are due for one?" Gabby said.

"Ha, no. It means they are safe and keep up their equipment."

"It's just, it's really high up there," Gabby said. She examined the wooden towers again, and her stomach did a little flip.

"Come on, there should be some amazing views from up there."

Gabby still wasn't sure. Since Jase was going to do it, maybe it was time for her to face some fears too. If Jase could do it, she could do it. Besides, she'd be able to keep a better eye on him from up there.

She took a deep breath and said, "Alright, let's go."

Gabby stepped into her harness, fastening it tight. Luke had grabbed a helmet for her. He put it on her head and tightened the strap under her chin.

"There you go," he said, smiling at her.

She couldn't help but smile back at him. She slowly followed everyone over to the wooden staircase to ascend up the tower. Ferdinand inspected her harness.

"Muy buena," he said, handing her a pair of orange gloves.

She gave him a nervous smile, replying, "Gracias," then started up the stairs.

About halfway up, she made the mistake of peering over the side, sending her heart into her throat. *Note to self: don't look down again.* Gabby told herself. Arriving at the top of the platform, she had felt the wood creaking beneath her. She wondered if seven was too many people and worried that the tower might topple over with them all on it.

Seth stepped up to go first. With a huge smile on his face, he was obviously excited.

"Honey, maybe you should let Jase or Gabby go first," Olivia said to her youngest.

"No!" Gabby and Jase practically shouted in unison, making everyone stare at them.

"No, it's fine," Gabby said with an embarrassed giggle. "He's so excited. He should go first."

"For sure," Jase agreed.

"Thanks," Seth said as he jumped to the front and started hooking up to the zipline. Ferdinand asked if he was ready.

"Ready!" Seth shouted. He jumped off the platform and glided down the line. They all watched as he let go of the line with one hand, leaning as far back as he could. He hollered with excitement as he whizzed over the jungle and drifted effortlessly into the next tower.

"Wooo! Yeah, baby!" Seth cheered, and they could hear him from the next tower. Gabby smiled and clapped along with everyone else, but her heart was beating like a drum in her chest.

"Who is next?" Ferdinand asked.

Ben went next, followed by Olivia and Sophie. They all seemed perfectly at ease flying through the sky. Gabby prayed she looked that graceful when it was her turn but would settle for not passing out.

"Jase, you ready?" Luke asked him.

Gabby recognized the scared but determined expression on Jase's face. Luke seemed to notice as well.

"It's cool, man, if you don't want to," Luke told Jase.

"No, I can do this." Jase gripped the cable. While the big orange gloves covered his hands, Gabby was sure his knuckles were white underneath. Jase closed his eyes, dropped his head for a long moment, took some deep breaths, and jumped. Gabby's stomach dropped as Jase lunged off the platform and hovered over the earth.

When Jase landed safely at the next tower, Gabby realized she had been holding her breath the whole time.

Jase let out a big "Woohoo," and everyone on the other side clapped and cheered. Gabby could see that he had a huge smile, and that made her smile too.

"Gabby, you're up next," Luke said.

Her stomach dropped again, and she thought she might faint. She went to take a step forward and tripped over her own feet. Luckily, Luke caught her before she fell.

"Whoa, that was close," she said and laughed nervously.

"I told you I had you," he said.

"Thanks," she managed. She was still shaking.

"I didn't realize you and Jase were afraid of heights," Luke said quietly.

"We're not afraid," she defended. "It's more of not a fan."

"If you really don't want to do this, we can go back down and just watch them," Luke said and put a hand on her shoulder.

Gabby thought about that. Then she decided that as much as she loved the thought of solid ground under her feet again, she had to do this. Jase had done it. Plus, she didn't want Luke to miss out on something he was obviously excited to do.

"No, I got this," she said, trying to sound confident.

"Then let's get you up there."

She stepped up to the opening, watching closely as Ferdinand connected her harness to the zipline.

"Is this payback for the shark?" She asked Luke, who just laughed. And shook his head. "Because, remember, you actually came into the water on your own."

"You can do this," Luke said as he put his hand over her gloved hand.

She was about to change her mind as her eyes measured just how far the earth was below her. Then she stopped and prayed silently. *Lord, please get me through this safely.*

Gabby wasn't sure if it was God or Luke, but she heard clearly in her ear, "Let go and jump." So, she did.

She felt her feet leave the platform to find nothing beneath them. The air rushed against her face, and she could hear the whizzing of the hook against the zipline. She heard someone screaming. She wondered where it was coming from then she realized it was her own voice. She screamed the entire way to the next tower, but she had to admit, it was exhilarating.

After she landed, her brother immediately wrapped her in a big hug.

"We did it!" she shouted at Jase, who was still smiling.

"Mom and Dad would be so proud of us," he said, hugging her again.

When Jase released her, she turned to see Luke gliding down the line with one hand on the cable, leaning backward and enjoying his ride.

After Luke landed and unhooked from the cable, he patted Jase on the back. Then turned and hugged Gabby.

"Look, you survived," Luke exclaimed.

"I did!" She smiled. "I think God helped."

"He always does. You just need to ask," Luke replied with a big smile.

"That's right," Gabby said.

She glanced at Jase, who scoffed at their statements. Luckily, Seth pulled him into a conversation, and Jase bounced back into a good mood.

Gabby had to admit, this was more fun than she had thought. But still grateful they were on the last leg of the course. Jase had even let go with one hand on the last one. Gabby kept a firm grip with both of her hands on all of them, but she was still proud that she had done it. The grin on Jase's face said that he did too.

Gabby was the first to descend the stairs to return the equipment to the hut. Unhooking and unlatching the harness and helmet, she heard the words whispered in her ear again, "Let go and jump." *Let go of what?* she thought.

Chapter 25: Jase

After ziplining, Jase was pumped up. That had been an adrenaline rush he hadn't expected. He wasn't in a hurry to do it again but had had a good time. Everyone returned their equipment and said their goodbyes to Ferdinand. Jase thought his name was fitting, as it had been a great adventure. And it had been very brave of him and Gabby to do those ziplines. As Jase climbed into the bus, he was still amazed that they had done that.

"Did everyone have fun?" Diego asked.

"Oh, yeah," Seth declared.

"I thought I would pass out up there," Gabby admitted to everyone with a beaming smile, obviously proud of herself too.

"How about you, Jase? Did you have fun?" Ben asked him.

"Yeah, today was good. I wasn't sure about the ziplining, but it was fun."

"It was brave of you guys to join in, especially since you're not big on heights," Olivia said.

Jase eyed his sister, who smirked at him. "Heights aren't our favorite thing, but our parents tried to make it one," He added.

"They really did," Gabby added. "For Jase's 21st birthday, we all went to Vegas. Our parents took us to the top of the Stratosphere. It's the tallest building in Las Vegas. It's like a needle with a space-ship balancing on top. There's a roller coaster that goes around the outside of the UFO part that Mom and Dad thought would be awesome."

"Like either of us really wanted to dangle over the Vegas strip in a roller coaster," Jase added.

"Right, so we passed on that. But somehow, they talked us into the Big Shot. It's another ride up the top. It sits four across and shoots you straight up into the air on a giant pole. It was ter-rifying."

"It was," Jase continued. "After it was over, we went to the souvenir booth to see our photos.

There was a big TV displaying all the photos. And there we were. Mom and Dad were laughing with their hands up. Me and Gabby were gripping onto the restraints like our lives depended on it, screaming like toddlers. Mom and Dad loved it so much they bought a copy."

"Yeah, it was also so thoughtful of them to use that as our Christmas card that year," Gabby said sarcastically.

"No! They didn't," Sophie exclaimed while everyone laughed.

"Yeah, they did," Jase said. "I had just been called up to play with the Defenders, and our family Christmas card had me crying like a baby on a ride. It was fantastic."

Jase chuckled as he rolled his eyes.

"That wasn't your best photo op," Gabby teased him.

"Maybe not, but remember when we went to Toronto? The CN tower? The glass floor?" Jase asked his sister in a teasing tone.

Gabby groaned and covered her face.

"The CN tower kind of reminds me of the Stratosphere now that I think about it," Jase said. "But there's this huge glass floor at the top that you can see 1500 feet to the ground below. Everyone was laying on it and having their pictures taken," Jase laughed. "Gabby was 19, and she was not about to lay on that glass floor to take a photo. Mom accidentally tripped her, and Gabs fell and started sobbing. Crawling off the glass floor back to safety, crying, 'Why would you do that? Why would you do that?'"

"I still say Mom pushed me down!" Gabby pleaded her case.

"She might have," Jase shrugged. "She had that camera out taking pics of you pretty quick for someone who claimed it was an accident."

Everyone joined in with laughter. Jase couldn't remember the last time he'd laughed so hard. It felt good.

When they arrived back at the resort, it was almost 3:00 pm. Jase knew he needed a shower and change of clothes. Everyone agreed they did, too, and decided to meet for dinner at 6:00 pm.

Jase and Gabby both flopped onto the couch when they made it back to the safety of their room. Jase appreciated sitting on solid furniture with a floor firmly under his feet, though he and Gabby were still laughing about the outing.

"I thought I was going to pee my pants on that zipline," Gabby admitted.

"Me too," Jase confessed.

"If only Mom and Dad could have seen us," Gabby said.

"I think they would have been shocked," Jase chuckled.

"You think?"

"I know," Jase said. "But can we agree on something?"

"What's that?"Gabby asked.

"No more surprise adventures."

"Deal," Gabby agreed, still laughing.

They both sat silent for a moment.

"You know, just before I jumped off on that first zipline," Jase paused.

"Yeah?"

"I prayed."

"You did?" Gabby sounded excited.

"Yeah, I did. That was terrifying," Jase said.

"It was," Gabby said. "I prayed too, but I also heard a voice."

"A voice?" Jase asked, confused as to where she was going with this. "Like God's voice?"

"I don't know, maybe," Gabby said sheepishly. "It said, 'Let go and jump.'"

"We were ziplining..." Jase tilted his head to the side. "That's what you were supposed to do."

"I felt like it meant more," Gabby said.

"Like what?"

"I'm not sure yet, but I guess I'll find out."

"Well, no more mystic Mayan adventures for you; you come back hearing voices," Jase said, trying to keep the mood light.

They both chuckled, but Jase could see that he'd hurt her feelings. "I'm sorry, Gabs. I'm just not sure God is talking to us...or if he's even real."

"What?" she exclaimed.

"Nothing, just forget about it."

"Jase," Gabby turned to him and made sure he was paying attention. "Of course God is real, and he loves us."

"He sure has a funny way of showing it," he mumbled.

"I know it seems like that right now, but..." Gabby stopped. "Who did you pray to if God isn't listening?"

She had him there. He wanted to believe...he just couldn't understand. Why would God take so much from him? From them? His sister had been a strong believer their whole lives. He knew God loved him at some point because his life had been perfect. Maybe he hadn't appreciated it, so God took it all away. Jase didn't know.

"Today was fun, Gabs, but I'm exhausted. I think I'm going to chill for a while."

"Okay," she said.

Jase slapped his knees and forced himself off the couch. He closed his door and crashed onto the bed. It had been a good day. He might even consider hanging out with the Andersons tomorrow. *We'll see*, he thought. Right now, he had earned a nice long nap.

CHAPTER 26: GABBY

After Jase went to his room, Gabby wandered out to the patio and sat with her feet in the water. *What a day.* Gabby felt ready for a nap herself.

She was still thinking about the voice she had heard. "Okay, God, I heard you. But let go of what? Jump into what?" she said out loud.

Was she supposed to let go of the business or the house? Of Mom and Dad? Of Jase? Of trying to control everything? Or had she really just heard someone say jump because she was ziplining? Did she make up the voice?

Maybe Jase was right, and she was just hearing things. What about him praying? Wow, she was so excited to hear that. She felt sad that he was questioning if God existed, though. She didn't know why God took their parents, but she knew there was a reason. It was all in God's master plans - the blueprints that we don't get to see. Someday, it would all make sense.

Maybe it was so she could meet Luke? Although that didn't make sense. God wouldn't take her parents so she could get a date. But there had to be some sort of divine intervention arranging for Luke and his family to be here and take Gabby and Jase under their wings.

Gabby sighed. Then her phone rang. Could it be Luke? It had to be. Who else would be calling?

"Hello?" she answered sweetly, expecting to hear Luke's voice.

The voice on the other end was not what she expected. It was a woman. "Hello, Gabby?"

"Yes?"

"Hi, sweetheart. It's Olivia."

Gabby felt a little disappointed. "Oh, hi Olivia."

"Sophie and I were wondering if you'd like to join us at the spa after breakfast tomorrow."

Gabby thought for a moment. A spa day does sound nice. She hadn't treated herself to any kind of pampering in a long time.

"That actually sounds fantastic," she told Olivia.

"Wonderful, I was hoping you'd say that. Also, the boys wanted to know if Jase wanted to go fishing with them at 9:00 am."

"I'll have to ask him, but he already went to take a nap," Gabby replied.

"Not a problem. They chartered a boat, so he can let them know at dinner tonight," Olivia told her.

"Sounds good," Gabby replied.

"Great, we'll see you then," Olivia said.

"Oh, Olivia," Gabby said quickly, trying to catch her before she hung up.

"Yes?"

"In case I forget later, thank you again for inviting us today," Gabby said. She really did appreciate the Andersons inviting them along.

"You're welcome. We're so glad you both came," Olivia said.

Gabby smiled as she hung up. She was glad they had gone too.

CHAPTER 27: LUKE

L uke was stretched out on the couch in their villa with his eyes closed. Suddenly, a weight landed on his stomach, knocking the breath from him.

"Way to make a great impression, bro," Seth said. Luke pushed Seth off of him as he sat up.

"What do you mean?" Luke said, knowing full well what his brother meant. The day had been awesome... Right up until the zipline.

"Let's see, what do Gabby and her brother absolutely love? Heights?" Seth asked, "Oh yeah, they actually hate them."

"Maybe ziplining wasn't the best choice. But I wouldn't have ever guessed they were afraid of heights?" Luke asked.

"Yeah, I wouldn't have thought Jase Jackson would be afraid of anything," Seth admitted.

"He's human just like the rest of us," Luke reminded his slightly starstruck brother.

"He wasn't human like the rest of us when he won the All-Star Home Run Derby last year. He was a beast," Seth said.

"He was," Luke remembered thinking Jase was superhuman when they watched that game. It was odd to think that the guy who had crushed home runs and helped his team win the all-star game, who had so much confidence on the field, would be scared of heights. It wasn't the fact that Jase was scared of heights. Everyone was scared of something. Luke didn't like to admit his fear of the ocean. Jase just wasn't at all the confident man he'd seen on the field and in interviews. He recognized the deep sadness in Jase. He'd seen it before. He'd felt it before.

Luke decided to pray for God to restore Jase's confidence. Maybe there was even a way he could help with it. He had seen a glimpse of that confidence again when Jase landed at the first zipline platform. Jase had looked so proud afterward, standing tall with his head held high. Gabby had that same excitement when she landed. Luke could tell it was a real accomplishment for them.

He wanted to call and see what Gabby was doing, but he'd just heard his mom call her. He had to figure out something he and Gabby could do together, just the two of them. He did want to ask Jase first; Sophie was right about that. He could ask Jase tomorrow while they were fishing. For now, he was starving and ready for dinner.

CHAPTER 28: GABBY

She and Jase met the Andersons for breakfast at the buffet. Both had come packed and ready for the rest of their day. Gabby had chosen a light sundress for her spa day. Since she was sure Jase wouldn't think of it, she packed him a bag with water, towels, and sunscreen.

After breakfast, Gabby followed everyone to the lobby where they were saying goodbye and parting to go their separate ways for the day. Gabby's heart was filled with joy that Jase seemed excited about going fishing with the Anderson men.

"Have a good time," Gabby said to her brother.

"Thanks. I actually think I will. I know you'll enjoy the spa," he said.

"I'll try," Gabby said with a big smile. "See you later; be careful."

"Have fun today. You deserve to relax," he said with a final wave as he followed Seth and Ben towards the doors.

Gabby had turned to see Luke still standing there. "Hey," she smiled at him.

"Hi," he smiled back at her,

"Thanks, you have fun too."

"I'll see you later?" he said, with a look in his eyes that melted her heart.

"I hope so," and she really did.

He took her hand and gave it a squeeze. "Me too," he said before turning to catch up with the rest of the men.

Olivia called after the men, "You boys behave. I don't want to hear that anyone was thrown overboard."

"Yes, ma'am," Luke and Seth answered.

"Jase, I expect you to keep them in line," Olivia said.

"Jase is more likely to spur them on," Gabby laughed.

Jase gave a slight smile. "I'll do my best, but I've never been opposed to seeing someone thrown overboard."

Once the men had left, Olivia took Gabby and Sophie by the arms. "Well ladies, are you ready for a day of pampering?"

"I'm not sure I've ever needed this more," Gabby said.

"I think we could all use it," Olivia told her.

After they checked in at the spa, they were escorted to small changing rooms to change into the spa robe and slippers. Olivia had reserved them each a half-day spa package. It included a thirty-minute massage, a facial, a sea salt hot soak, and a mani/pedi, followed by lunch.

The little room had some cute shelves and a closet for Gabby to keep her clothes and personal items in. She changed quickly into her bikini and wrapped the soft robe around her. She locked the room behind her and met Olivia and Sophie before being escorted to the massage area.

Gabby followed the massage therapist out a side door into the bright sunshine. She caught her breath at the beautiful setting before her. The ocean glistened nearby, while a lush garden surrounded the massage area. A pergola sheltered three massage tables, divided by thin curtains. The sea air and fragrances of various flowers enveloped her. A gentle breeze cooled her skin. She felt like she was entering an enchanted garden.

"Wow," Sophie exclaimed. "Just looking at this place is relaxing."

"No kidding," Gabby agreed.

Gabby rested on the massage table, running her hand over the silk sheets. It's *like laying on a cloud*, Gabby thought.

Gabby couldn't remember the last time she had taken time for some pampering. Stopping at Holly's coffee shop for an espresso had been her idea of pampering for the last few years. At home, she wouldn't even get a full manicure, settling for the thirty-minute express one. She wasn't even sure she knew how to relax anymore. She wondered when that had happened. When had she become so busy that she couldn't enjoy some Gabby time?

In high school, she had worked hard at school, swimming, and gymnastics. In college, even swimming and gymnastics took a back seat to her studies. Then, after college graduation, she went right to work for her dad. The only thing she did for herself anymore was to go work out or read her books at night. Her social life consisted of different charity events and dinners out with Holly. She only had an occasional first date. No wonder she never went out on second dates. Her life lacked some excitement and variety.

And now, with her parents gone...well, now she had focused her energy on Jase to make sure he was doing okay. She had been trying to get him to refocus on baseball or whatever the next step was going to be for him.

The masseuse's hands were working out the knots in her shoulders and back. It was definitely helping her relax, and the ocean breeze was lulling her thoughts away. The tension that normally resided in her shoulders and neck was absent. She couldn't remember the last time she'd felt this light. She was going to have to remember to book a regular massage when she got home.

After her massage, Gabby was led to the soaking room, with Sophie and Olivia right behind her. Oversized soaking tubs and soft music welcomed them. Apparently, Olivia and Sophie must have been feeling as relaxed as Gabby because no one spoke for at least five minutes once their soaking experience started.

With her head leaned back on the edge and eyes still closed, Sophie sighed, "This is so amazing."

"It is," Gabby agreed. "I don't know if I've ever felt so tranquil in my life."

"We should all get together and do this when we get back home," Olivia said.

"We should," Sophie agreed. "Especially to escape the snow and ice."

"I forgot about the snow," Gabby groaned. "It's so weird to think we were walking around in a foot of snow just a few days ago."

"And that we have to go back to it," Sophie said.

"I could stay here all day." Gabby leaned back, shutting her eyes and skimming the warm water with her hands.

Thirty minutes went by too quickly. The attendants came to collect them for their mani/pedi appointments. They dried off and wrapped up in the white, fluffy robes. Then they relocated to the ergonomical spa lounges for the completion of their spa day.

Gabby chose a teal green color and noticed Sophie and Olivia chose tropical colors too.

"It seems like a waste to wear a summer color when I'll have to change it for winter again when we get home," Sophie said, admiring the bright pink hue covering her nails.

"I think it'll help remind us of how relaxed and wonderful vacation was," Gabby said, delighted with the teal color she had chosen.

Olivia was obviously thrilled with the bright orange she had chosen, which complimented her already tan skin. "I might keep this color going all year."

"I'm sure, Mom," Sophie said while rolling her eyes. "You'll go back to your standard French manicure."

Olivia wiggled her toes which sparkled with orange polish.

"You're probably right, but maybe I'll keep it for the toes," she said and smiled at her daughter.

After they were done, they quickly changed and were escorted to a seaside terrace just outside the spa for lunch.

Seated at an oceanfront table, Gabby gazed at the crystal blue water as the gentle waves tumbled onto the shore. She thanked the waiter who placed glasses of lemon cucumber water in front of them. After ordering seafood Cobb salads, they sat in a comfortable silence, enjoying the view.

"I wonder who was pushed in first?" Sophie said, grinning mischievously and breaking the silence.

"I'm sure they're fine," Olivia chuckled.

"Are they all really that competitive?" Gabby asked.

"Yes," Sophie and Olivia answered.

Olivia continued, "We all are to some extent, but you know how men are. They take competition to a whole new level."

Gabby thought about all the things her family would turn into competitions. It wasn't just sports, but who could clean their room the fastest, who could get their homework done first, or who could fall asleep first. She gave a little laugh that made Olivia and Sophie glance up from their salads.

"I was just thinking about how competitive we were growing up and how well my parents took advantage of that. Who could clean up the dinner table fastest, who could clean their room the best, who could fall asleep first."

"Smart parents," Olivia said with a grin.

"Yeah, they were the best," Gabby said.

"I'm sure it's hard without them." Olivia took Gabby's hand in hers. The gesture startled Gabby. When her gaze met Olivia's, she fully expected to see that sympathetic face she hated. Instead, she saw love and caring.

"Thank you." Gabby nodded at her. "It's been a rough year."

"I know it has," Olivia said.

Sophie sat silently with her hands in her lap, fidgeting with her napkin.

"Luke told you all before we did, didn't he?" Gabby asked, feeling a little betrayed.

"He did," Olivia said cautiously, "but he was concerned for you guys. And actually, I already knew. I recognized your names from the paper."

"You did?" Gabby asked. Sophie also appeared confused by this.

"Yes, I just didn't want to say anything unless you wanted to talk about it," Olivia said.

"Thank you, most people can't wait to remind Jase and I about it," Gabby said.

"In fact, Ben and I were at the same charity event your parents attended the night of the accident."

"You were?" Gabby flashed back to that first dinner when she confessed the real reason for their desire to escape Christmas. The look Olivia had given her that night made sense now. They had already known.

"We met your parents, Vincent and Jillian, at that dinner. We were seated at the same table. Jillian and I got to talk for a while, and she was really something. She seemed to care about her students and loved her job."

"She did." Gabby smiled. "Mom was a special ed teacher at the high school. Her students had more emotional issues than mental ones, but she taught them how to read, and they adored her. I would stop by the classroom to bring her lunch. Just one glance at their faces showed how much they loved and respected my mom."

"And she was so proud of you and your brother," Olivia continued.

Gabby's eyes went wide, "Really?"

"Oh yes! She hoped Jase would complete his therapy and get back to baseball."

That wasn't surprising to Gabby. Mom had always been Jase's biggest fan.

Olivia went on. "And she was so impressed with you."

"She was?" Gabby nearly whispered. Her mom never seemed as open about how proud she was of her as she was of Jase.

"Oh yes, darling. Both of your parents were. Your dad kept bragging about how you were taking his business to places he hadn't even imagined. Mostly, he just hoped you loved it as much as he did. It was obvious how much your parents loved both of you."

Gabby couldn't speak, but she nodded and smiled. It was one thing to hear how much her parents loved them from their friends, but another thing to hear it from someone who had only met her parents once.

"I can't imagine how hard this year has been for you. I know nothing is ever going to be the same again, but you can be assured that your parents loved you and your brother more than anything else in this world," Olivia said earnestly.

"I'm not sure how I'm going to live without them," Gabby sniffed.

"One day at a time, sometimes one breath at a time. You will find your way," Olivia said, squeezing her hand.

"And Jase, I just..." Gabby trailed off. She wasn't sure what to say.

"Jase will find his way too," Olivia assured her.

"But how am I supposed to help him?" Gabby asked.

"Just pray for him, love him, and be his sister," Olvia told her.

Something in Olivia's words gave Gabby new hope that things might be okay.

"I will keep praying for both of you," Olivia said.

"We all will," Sophie added, taking Gabby's other hand. "And you and Jase are part of our family now. We'll be here for you."

Gabby felt overwhelmed with gratitude. These people, who had been strangers just days ago, had given her a renewed faith that most of her friends and family hadn't been able to give over the last six months. *Wow, God really does put the right people in the right place at the right time*, she thought.

CHAPTER 29: JASE

Jase was feeling pretty content. Kicked back in a padded seat, feet propped up, having a drink with the guys, watching his fishing pole mounted to the side of the boat for any movement. Yes, life was okay at the moment. Not a single fish had been caught yet, but he was enjoying the view and the easy conversation.

As the boat rocked with the waves, Ben leaned back. "I could get used to this."

"Are you going to buy us a boat, Dad?" Seth asked.

"I might buy your mom and I a boat," Ben told his youngest.

"Is that how you're going to spend retirement?" Luke asked his dad.

"Maybe," he replied, tilting his face to the sun.

"Are you retiring, Ben?" Jase asked.

"No, I'm only 58." Ben laughed. "But it's always fun to think about."

"Maybe I'll retire with you," Seth said.

"You have to retire from something Seth," his brother reminded him, flicking his hat off his head.

"Hey," Seth shouted, managing to grab the hat out of the air before it blew overboard.

All this talk of retiring was making Jase a little nervous. He knew he wouldn't be able to play ball forever. Baseball definitely had a shelf life, and he was getting close to the expiration date. Unlike Ben, he wasn't sure what else he would do. At twenty, you think baseball will last forever. At 27 and with an injury, he realized his career wouldn't last forever. Maybe it was already over.

"Hey, Luke," Seth said, "did you figure out what you're going to do with the kids after Christmas?"

"Kids?" Jase asked.

"My students," Luke replied. "I really should spend some time planning lessons for after break, but there's so much to do here. It's nice just kicking back for a change."

"I'm sure you'll come up with something awesome," Seth said.

"I hope so," Luke said. "It's hard to get high school kids interested in history. With all the tablets and smartphones, they have the attention span of squirrels."

They all laughed at that.

"Luke is awesome, though. You should see the ideas he comes up with to keep the kids interested in his lessons," Seth said.

"Like what?" Jase asked.

Luke described some of his attempts to entertain while teaching. One time, he had the students recreate historic court cases to see if the jury would still have the same verdicts. Other times, he dressed up as former presidents or generals and gave their famous speeches.

"My favorite was close to Halloween," Seth said. "Luke had them research historical mysteries and present them like they were a mystery show on YouTube. The kids had to present the information and come up with conclusions of what might have happened."

"That's cool," Jase said. "I wish my teachers had tried to do something like that. I may have paid more attention."

"Thanks. I like when the kids get engaged and have fun with it," Luke said. "Seth would make a good teacher too."

"Let's not start on this again," Seth grunted.

"I'm not starting anything. I was just saying," Luke defended.

Jase wanted to save Seth from an inquisition. "What do you want to do, Seth?"

"I'm not sure yet," Seth said.

"Seth is still finding his path," Ben explained. "But I'm sure he'll find it soon."

Ben focused his eyes on Seth. Seth replied with an exasperated sigh and an eye roll.

"I get it," Jase said. "I don't know what I'd do if baseball hadn't worked out for me."

"Really?" Seth asked.

"Yeah, I'd probably be trying to play video games for a living or something," Jase joked.

Seth and the other guys chuckled.

"I have a business degree, but I don't want to just take a job," Seth explained. "I want to be like the rest of my family. I want a job that makes a difference in people's lives."

"But not in teaching?" Jase asked him.

"I don't think teaching is for me," Seth said, shaking his head

"What do you like about the jobs you've had? You said you've been a lifeguard, ski instructor..." Jase asked. He saw a lot of potential in Seth.

"I don't know." Seth considered the question. "I guess I liked that I kept people safe, taught them things, and they were fun," Seth replied.

"Maybe you need to research opportunities or careers that can give you that," Jase said.

Seth nodded, and Jase could see the wheels turning in his head. He glanced at Ben, who smiled and gave him an appreciative nod.

"Thanks," Seth said after a few moments. "I never thought about careers that could be fun too. Business seemed like it would be a life of suits and offices with no windows."

Jase laughed, that's what he had always thought too. "Then why did you pick it?"

"I don't know. I was good at the classes, and I had to pick something." Seth shrugged. "Everyone said it was a good idea that could open a lot of doors."

Jase noticed Ben and Luke shaking their heads with a little laugh.

"Well, I guess that's true," Jase chuckled. "You just have to pick a door that's good for you. You can find a company who matches what you're looking for or start your own company."

Seth seemed to contemplate that for a while but then spoke up again.

"So what are you going to do, Jase?" Seth asked, suddenly changing the subject. "You think you'll play again?"

Jase was taken aback by the question. He hadn't expected the conversation to circle back to him. He still didn't know how to answer it.

Ben peered sharply at his youngest son and grunted. "Seth."

"It's fine. I have to think about it sometime," Jase said. "I'm really not sure. My knee is feeling better. I just don't know if I want to play anymore. But if I don't, I don't know what I'll do. All I've ever done is baseball."

"Dude, you have the greatest job in the world," Seth said. "Why would you give that up?"

Luke poked his brother and gave him the same glare that he must have learned from his father.

"It's just not the same now," Jase shook his head.

"Since your parents?" Ben asked gently.

Jase raised his eyes to meet Ben's. "Yeah, between losing them and hurting my knee, I think I lost the heart to play. Even if I wanted to, I'm not sure my team wants me back."

Jase was surprised he was able to open up like this. Once he had started, he couldn't seem to stop.

"My parents were my biggest fans. Them and Gabby. They came to every game from the time I hit my first ball off a tee. Dad coached most of my teams until high school, and even then he volunteered with the team. Without Mom and Dad, the passion and the drive that I used to feel is just...gone."

"It's not gone, son. It's just buried deep below all the other emotions right now," Ben said.

Jase shrugged. It sure felt like it was gone and replaced with all the other emotions.

"You know, Olivia and I were at the same charity event as your parents and sat at the same table with them. We were shocked and saddened to read about the accident the next morning. We really enjoyed their company and even made plans to all go out to dinner sometime."

"You were there?" Jase said while Luke and Seth stared at Ben in surprise.

"We were, and they were both so proud of you and Gabby," Ben assured him.

"Well of course they were proud of Gabby. She's their perfect child." Jase scoffed.

Ben laughed. "They seemed proud of both of you. They hoped you'd go back to playing baseball. They just weren't sure if your heart was still in it either. But they loved watching you play."

The memory of his parents cheering in the stands made Jase smile.

"I know it won't be the same without them. People will tell you that they are there watching over you, and I believe that too. But you have to decide for yourself if you want to play again. You have to do it for yourself, whatever you decide," Ben said.

Jase turned his focus to the ocean. He wasn't sure what he wanted. He tried to sort through the storm of thoughts thundering through his head. He believed his parents were watching over him too. But it wasn't the same as them actually being there.

"I don't know what I want anymore," he finally confessed.

"That's understandable," Ben agreed, "but you can't hide from life forever."

"I'm not hiding, I just..." Jase thought for a moment before admitting, "Maybe I've kind of been hiding."

"And that's okay for now. Life just turned upside down for you and Gabby," Ben said.

Jase nodded. "I feel guilty that Gabby moved home."

"Why's that?" Ben asked.

"She had her whole life going for her, graduated college, took over Dad's business, and bought her own cute little house that was totally her. And then she sold it or rented it, something, I don't even know. Then she moved back home with me."

"And you feel guilty that she wanted to be near you?" Ben asked.

"No," Jase started. "I feel guilty because I'm glad she did. Now I can hear her and see her and know she's there, know that she's safe. I worry that something will happen to her all the time. She's all I have left. Even her fifteen-minute drive to the office seems too far. What if something happened and I couldn't get to her in time?"

Ben leaned forward and looked into Jase's eyes. "Jase, you can't live in fear that something bad is going to happen."

"But it already has happened," Jase scowled.

"You're right, it has," Ben said. "But constantly worrying that something else will happen isn't going to do you any good."

Jase considered that for a moment.

"I don't know your sister well," Ben added, "but I don't think she is someone who does things she doesn't want to do."

"Yes, she would," Jase replied. "She is all about duty and obligation. Do you think she dreamed of running the family insurance business? She just didn't want to let Dad sell off something he spent a lifetime building."

"I think she loves you, just like you love her. I'm sure she doesn't see you as an obligation," said Ben. "She is probably just as happy right now being near you."

Jase nodded as he let Ben's words sink in.

"Listen, Jase," Ben said. "Life spins out of control sometimes; it knocks us down. It's okay to sit and regroup for a bit. Then, one day, you stand up and grab control again, even if it's little by little. But you can't lay down and die. Eventually, you have to get back up and live the life you are supposed to."

Jase raked his hand through his hair. "Yeah, I don't even know where to begin, though."

"With prayer," Ben said.

Jase rolled his eyes. "Like God's even listening."

"God is always there and always listening," Ben said gently.

"He has a funny way of showing it," Jase mumbled.

"Son, we don't know why things happen the way they do, but we can choose how we react to them," Ben said. "The fact that you woke up this morning means that God isn't done with you."

Jase let Ben's words circle in his head. He just didn't understand how God could take such good people like his parents. How could that have been part of God's great plan? Didn't God see the world was a better place with them in it? He could have saved them, but he didn't. Didn't God realize that he was better with his parents here? He needed them. Jase couldn't see past the pain of today to any sort of future.

His thoughts were interrupted by a sudden whirring sound as his reel started spinning.

"Whoa! We got a live one!" Ben shouted, and they all jumped to their feet.

Jase grabbed the rod and started reeling in whatever was on the other end. Seth jumped in, and the two battled with the line for what seemed like forever. Ben and Luke were watching over the side, with nets ready, cheering them on. Finally, they pulled it onboard. No one could believe what they were watching flop around on the boat's floor.

"Is that..." Jase started as he stared at the large, flat, black creature.

"That's a stingray," Seth shouted excitedly.

"It sure is," Ben said, taking his ball cap off and rubbing his head.

"What do we do with it?" Jase laughed.

"Can we keep it?" Seth asked. "I can get a big tank at home."

"Seth, how would you explain that at customs?" Luke asked.

"I don't know yet," Seth said. Jase could see Seth's wheels turning, trying to figure out how to make this work.

"We need to get it back into its home guys," Ben said.

"Can we at least take some pics first," Seth asked, already searching for his camera. "No one will ever believe this if we don't have photographic evidence."

"Okay, but let's make it quick. We don't want him to get hurt out here," Ben said. He lifted a flipper and started to remove the hook from the stingray.

"It doesn't look like he was injured." Ben smiled.

After posing for a few quick photos, the four of them struggled to lift the flapping ray and heave it over the side of the boat. It landed with a splash. They watched as the ray disappeared quickly into the deep water. Jase still couldn't believe what had just happened and agreed when Ben asked if they were ready to call it a day, and they started back to shore.

Jase sat at the back of the boat, staring at the horizon. Ben's words rolled through his head like thunder. He knew he couldn't stay where he was but didn't know how to get away from it either. He wasn't sure he wanted to. He had become comfortable in his misery, accepting that this is just how life is now. What would happen if he tried to step away from it?

With the boat bumping up and down with the waves, he was startled by Luke's voice right behind him.

"Sorry, I didn't mean to startle you," Luke said.

"All good man. What's up?" Jase noticed Luke had an odd expression.

"I've actually wanted to talk to you about something all day, but I wanted to make sure you were good," Luke said. "I've been on the receiving end of Dad's pep talks many times. I know they can leave you with a lot on your mind."

"Yeah," Jase said. Luke was right about that; Ben's words had left him feeling emotions he'd been trying to avoid. Jase wasn't sure he wanted to dive any deeper into that right now, so he just said, "I'm good, but thanks."

"You sure?" Luke asked skeptically.

"Yup, all good," Jase said. "So, what did you want to talk to me about?"

"I wanted to talk to you about Gabby," Luke said.

Jase grinned. Luke liked Gabby. Jase could see it, and he thought Luke would be good for her. He decided to put Luke out of his misery. He said, "I think she likes you too."

Luke turned towards Jase. "What?"

"My sister, she likes you too."

"You think?"

"Yeah. She doesn't normally get all goofy around guys, but you have her tripping over her own feet." Jase gave a small grin.

"I wanted to see if you were cool with me asking her out on a date."

"I think it would be good for her, and you seem like a good guy," Jase smirked.

"Thanks, I appreciate that," Luke said. "Well, I'll let you get back to your thoughts."

Luke stood and walked over to help his dad steer the boat. Jase stared off to the horizon. *It's been a strange day*, he thought. Not bad, just not what he had expected.

CHAPTER 30: GABBY

G abby was sitting on the patio soaking in the sun with her feet in the water and reading a book when Jase came back to the room. She put down her book, anxious to hear how fishing with the guys went.

"Hey, how was fishing?" She asked her brother.

"It was fine," he said. He walked past her and went directly into his room.

"Okay?" She was confused. He wasn't mad, not happy. She wasn't sure what he was. What could have happened?

Gabby waited for Jase to come back, wanting to give him his space. *Ben probably talked about Mom and Dad too*, she thought. Maybe they decided that they would each mention it today. She hoped this didn't make her brother spiral downward after he seemed to be coming out of his shell. She also hoped it didn't mean that they wouldn't be able to see the Anderson family anymore. She enjoyed their company.

Jase came back out and sat on the lounge chair.

"You okay?" she asked.

"I don't know," he replied, but his voice was gentle.

"Want to talk about it?"

"I don't know. Ben talked to me about Mom and Dad...and I don't know."

"Olivia talked to me today, too," Gabby confessed.

"Ben told me how proud Mom and Dad were of me and how they hoped I wouldn't quit baseball," Jase said pensively.

"Yeah?"

"I just don't know if I want to," Jase said. Then quietly added, "Or if the team even wants me back."

"One day at a time, sometimes one breath at a time," Gabby said, hoping Olivia's words would have the same impact on Jase that they had on her.

"I don't know." Jase shook his head.

"The good news is you don't have to decide anything today," Gabby said. "We can just enjoy the time we have here. Like we said on the plane."

"Yeah, we have a lot to figure out when we get home," Jase said.

Gabby wasn't sure what all he meant by that. She also wasn't sure if she wanted to know right now, either.

"So, how was fishing?" Gabby changed the subject.

Jase grinned. "I was the only one who caught anything."

"What? That's awesome! What did you catch?"

"A stingray," he chuckled.

"A stingray?" Gabby gasped.

"Yeah, it shocked us all too." Jase's mood started to lift as he described reeling in the line, only to find a huge stingray at the end of it.

"We aren't eating it for dinner, are we?" Gabby laughed nervously.

"No," Jase said, shaking his head. "We tossed it right back after we got it off the hook and took a photo. That thing was heavy and strong."

"Oh good." Gabby sighed. "Did anyone get tossed overboard?"

"No, just the stingray," Jase said glumly. "I was really hoping to see someone get chucked over."

"Of course you did." Gabby laughed at her brother. "Do you still want to have dinner with the Andersons?"

"Why wouldn't I?"

"I don't know, I just thought after today you might feel..." Gabby trailed off, not really knowing what he would feel.

"I like them, and I like being around them. They're good people," said Jase. "It's just hard sometimes to see them together. They are a lot like we were as a family."

"They are, aren't they?" Gabby stood up and hugged her brother.

"Besides," he said, "I'm not going to miss out on the steakhouse."

That made Gabby laugh. "No, the Jacksons are not people who turn down steak."

As she hugged him tighter, she caught a whiff of his activities that day. She added, "Maybe you should take a shower before dinner. You smell like fish bait."

Jase sniffed himself. "I kind of do."

Jase turned to go to his room, then he stopped and turned back to Gabby. He seemed to be examining her. *Why is he looking at me like that?* she wondered.

"Did you have a good time at the spa?"

"It was amazing," she sighed.

"You look so... relaxed."

"It was amazing."

"Good for you. You needed that." He was just about to leave but stopped again and said, "By the way, I think Luke wants to talk to you later."

"About what?"

"I don't know, but I told him it was a good idea." He shrugged with a smirk.

"You told him it was a good idea to talk to me about something, but you have no idea what that something could be?" She asked.

Jase winked at her. "Yup." Then he headed inside.

That's a little odd, even for Jase, she thought. Then she went to change for dinner as well.

As she was getting ready, she prayed that Ben's words had impacted Jase the way Olivia's words had impacted her. Maybe she and Jase were both ready for the next step, whatever that was supposed to be.

CHAPTER 31: LUKE

Luke sat on the patio with his sister, telling her about the day's adventures.

"I can't believe Jase caught a stingray," Sophie said.

"Neither could any of us," Luke said.

"I also can't believe he was the only one that caught anything," Sophie teased. "He needs to come around more often and put you guys in your place."

Luke thought back on the conversation that Jase and his dad had. "I hope he still comes around at all after Dad's little chat with him."

"Dad's chat?"

"Yeah. One of Dad's chats," Luke said. He gave his sister a knowing glance.

"Oh, one of his 'get to the heart of the matter' chats," Sophie said.

"Exactly. Did you know Mom and Dad met Jase's parents the night they had the accident?"

"I found that out over lunch. I couldn't believe it," Sophie said, shaking her head.

"Me neither," Luke said.

"So, you don't think Jase will want to come back around because Mom and Dad met his parents?" Sophie asked. "I mean, they didn't cause the accident. They didn't even know about it until the next day."

"No, not because of that. Jase seemed unsettled after Dad's pep talk."

"Ah," Sophie said knowingly.

"Yeah. I hope Dad didn't push him too hard. Jase might not have been ready for that. It's still all so fresh."

"Or maybe it was the perfect time to hear it," Sophie said hopefully.

"Maybe." Luke shrugged.

"Luke, do you remember when you got out of the Army?"

"Yeah?" Luke wondered where she was going with this.

"You were miserable and lost," Sophie said.

"No, I wasn't," Luke defended, even though he knew he had been.

"You were miserable, and you were making the rest of us miserable," Sophie said.

This made Luke wince. He hated that he'd caused so much pain to his family.

"Luke, we didn't blame you. You'd gone through things that we couldn't relate to. You lost friends in the most horrible way," Sophie said empathetically. "None of us knew how to help you. You'd stay locked in your apartment for days. We didn't know from day to day how you were going to be or if you would stay that way forever. It was like Luke was gone and replaced by some zombie Luke. Like you were there physically, but not mentally."

Luke remembered. It wasn't a time he wanted to revisit.

"Dad prayed for you. We all did. Then, after a few months, what did Dad do?"

"He gave me a pep talk and dragged me to church." He said, nodding his head.

"That's right. He knew it was time that you came out of the darkness to see the light."

Sophie was right. He had sat in darkness for months, reliving the unthinkable things he had seen, unsure of what to do. Every moment of every day had been planned for him for eight years. Then suddenly, he had nothing to do. And his family and friends couldn't understand what he was going through. He didn't realize that his depression had affected his siblings so much. His dad had finally sat him down and given him a similar speech to what he gave Jase this afternoon.

Sophie continued. "What happened after weeks of church and Bible study?"

"I started talking to Dad, to Mom, to other vets from the church. Gradually, I realized that what I loved most about the Army was coaching and encouraging the younger guys. I enjoyed watching them grow and accomplish things they didn't know they could. Then I enrolled in college and got my masters."

"Right, and now you're an amazing teacher and an amazing man of God. You had to go through everything you did and needed that push from Dad to come out the other side. That's what Dad is trying to do with Jase since Jase's dad can't. Honestly, I think it was God's work that we are all here together."

Luke stared at his sister. "How did you get so smart?" He was continually amazed at her wisdom.

"You're welcome." She smiled at him. "Since you think I'm so smart, maybe you'll listen when I say I think it's time for you to ask Gabby out for a real date."

"Oh yeah?" Luke laughed.

"You did ask her brother if you could ask her out, right?" Sophie asked pointedly.

"I did." He smiled at her.

"And he thought it was a good idea too, right?" She grinned like she already knew the answer.

"He seemed to."

"Perfect! Then ask her," Sophie said. "I've gotten to know her, and I just know that something special could happen between the two of you."

"You think?" Luke asked.

"I do. She's a wonderful person. She's smart, funny, and has a strong faith too. Not to mention, she's beautiful." Sophie said enthusiastically.

Luke agreed. Gabby did seem to be all that. "What should I ask her to do?"

"Funny you should ask...." Sophie reached into the back pocket of her shorts and pulled out one of the resort brochures. Luke took it and read it over.

"This could be perfect. I'll make a reservation for tonight after dinner." He said with a smile.

"Tonight, then?" Sophie asked expectedly.

"Yeah, tonight."

Sophie clapped her hands. "Go call her, and I'll call and make the reservation for you."

"Thanks! And thanks for the pep talk. Dad would be proud." He nudged his sister's shoulder.

That made Sophie smile even more.

Luke picked up the phone to call Gabby.

The phone was ringing, and his heart was pounding. It rang again and again.

"Hello?" Gabby answered.

"Gabby?"

"Luke?"

"Yeah, hi."

"Hi," she replied. He could hear the smile in her voice.

"I wanted to make sure you guys were still coming to dinner?"

"Of course, neither of us would miss out on a steakhouse." She said enthusiastically.

"Great," he said. He gave himself a mental pep talk. *I can do this. I can do this.*

"Luke, are you there?"

"Yes, sorry. I was just wondering if, after dinner, you wanted to go do something?"

"I'll see if Jase has plans, but I'm sure we are free."

"Actually, I meant just you...like me and you could go do something."

"Oh," was all she said. Luke waited what felt like an hour before she spoke again.

Finally, she said, "Yes."

"Yes?"

"Sure. What did you have in mind?"

"It's a surprise," Luke said, hoping she liked surprises.

"I like surprises," she said.

"I thought you might," Luke said, feeling relieved.

"What should I wear?"

"Anything will be fine."

"No more heights though, right?" She asked anxiously.

"No, I promise I won't do that to you again."

"Then yes." She laughed. "I'll see you in a little while then."

"Great. I'll see you at dinner," Luke said with a wide grin.

Luke couldn't help but smile as Sophie walked back into the room.

"She said yes, I see," Sophie smirked.

"Yes, she said she'd go. I told her it was a surprise, so don't ruin it at dinner."

Sophie feigned hurt feelings. "I would never! I have everything all arranged for you. They'll have blankets and pillows on board, and I'll have a goodie bag delivered to the boat."

"You thought of everything," Luke said.

"It's what I do. I'm proud of you trying to live a life you coach others to live."

His sister, as usual, was right. He was good at pushing the veterans in groups to live outside their comfort zones. Be bolder in their choices. Live with no regrets, be intentional in their actions, resolve old wounds, be their authentic selves, engrave discomfort, and be vulnerable. But he's been living a safe life. There was a steady routine, and he liked that. He hadn't let anyone in since Priscilla, and frankly, he hadn't even let her into his heart. He realized it was time to put into practice the things he was preaching.

Luke wrapped his arm around his sister. "Thanks for the push."

"You're welcome. Now please get ready and don't take forever." Sophie said and shooed him off to his room.

CHAPTER 32: GABBY

Gabby was so grateful Holly had talked her into packing some of her nicer dresses. They were all going to the steakhouse for dinner. Then she and Luke were doing something together...alone. She felt both excited and nervous. Was this a date? It had been so long since she'd been on one. She didn't know how to act or what to say. Or was this not a date? Was he just being nice?

Gabby decided on a white maxi dress with a delicate pink floral pattern and cream wedge sandals. She scrutinized herself in the mirror. Why was she so nervous? And what did Luke have planned for them? She was so distracted, she barely heard Jase knock on the door. He came in without waiting for her to answer.

"Wow!" Jase scanned his sister. "You look nice."

She turned to him. "Is it too much?"

"Not at all. Luke will love it," Jase said with a nod.

Gabby rolled her eyes at him, but she couldn't wipe the smile off her face.

"Luke asked me to do something with him after dinner."

"I hope you said yes," he said with a raised brow.

"I did," Gabby said. Her smile spread even wider.

What are you guys doing?"

"I don't know, it's a surprise." Gabby noticed concern cross his face. She continued, "Luke said no heights and nothing dangerous."

"Good," he said, and Gabby noticed he relaxed a little.

"By the way, you look nice too," she complimented him. She was impressed that his khaki pants were pressed and paired with a blue linen button-down shirt.

"Did you brush your hair?" she teased.

Jase ran his hand through his wavy brown hair."Yeah, it was all...you know, tangled from being out on the ocean all day."

"It looks good." She nodded an approval. She refrained from mentioning it could use a trim and chose to just be grateful that he was taking an interest in himself again. The past few months, he'd let his hair grow and stuffed it under a ball cap. *This is a good sign*, she thought.

"We clean up pretty good, little bro." Gabby admired their reflection in the mirror and looped her arm around his waist.

"We sure do," he agreed.

As they walked out the door, she asked, "Are you sure you're okay on your own tonight?"

"Of course," Jase replied. "Seth and I will probably grab some drinks, maybe see one of the comedy shows."

"That sounds like fun."

"I see a bit of my younger self in Seth," Jase said thoughtfully.

"I'm sure it's good for him to be around you."

"Yeah, because I'm an awesome role model," Jase stated, rolling his eyes.

"You are!" Gabby smiled at her brother and prayed he'd realize someday what an amazing human he was. Seth was nearly five years younger than them. Gabby could see that he really idolized his brother and now Jase too.

They arrived at the restaurant before the Anderson Family, which was a first. The hostess told them it would be a few moments while they finished getting their table ready. Gabby watched the tropical fish swim in the floor-to-ceiling aquarium. She could hear Jase pacing behind her. Then heard him say "Gabs" and nudged her arm with his.

She turned to see the Anderson family appear at the entrance of the restaurant. It was like a movie scene started playing in Gabby's mind. Like she could hear theme music playing and swore they were walking in slow-motion. They were all stunning. The three handsome men wore button-down shirts in different shades of blue. The two tall, slender women wore white and blue dresses with different floral patterns.

"Do you think they do cover shoots for GQ in their spare time?" Jase whispered to his sister as if he was reading her mind.

"They must," she whispered back.

Luke caught Gabby's eye and smiled. He looked amazing.

"Hi," she said, feeling suddenly shy.

"Hi." Luke smiled back. "You look really beautiful."

"Thank you," she smiled shyly.

They all walked to their table, and Luke pulled out her chair.

"Thank you again," she said. "And they said chivalry is dead."

"I tried to raise my boys right," Olivia said with a smile.

"I'd say you did a good job," Gabby assured her.

Everyone ordered some version of surf and turf. The conversation turned to their outings that day.

Their meals arrived just as Seth pulled out his phone and showed photos of the stingray and their fishing excursion. Everyone laughed as Seth gave an animated recount of the stingray story. When Gabby saw the photo, she noticed that Jase genuinely appeared to be having a good time. She hadn't seen her brother smile that much in a long time, even before the accident. It made her heart smile. She said a silent prayer. *Thank you God, for giving him a good day.*

There were photos of each of the men posing with the stingray and photos of them releasing it back to its watery home. Gabby paused on a photo of Luke. He was shirtless, with his baseball cap on backwards, and leaning back in his chair. She couldn't help but stare at how handsome he was. Even the funny face he was making at the photographer made him more endearing to her.

"Let me see." Sophie reached for the phone. The guys were laughing at Seth's retelling of what sounded like a scene from Three Stooges. Feeling embarrassed, Gabby quickly swiped to the next photo before passing the phone to Sophie.

Gabby glanced up and caught Luke's eyes on her. Did he know she was just checking him out in a photo? *Why does he have to be so ridiculously handsome?* she thought.

"Seth, can I get copies of all of those?" Gabby asked Seth.

"Sure! I'll post them and send you the link."

"Thanks," She said.

"We should all post our vacation photos there," Seth added.

"What a great idea," Sophie agreed. "I can't wait to see them all."

Gabby was excited to see all the photos too. She knew this was a trip she would remember forever, with or without the photos.

As dinner came to a close, Gabby felt both nervous and excited about her outing with Luke. She wondered what they were going to do and what they would talk about. They'd had easy conversations since they met. What if they ran out of things to say? If they didn't have a good time, would it make it awkward to see the Andersons the rest of the trip?

Her stomach was starting to react to her emotions. She put her hand over it to try to calm the butterflies.

"Relax," Jase whispered to her.

"I'm fine. I think maybe my stomach is acting up. Maybe I should go back to the..." She whispered. Before she could finish, Jase touched her arm. "Gabs, you will go, and you will have a good time."

She moved her eyes to meet her brothers.

"It's one night. You don't need to marry the guy," he whispered even lower.

That made her laugh. She hadn't even tried to think that far ahead.

"So, you're good?" he asked.

She nodded, feeling herself relax. "Yes. I'll be fine."

"You'll be more than fine. You'll have a great time," he said, offering her a grin.

Her nerves were settling a little. Jase was right. No one was proposing marriage. It was one night. What's the worst that could happen?

CHAPTER 33: GABBY

Gabby stood just outside the restaurant. It seemed like everyone was talking at once, planning what they would each do for the evening and trying to decide on plans for the following day. Gabby mentioned she hadn't had any beach time yet, so they all agreed to have a beach day tomorrow. She noticed Luke glancing at his watch and then at her. Pulling her away from the group, he asked if she was ready to go.

"Yes," Gabby said. "Are you sure I'm dressed appropriately for... whatever we might be doing?"

Luke stood back, examining her outfit. "You are perfect."

Gabby felt heat climb into her cheeks and thanked him. "I'm ready then."

"Great! Wait here, and I'll be back in a few minutes," Luke said.

Gabby watched Luke walk off. She wondered what he could be up to and what they could possibly be doing tonight. She heard someone approaching behind her and turned to see her brother smirking at her.

"What are you going to do now?" Gabby asked her brother.

"I'm not sure yet," Jase replied.

"Are you sure you're good with me going to hang out with Luke?"

"Yes!" Jase laughed. "Please go enjoy your date."

Gabby smiled. "Thank you, but if you don't have something to do or don't want to be alone, I can..."

Before she could finish, Seth and Sophie approached, each taking one of Jase's arms. "Hey Jase, we are kidnapping you for the evening."

Jase smiled and shrugged at his sister. "Look at that. I guess you're out of excuses."

"Haha," Gabby replied with a hint of sarcasm. "You go have fun too."

She watched as her brother strolled off with the other two Anderson siblings. She smiled, thinking how grateful she was that God had sent this family to them. The Andersons truly had made this vacation special for her and her brother. And to think that she and Jase had judged them so harshly when they first laid eyes on them. She couldn't help but feel these new friends would be a part of their lives for a long time to come.

"I'm back." Luke's voice interrupted her thoughts. "Ready?"

"Yes," Gabby said.

"Then let's go," Luke said, holding out his arm for Gabby to take.

She looped her arm through his thinking. *It has been a long time since I've met a man that was such a gentleman.*

"So where are we going?" She asked as they walked out the doors to the beach.

He gazed down at her. "I told you, it's a surprise."

"Can you at least tell me where we're going yet?" She asked after some time walking together.

"We're almost there," Luke told her.

They walked along the waterfront boardwalk, then turned onto the wooden dock. She tried to locate any signs for an activity, but she saw nothing but the marina.

"Alright. Here we are," Luke said.

"Of course, the end of the dock," Gabby said. "It was the highlight of all the resort brochures."

"Just wait a minute," Luke said with a laugh. Peering to the left and waving his arm.

Moments later, a sailboat came drifting up. It came to a stop in front of them. It was just like the one that had taken them out snorkeling. Just as Gabby was about to ask, she noticed Captain Rivera was standing on the side of the boat. He jumped off when he was closer to the dock and started to tie up the boat. "Buenas noches, amigos!," The captain greeted them. He shook Luke's hand and then Gabby's.

"Hola, Captain," Luke said.

"Well, hello there," Gabby was happily surprised to see the captain again.

Gabby felt confused. It was too late for a sunset cruise. It was already dark. She smiled up at Luke and asked nervously, "What are we doing?"

Luke replied with a mysterious smile.

"It is a lovely evening, bonita, si? You are ready for an adventure?" Captain Rivera said.

Gabby looked back at Luke. "An adventure?"

"I heard that out on the ocean, it's dark enough that we can see the stars in the heavens," Luke said.

Gabby stared at him in wonder. "Stargazing?" She squealed in excitement.

Could he really be this sweet and thoughtful? Stargazing used to be one of Gabby's private escapes. She used to take her camera to the dark sky park near their home and take Milky Way photos.

"Is this okay with you?" Luke asked, sounding unsure.

"Yes," Gabby said excitedly. "It's amazing!"

Luke sighed and smiled. "Oh, good."

Captain Rivera helped them both climb on board.

"Gracias," Gabby said to the captain as he took her hand to guide her onto the boat. Once Luke was aboard, Captain Rivera led them to the front of the boat. The front had cushioned seating and then a few steps up from there led to a sun deck. As they were making themselves comfortable, Captain Rivera continued on about their evening voyage.

"We will head out to the sea for about a twenty-minute journey," Captain Rivera explained very animatedly. Using his arms while he spoke. "We will make sure the city lights won't block the stars. The waves un poquito, very small. So it will be a smooth sailing."

They both thanked the captain who left them and started yelling orders to his crew in Spanish.

They looked at each other and laughed. Then Luke pulled a light blanket out of a big bag and wrapped it around Gabby's shoulders.

"Thank you," she said

"I don't want you getting cold."

"Where did you get a blanket from?"

"Honestly, Sophie helped set this up. She packed a bag and sent it down here. She even booked the boat for us, although I didn't realize she'd booked a private tour."

"That was so sweet," she said.

Moments later, they had pushed off and were heading into the darkness. They sat in a comfortable silence for a while. Gabby watched the lights from the island shrink till they were barely noticeable. Then she turned to see the darkness in front of them. As much as she loved the water, being so far from shore and it being so dark, was a little unsettling. It made her shiver.

"You okay?" Luke asked

"I'm fine," Gabby replied, "I'll be honest. I'm afraid of water that I can't see the bottom of."

"Seriously?" Luke asked, sounding surprised.

"I've been scared of it since I was a kid," she admitted, a little embarrassed.

"Want me to have them go back?"

"No," Gabby said quickly. "I mean, no, this is great, and I'm fine."

"I'll keep you safe," Luke said, putting his arm around her.

Gabby knew he would. His arms were strong and warm. She felt safe with him. She was surprised that she even felt comfortable with him, as if they had known each other forever. She wasn't sure she had ever been on a date when she felt so at ease.

The boat slowed, and the engine sputtered. The sudden stop pushed her closer to Luke. She could smell his cologne and the salt air. She loved the mix of those two scents. She took another deep breath to capture it all. She closed her eyes, wanting to remember all of this.

Her thoughts were interrupted by Captain Rivera.

"We are dropping the anchor now. We will turn the lights off in a few minutes so you can see the star show." Captain Rivera said. "Extra blankets and pillows are under the seats if you want them."

"Sounds good," Luke said with a salute. "Thanks, Captain."

"No problemo," the captain said, giving them two thumbs up. "Me and the crew are in the back if you need anything."

After the captain left, Luke walked over to the other benches and pulled out a blanket. He spread it over the sun deck. Gabby grabbed two oversized pillows and handed them to Luke, who placed them on the blanket.

"Here," Luke said, holding out his hand and helping her up the narrow steps to the deck.

"Thank you," she took his hand and climbed up.

Luke reached into his bag and pulled out two plastic wine glasses and a bottle of wine.

"Stella Rosa?" Gabby said, surprised. "It's my favorite."

"I had a feeling it might be," Luke said with a grin, pouring them each a glass.

"Really? How?" She asked, raising an eyebrow at him.

"Maybe because I asked your brother, and he told me," Luke confessed.

Gabby laughed. "I'm impressed."

"Impressed that I thought to ask what your favorite wine is?"

"That," Gabby said, "and that my brother actually knew what my favorite wine is."

"You two live together. It can't be that big of a surprise."

"He's just so much in his own world with his video games and virtual buddies these days. I didn't think he noticed anything I did or like."

"I think he's more observant than you think," Luke said.

"Oh yeah?" Gabby scoffed.

"Yeah, I do," he said gently.

"What makes you think that?" she asked.

"He knows that you do a lot for him and that you give a lot of yourself, not only for him but for everyone."

"He said that?" her eyes raised.

"Yes, and he thinks you need to do more for yourself."

"Really?" she quietly said.

"He does. He told us that you do everything for everyone and carry out a lot of obligations."

Did her brother actually realize all Gabby did for him and for the people in the community? Did he actually appreciate any of it? She would do it anyway, but it was nice that he actually recognized it. Jase was always saying she needed to do things for herself, but she thought that was just to stop her from nagging him about anything. Tears came to her eyes, and she turned her head, not wanting Luke to see her cry. What was wrong with her? She wasn't a crier.

"I'm sorry," Gabby sniffed the tears back, "I don't know what's wrong with me. I never cry."

Luke took her hand. "Don't apologize. You don't always have to be strong. Sometimes, you just need to let go and let God in to do his work."

"What?" Gabby asked. She remembered the voice that had said, 'Let go,' and it gave her goosebumps.

"Let go," Luke repeated.

"What do you mean? I pray to God all the time," Gabby asked.

"I'm sure you do. But after praying about something, do you actually hand the sadness, stress, grief, whatever it is, over to God to let him take care of it? Or do you continue to try to take care of it yourself?"

Gabby realized she never let go. She always had to feel in control.

She smiled sheepishly at Luke. "Sometimes I just like to help God out."

"You think God, who created all of this," Luke's hand swept across the sky full of sparkling stars, "needs assistance in his plans for you?"

That humbled Gabby. She wasn't good at handing things over. She liked knowing what was happening, what was going to happen. She liked to have a plan. But she knew God had even better ones.

"I guess you have a point. He's been doing this a while, and he probably has a handle on things." She gave a small grin, knowing full well God didn't need her help. "It's just hard letting go."

"Of course it's hard," Luke agreed. "We want things to go a certain way, and when that doesn't work out, we try something new. But trust me, lay it in his hands and breathe. He's got you."

"Just like that, huh?"

"No." Luke laughed. "It takes practice, for sure. It took me years of practice, and I'm still not always great at handing everything over to God. But I can tell you that when I've let God lead the way and take over, things ended up even better than I thought they would."

Gabby gazed into Luke's eyes. She didn't see the pity that she was used to seeing from people. Instead, she saw caring and his willingness to be there for her. Rather than patting her shoulder and saying it would all be okay, Luke was giving her a path and plan. For the first time in a long time, maybe even ever, Gabby felt like she could let down her guard. She didn't have to be the rock that everyone leaned on and depended on. It felt nice.

Gabby wanted to sit here with Luke forever. Even more importantly, she wanted to have this feeling forever. She felt lighter with Luke. She could just be herself, and he didn't need or want anything from her.

Gabby and Luke laid back on the pillows and watched the night sky. The water lapped the sides of the boat, gently rocking them. Luke took Gabby's hand in his, brought it to his mouth, and gently kissed the back of her hand. Sparks shot from her hand, causing her whole body to tingle. She almost felt like she was waking up after hibernating for a long time. *This isn't just the best date I've ever had...this might be the best night of my life*, Gabby thought.

"I'm really glad you agreed to come with me tonight," Luke said.

"I'm glad you asked," she replied. "This has been a great night."

"It has been one of the best nights I've had in a long time," Luke said, giving her hand a squeeze.

"Me too," Gabby admitted. Smiling, she turned her attention back to the stars glittering above them. *This truly has been an amazing night.*

CHAPTER 34: LUKE

This is going great, Luke thought. He couldn't believe how lucky he was that he happened to be at the same resort at the same time as this amazing woman. What were the chances? It seemed unreal that his crazy family and her and her brother all lived in the same area in Michigan, and they got along so well. She was adventurous enough to agree to come with him tonight, not even knowing what she was getting into. Now he just needed to not screw it up.

Holding her hand in his felt right. He had been worried that the stargazing would be too over the top. When he saw how excited she was, he knew he, or at least Sophie, had made a good choice. He barely knew anything about Gabby. At the same time, he thought God had put Gabby directly in his path for a reason. Luke wanted to get to know her better. He had this feeling that she needed someone to talk to. She obviously was used to being the one that held things together. He wanted her to know that she could trust him, and he could be strong for her.

"So, Gabby," Luke started.

"Yes?" She replied.

"Tell me about you," Luke said, leaning on his elbow to face her.

She smiled, leaning on her elbow to face him in return. "What do you want to know?"

"Everything," he said, smiling back at her.

"Everything?" She laughed. "That might be a little boring."

"I can't imagine that you could ever be boring," he said.

"How about you narrow it down some?" Gabby said.

"How about growing up," he said. "What were things you and your family liked to do? Or vacations you used to take."

"Growing up," Gabby pondered that. "I'd say it was a pretty standard happy childhood. It wasn't until I was older that I figured out our lives were a little different from the other kids my age."

"How so?" Luke asked.

"Well, when I was almost ten and Jase was eight, he started playing travel baseball, and we had a summer family." Gabby explained..

"A summer family?" he asked.

"Yes. There were about ten families that traveled together all summer long. Sometimes for long weekends, sometimes for a week, going from tournament to tournament all across the country. We did that for eight years until the boys graduated high school. A few even played together a couple years after that. It was like having ten brothers, and their families were like aunts and uncles."

"Didn't you miss out on doing your own things?" Luke wondered if she had ever done anything for herself.

"Oh no, I loved it. I didn't know any difference anyway. I still did gymnastics and swimming during the week when we were home. Sometimes Holly, my best friend, would come to tournaments with us. Mom and Dad would get Holly and me our own hotel room, and we'd feel so grown up," Gabby explained.

"That sounds like fun," Luke said.

"It was. Holly's mom and my mom were best friends and both stay-at-home moms at the time. During the summer, we would go to each other's houses. We would swim, have picnics at a park, or our moms would take me, Holly, and our siblings on adventures."

"You and Holly have been friends a long time," Luke observed.

"Since we were four years old. Our moms met in church, and we were in the same Sunday school class," she said. "Then the following year, I started first grade at St. Michaels with her."

"It's great having such close friends for so long. Most people don't get that," he said. "I have to admit, I'm a little jealous."

"I've been very blessed in the friends department," Gabby said. "How about you?"

"My mom stayed at home with us until Seth started middle school. Then she went back to work."

"My mom started teaching when Jase was in high school."

"I hated it back then," Luke said. "I had friends that got to stay home alone, but my mom was always around. I'm really grateful for it now, though. I know it was a huge blessing that she was able to be home with us; it probably kept me out of a lot of trouble."

"I felt the same way about my mom always being there," Gabby agreed. "Are you still friends with people you grew up with?"

"I still know the people I grew up with." He laughed. "Most of them are just people I used to know at this point."

"I think that's how it goes. People grow up and apart," Gabby said. "Did you have a best friend?

My best friend, he thought. Luke was silent for a moment, gazing up at the stars while the boat rocked gently. He wasn't sure if he wanted to continue. He didn't want to ruin the night, but if he wanted Gabby to let him in, he had to be willing to be open about himself and what he had gone through too. *I can do this*, he said to himself, taking a deep breath before continuing.

"My best friend was Kyle. We were like you and Holly. We did everything together. Kyle even decided to join the Army when I told him I wanted to enlist."

Luke winced as he had a flashback to that day, but he continued on. "We thought it was going to be this big adventure, and we would see the world together."

"I bet that was fun," Gabby said, smiling at him.

"As fun as the Army can be, I suppose." He gave a short chuckle. "It was a lot different than I thought it would be."

Gabby watched him intently. When she gave him a small smile, he felt safe to continue.

"Kyle and I made it through basic and knew we wanted to be Rangers. So after advanced training, we took the ranger assessment. Somehow, we both got accepted," Luke explained proudly.

"Wow! I didn't realize you were a Ranger," Gabby said with wide eyes.

"It was the hardest thing I've ever done but the most rewarding," he said.

"I bet," she said.

"I thought I would make a career out of it. I loved my time with the Rangers. I rose to a Master Sergeant, and I had an amazing team. It was intense, exhausting and stressful...but my co-workers were also my brothers. We experienced things that most people wouldn't even think could happen. That forms a bond that civilians wouldn't understand."

"It sounds like you really loved it," Gabby said. "What made you decide to leave?"

Luke paused, taking a deep breath. He sat, crossing his legs in front of him.

"We were deployed for a raid. We were ready. Two teams were ready to breach the building. Our recon team had good intelligence that we were following." Luke stopped, his chest tightening as he recalled the tension he had felt getting ready to breach the building.

"We entered the building and cleared it with surprisingly little trouble. As we were exiting, I heard a loud popping. I saw a kid coming out of a trap door. The kid had a gun in his hands, aiming around the room," Luke's jaw clenched. "He was just a kid! He couldn't have been more than ten. And he started shooting."

Luke could feel the rage inside of him scratching its way to the surface, but he went on. "I turned and saw Kyle standing there, his face frozen. I knew something wasn't right. Then it felt like everything was moving in slow motion. I watched as Kyle dropped to his knees. I caught him as he fell forward."

Luke was shaking and could feel tears in his eyes. It had been a long time since he had spoken of that night. "I couldn't make sense of what was happening. There were some more pops, and someone on my team was yelling at me to grab Kyle and go. So I did." He paused, trying to keep his emotions in check. Gabby sat there silently, staring at him and hanging on his every word.

"What happened?" she whispered.

"We got Kyle out of there, but we couldn't save him," Luke whispered. Even six years later, the feelings could come back like Kyle had just died.

"So you left the Army because your best friend was killed?" Gabby asked softly.

"I left because it was my fault," Luke grunted. "I had seen the kid and the gun, and I froze. I couldn't shoot a kid. Instead, he shot my best friend."

Gabby seemed like she didn't know what to say. That was a common reaction from those who had never been in battle. People saw war on TV and in movies, but it couldn't compare to living it in real life.

"After that, I served out the last six months of my contract and didn't reenlist. I came home. I was a mess. I was so angry, and I felt lost, guilty, sad, and everything in between."

"You seem like you're in a better place now," Gabby said, giving him a little smile.

"I am," Luke agreed, grateful that he was. "My dad gave me one of his famous pep talks. He wasn't going to let me waste the life that God felt the need to spare. Dad took me to church and made me join a veterans therapy group. There, I could talk with people who had been through what I had."

"And that helped?"

"Not at first. At first, I just sat in church to appease Dad. I went to the groups and said nothing. Then one Sunday, our priest gave a sermon on forgiveness. He explained how we often need to forgive ourselves because God already had. His words really stayed with me and got me thinking. I started actively listening and participating in both church and my veterans group. I got into coaching at the high school. I realized that I missed leading a team, and coaching gave me that."

"Sounds like you have things figured out." She tilted her head and smiled.

"Letting go of anger and grief is a work in progress, but leaning on God, my family, and my friends helps. I was in a dark place, but I went through the grief process and came out the other side."

"So you're okay now?" Gabby asked.

Luke laughed. "Okay is relative. There are still days that I struggle with sadness, guilt, pain, or anger. I know how to manage it better now, though."

"Does it ever go away?" Gabby asked.

Luke recognized the earnestness in the question. *You want to feel normal again. You want the pain and anger and hurt to disappear.*

"I'm not sure," Luke admitted. "It's learning to live with the pain and managing it. Making the best out of things."

"I'm worried that Jase will never be the same," Gabby said with concern in her voice.

"I'm sure you are. You love him and worry about him. But what about you?" Luke asked as he took her hand.

"What about me?" Gabby asked. Sitting up and crossing her arm across her chest.

"How are you going to deal with your grief?" he asked gently.

"What do you mean?" she asked with a nervous smile.

"I mean, what are the steps you are taking to handle your own grief?"

She stared at him for a long time, and Luke worried that he'd gone too far. *Why did I push? Did I ruin everything?* It had been a perfect night. Why couldn't he have just enjoyed the stars with her? He could have talked about normal things like food or movies. Luke was about to apologize and change the subject when Gabby opened her mouth as if she was about to say something.

CHAPTER 35: GABBY

"I really am fine," Gabby told Luke.

She didn't mention that her head was spinning and not from the motion of the boat. Luke had been so open, sharing his story with her. Now, he wanted to know more about her. He sat quietly, patiently watching and waited for her to continue. Whether he believed it or not, she was fine. Right?

"At least mostly," she added after a long pause. She uncrossed her arms and laid her hands in her lap.

"You know it's okay not to be okay, right?" he asked and gently placed his hand over hers.

"Of course. But I know my parents are in a better place and death is a part of life. Jase and I were raised to know that. Our parents gave us a solid spiritual upbringing. That's why I'm so confused about why Jase is struggling so much." Gabby knew she sounded more defensive and accusatory than she meant to.

"Even Christians need to grieve," Luke said.

Gabby appreciated what Luke said, but grieving seemed like such a waste of time and energy. She was fine. Sure, she had kept herself as busy as possible so she wouldn't have time for sad thoughts. She had to concentrate on Jase and keep the business going. Besides, giving in to the grief meant admitting her parents were really gone. The first few months had been easy; she had felt nothing at all. Convinced herself her parents were just on vacation or something. The last few months however, had been harder. She had to compartmentalize and put the sadness and anger into boxes to deal with later. But she hadn't dealt with them later. She hadn't dealt with them at all. Maybe Luke was right. She had worked so hard on ignoring her own emotions and worrying about Jase that she hadn't let herself grieve. *I'm fine, right?* But if she were really fine, then why were tears coming? She didn't want to cry in front of him.

"I'm sorry," she sniffed them back.

"Don't be. Let it go. You've been so busy worrying about everyone else and trying to be strong that you haven't given yourself the grace to let yourself feel all of the emotions."

"I'm afraid of feeling them," she confessed, surprising even herself.

"You don't have to be. You aren't alone." Luke said, looking her in the eyes.

"For months after they died, I felt nothing at all. No happiness, no sadness, nothing. It was like a never-ending void. When anger or sadness would creep in, I'd busy myself with something to avoid them. I'd try to thank God for all the blessings he has given us. I paint a smile on and go about my day, showing the world what a faithful Christian woman can do through tragedy."

Luke gave her a sad smile. "God never said don't be sad or that life won't be hard. He actually tells us the opposite. There are going to be challenges and struggles. We'll want to give up and give in, but that's when we lean on him. He will never leave us. He will always be by our side, getting us through the hardest parts."

Gabby couldn't hold the flood back any longer. With a soft cry, she burst into tears. For the first time, she didn't try to stop them. She just sat there and ugly cried.

Luke wrapped her in his arms and stroked her hair.

When the tears had come to a slow roll, she sat up. She was somewhat embarrassed by her emotional outburst. But she also felt lighter, like all the weight she'd been carrying around had been lifted from her shoulders.

"Thank you," Gabby said when she could speak again. "I'm sorry. I'm sure this is not the night you imagined."

"It was a great night," Luke assured her, wrapping his arms around her.

"Thank you." Gabby leaned into him. "I've had six months of people telling me how they admired my courage, while others said maybe I wasn't grieving enough or that I was in denial. People have all sorts of opinions that they are happy to pass on. But you and your family have managed to help more in a few short days than all those people have in six months."

"As my mom says, there are no mistakes. God puts the right people in place at the right time." Luke said, resting his chin on the top of her head.

"He seems to be doing a really good job of that this week." Gabby smiled.

"I couldn't agree more," he said, releasing her and reaching forward.

Luke poured them each another glass of wine. Then they leaned back against the pillows again and gazed up at the stars. Gabby leaned into Luke as he put an arm around her.

"Look! A shooting star," Gabby said, pointing at the rush of light that traced across the night sky.

"Make a wish," Luke said.

Gabby closed her eyes and made a silent wish.

"Did you make one too?" she asked.

"Of course I did. You can't waste a shooting star in the middle of the ocean," he said with a grin.

Gabby laughed. She had to admit, she felt a peace that she hadn't felt in a while. Maybe she did need to talk about her feelings more often.

Gabby couldn't remember a better night, even with the strange and unexpected way it had unfolded.

CHAPTER 36: JASE

J ase had been hesitant to accept Seth and Sophie's invitation
to the comedy show. For one thing, he hadn't done this much
socializing in months. He would rather be back in his room.
Secondly, he figured a free show was going to be worth about the
price they paid. The comedian surprised him. He had even made
Jase laugh out loud a few times. The real entertainment was watching Sophie and Seth. They had laughed through the entire show
without shame. Gabby was like that. Jase envied the way she could
get lost in movies, books, or any entertainment. She would laugh
loudly and freely. Sophie and Seth seemed really close. The whole
family did. It reminded him of his own relationship with his sister.
Or at least how it used to be. He missed that.

After the show, Jase joined Sophie and Seth on the lounge patio and ordered a few drinks. The setting was amazing. The beach,
the palm trees, the warm breeze, and the live music coming from
inside the lounge created a refreshing atmosphere.

"That was so much fun," Sophie said with a huge smile.

"That comedian was great," Seth agreed.

Seth and Sophie went back and forth with some of the jokes they'd heard, laughing again.

This is good, Jase thought. *It's nice to unwind and have a little fun.*

"Jase, I know you're a big tough guy, but it seemed like you were having some fun," Sophie said.

"I did. It was better than I thought it would be," Jase replied.

"He was spot on about the little brother getting away with everything," Sophie said, poking her brother.

"Hey, give him a break," Jase said with his hands up. "Coming from one little brother to another, it's not our fault."

"I forgot you are the little brother too," Sophie said. "Have you guys always been close?"

Jase was a little taken aback by this. "We used to be extremely close. We would fight, sure, but there was no one we'd rather hang out with than each other."

"But not anymore? You two seem close," Sophie said.

Jase felt a little uncomfortable. Sophie must have sensed it because she continued, "Sorry, you don't have to answer that."

"No, it's okay. This year has just been different. It's almost like Gabby and I avoid talking about anything more than food and who fed our dog, Tucker."

"You guys have been through a lot," Seth said.

"It's like neither of us want to admit the accident happened. Like somehow, if we don't talk about it, it didn't really happen," Jase said.

"So, the two of you are just kind of existing in the same space?" Sophie asked.

"Kind of. I mean, Gabby works a lot... like she's avoiding being near me," Jase grunted.

"Do you think she's avoiding you? Or do you think she's avoiding being in the house that surrounds her with memories of your parents?" Sophie asked.

Jase stared at Sophie. He hadn't thought of that. Maybe it was hard for Gabby to be at home. Maybe it was for the same reason he barely left the safety of his room.

"Maybe," he admitted. "I was staying at home before the accident so my parents could help with my physical therapy. Gabby had her own place, and she left it to be there with me."

"She left her place to live at home with you, and you think she's avoiding you?" Sophie asked gently.

"You don't get it," Jase said, feeling frustrated. "Gabby is fine. She always has a smile. Things are like rainbows and sunshine for her -they always have been. She doesn't want my black cloud of gloom and doom interfering with her sunshine."

"You really think she's fine?" Seth asked.

"She acts like it," Jase grunted.

"Of course she acts like it. She's worried about you, and she doesn't know what to do to help you. Neither of you have ever gone through anything like this, and neither of you know what to do. Maybe she thinks her sunshine will shine on you and help," Sophie explained.

"Well it's not! I want her to just stop and sit on the floor and curl up in a ball and cry next to me," Jase said through clenched teeth.

"Have you told her that?" Seth asked.

"Why would I tell her that?" Jase scoffed.

"How else is she supposed to know?" Sophie asked.

Jase could feel himself getting agitated. "Well, I don't know. She just should."

"Talk to her. She will understand," Sophie said with a soft smile.

"Maybe it's too late," Jase said. He leaned back and tightly crossed his arms.

"It's never too late to start being honest." Sophie smiled.

"I don't know," Jase said, shaking his head, "maybe you're right."

"Well, I am the smartest of my siblings." Sophie laughed. "I'll go get us another round."

Sophie got up and headed to the bar. Seth leaned in. "I will never admit this, but Sophie is almost always right when it comes to people communicating with each other. I think it comes from dealing with middle schoolers all day."

Jase uncrossed his arms and smirked. "My sister is smarter than me too, but I'll never admit to that either."

"You know she's right, though," Seth said, nodding his head. "You have to talk to each other. You guys remind me of us. You obviously love each other and care about what the other is going through. But you have to be honest with each other about what you are feeling. Otherwise, none of us are smart enough to figure it out. Trust me, I have to spell things out for my siblings all the time. It's like they don't get me, so I have to tell them."

"Thanks, man, you're pretty smart too," Jase gave Seth's shoulder a nudge.

"I know, right? More people should listen to me," Seth said with a laugh.

This made Jase chuckle again. Sophie arrived with the drinks and eyed the two of them suspiciously. "What are you two talking about?"

"Just how smart our sisters are," said Seth with a wide grin.

Sophie rolled her eyes. "I'm sure."

"Speaking of sisters, I wonder what mine is up to." Jase glanced at his watch. It was almost 11:00 pm.

"They're sailing," Sophie informed him.

"Sailing? At night?" Jase felt the panic in his chest.

"I booked them a private stargazing sailing tour."

"In the water? At night? In the dark? What were you thinking?" Jase grunted, lowering his voice.

"Well, it's easier to see the stars at night," Sophie laughed.

"What if she drowns out there? It's so dark they wouldn't find her!"

"First of all, that's what the boat is for. Second, there are life jackets. Third, if God forbid something did happen to the boat, she's a great swimmer. It's perfectly safe."

Jase was breathing hard.

Sophie took his hand, "Jase, she's safe."

"I thought my parents were safe," he said, feeling his heart race. He clenched his fists.

"Jase, you can't go through life worried that something bad will happen to her," Sophie said.

"I can't help it. God already took my parents, and I can't lose her too," Jase said.

"Unfortunately, we can't see God's blueprint plans for each of us. We have to believe and trust that he has a plan and live the life he planned for us. We can't just sit and worry that something else will happen or hide in a room and get lost in a different world." Sophie stated.

"God's plans suck." Jase grunted.

"God's plans don't always align with what we want, but it doesn't make them any less good for us," Sophie said softly.

"I'm sorry, did your parents die?" Jase nearly shouted at Sophie, causing her to retract in her seat. "No. Yours are happy and alive and waiting for you two to come back and keep celebrating what a great life you all have together."

Sophie and Seth were both taken aback by this outburst.

"Jase, I'm sorry, I didn't mean..." Sophie stuttered.

"No, you didn't. Come back to me with God's plans when you've been through something so terrible that you don't want to go on living. Then tell me how God's plans don't align with our wants, but they're still good plans." Jase shoved away from the table with such force their drinks nearly fell over and his chair flew back.

Stomping away from the bar with his fists clenched, he headed toward the beach. He walked away from the lights and into the darkness.

Fueled by adrenaline and anger, he started running. Harder and faster he ran, until his legs felt like they were going to give out. Finally, he collapsed to his knees in the wet sand. He yelled up to the skies, "Why? Why, God, why?" Tears streamed down his face. He couldn't form any other words. *Why? Why? Why would you do this to me?*

"God help me! Help me, please. I can't do this. I'm not strong enough. Take this pain away or just let me die too." Jase threw his head into his hands and sobbed. He wasn't sure he would ever stop. Finally, it did stop; it all stopped. The blind rage and tears subsided. A chill ran through him from the salty waves now saturating his clothes.

Gradually, the realization of what he said to Sophie and Seth sank in. They were only trying to be supportive; they hadn't deserved that. *I should go back and apologize to them*, he thought. *Is it too late?* Had he ruined this whole trip for everyone? Then he recalled Sophie's words, "It's never too late to be honest." He walked back to the beachside bar to apologize, but they weren't at the table anymore.

Jase started to head back to his room when he remembered he had seen their villa nearby. He changed his course to go there. Standing at the door, he hung his head, embarrassed at the way he'd reacted. He wasn't sure he could knock. As if some invisible force held his hand to the door, he heard knocking and saw that it was his own hand. Maybe no one was here. He was about to walk away when the door opened.

"Jase?" Ben asked as he cracked the door open.

"Hi Ben," Jase started, "are Seth and Sophie here?"

"They just got back." Ben opened the door for him to enter. "Come on in."

Hesitantly, Jase stepped through the door and removed his ball cap.

Olivia, Sophie, and Seth were sitting on the couch. They all stood when he entered.

"Jase," Sophie exclaimed, obviously taken aback by his arrival.

"Hi guys," Jase mumbled, not knowing where to start. So he just went with, "I'm sorry."

"Jase, I'm sorry. I shouldn't have..." Sophie started, but Jase interrupted her.

"Please don't. You were right and no one has ever made me listen to what I needed to hear, ever. People have always pandered to me my whole life and just let me do or say whatever I wanted. They tell me whatever they think it is I want to hear. They try to help me justify my thoughts and actions rather than help me see a better way and hold me accountable. I needed to hear those things. I just didn't know I needed to hear them."

"I wasn't trying to upset you," Sophie said softly. "You're right, I don't know what you're going through."

"No, but you cared enough to say the things that needed to be said. You all have," Jase said, scanning their faces, trying to gauge what they were feeling. "What you guys said gave me a lot to think about. And you didn't deserve my outrage, neither of you did. I truly am sorry."

"Thank you," Sophie said, and Seth nodded.

"I hope I didn't ruin your family's vacation," Jase said to all of them. "It's actually been really great being with you all, even though I didn't think I wanted that either."

Ben came up and put a hand on his shoulder. "You didn't ruin anything. I think God put us all here for a reason, and you have given us all something too."

"Road rash from my outbursts?" Jase tried to laugh.

"No." Ben laughed. "You made us realize how precious life is, that you never know what people are going through, and to be patient and understanding with everyone. You also showed us something that none of us had ever thought possible."

"What's that?" Jase scoffed.

"Well," Ben said before he got a big smile on his face, "that you can catch a stingray!"

They all laughed. *Maybe they're right,* Jase thought. *Maybe God's plan isn't what was expected or what we wanted, but he still has plans to get us through it.*

CHAPTER 37: GABBY

After her night with Luke, Gabby felt like she had opened the Pandora's box of her heart, letting all the hurt and pain out. To her amazement, the world was still spinning. God hadn't punished her for expressing those feelings. On the contrary, she felt like a weight had been lifted from her. Talking, really talking about things, had felt good. She hadn't even opened up that much to Holly, always insisting that she was fine. Gabby knew she and Jase needed to have these conversations, too. She was still nervous to make that effort with him, though. They would need to talk... sooner or later.

Today, however, was going to be a great beach day. Gabby was excited to see Luke again and to be at the beach, her happy place.

It was almost 10:00 am when she walked into the living room and didn't hear Jase. He hadn't been home when she arrived last night. She had been so emotionally drained that she went straight to bed.

Gabby busied herself packing a beach bag and cooler with water and snacks when Jase emerged from his room.

He looked... Well, she wasn't sure how he looked.

"Hey there, good morning," she greeted him.

"Good morning," he replied.

"How was last night?"

"It was good," he said.

Good? Good's a good thing, right? She wouldn't press.

"Want breakfast?"

"Not right now." He said, sitting down on the couch.

"Are you still up for the beach today?" she asked hopefully.

"I think so," he said.

"You know I'm always ready for the beach," she said happily, trying to get some sort of emotion out of him.

"Yes, I do," he chuckled. "So, did you have a good time last night?"

Gabby felt herself blushing again as she sat down next to him. "You know what, I did. It was..." she paused, searching for the right word, "delightfully unexpected," she said.

"Delightfully unexpected? Did you think it was going to be a bad time?"

"No." She laughed. "We went stargazing, and we talked, and it was just really nice."

"Good, I'm glad you had a good time. Are you ready to admit you like him now?"

Gabby rolled her eyes and sighed, "Fine, I like him."

"Was that so hard? Being honest with yourself?" He wrapped her in an unexpected hug.

What's this about? she thought. He showed no emotion when he came out of his room, and now he was hugging her?

"I'm glad you did something for you, and I hope this works out for you." He said sincerely.

"Thanks, I kind of am, too," she replied with a smile.

After putting their bathing suits on, they grabbed their bags and headed to meet the Andersons at the beach. Gabby scanned the beach and wasn't surprised to find the Andersons already there, setting up chairs and umbrellas.

"There they are," Gabby told Jase, pointing in the direction of the Andersons. She took a step forward, but Jase stayed put. She turned back and noticed he seemed a little hesitant to keep going.

"You okay?" she asked, wondering what his hesitation was about.

"Yeah, I just..." he paused, "Yeah, I'm good."

Gabby momentarily wondered what had happened last night, but the thought left as quickly as it came when Luke jogged up.

"Hi there." He smiled at her.

"Hi!" She smiled back as he led her to the blue cushioned lounge chair next to his.

"Ready to get wet?" Luke asked.

"I was born ready!" Gabby said excitedly.

Gabby kicked off her flip-flops and left her coverup on a lounge chair. She shouted, "Race you!" and took off running.

She and Luke raced to the water and dove into the waves. They were quickly followed by the rest of their siblings. There was splashing and playing and dunking each other underwater. Gabby felt so carefree and fun. It felt like they were a bunch of kids playing together.

After playing in the water for 30 minutes or so, she and Sophie decided to go lay in the sun while the boys tried out the skimboards Seth had brought.

The girls watched one boy after the other fall off the boards from their lounge chairs.

Giggling at the guy's efforts, Gabby said, "It's been forever since I've seen Jase have this much fun."

"I know, same for Luke," Sophie said. "For Seth, on the other hand, this is just another day."

"Must be nice," Gabby said, wondering what it would be like to have no worries or responsibilities, just living for the day.

"He makes it look nice," Sophie said. "I know my parents and brother give him a hard time about not growing up fast enough. Maybe if more people were like him and saw the world as their playground, it would be a better place."

"It probably would be," Gabby admitted.

Gabby smiled as she watched the guys playing. Apparently giving up on the skimboards, Jase grabbed a football and started tossing it with Luke. Seth rode the board a few more times and then joined in the game of catch.

"I'm a little jealous of Seth. I always wanted to get onto the next step," Sophie said, leaning on her arm to face Gabby.

"I was the same," Gabby confessed. "When I was in high school, I wanted to be in college. During college, I wanted to be working. Now that I'm working, I wish I could take a step back."

"Me too," Sophie said. "Would you make the same choices?"

Gabby felt a twinge of guilt just thinking about making different choices. If she were honest, she probably would want to do something completely different. She said, "I'm not sure. I don't know what else I would do. It was always just expected that I'd join my dad and then take over. How about you?"

"I would do the same thing. I love being a teacher and middle school is where it's at. Other teachers think I'm crazy for wanting to be a middle school teacher. Most of the people I work with are just waiting for an opening at the high school. But I love my students," Sophie said.

The cheerful smile Sophie wore told Gabby that she truly cared about her job and the kids. Gabby was slightly envious that Sophie was so sure and happy with her life.

"It's great that you are doing what you love," Gabby said.

"It is great," Sophie said. "And I would make the same choice. But I would have taken a longer time getting here. I would have enjoyed college more, traveled more, maybe done a semester abroad."

"I know what you mean. I took a lot of different classes and enjoyed them, but I never really thought about doing any of them as a career."

"It's not too late, you know?" Sophie smiled at her.

"What's not?" Gabby asked, confused.

"To change your mind. You could always go back and do something else," Sophie stated.

"Ha! I'm not sure that is really a possibility." Gabby shook her head.

"Sure it is. I work with a lady who is 45 and worked in marketing. She hated it and went back to school and became a teacher. She says it was the best decision she'd ever made."

"Maybe I could think about it," Gabby said.

What else would I want to do? She thought. *Teaching? Marketing? Photography? Scuba instructor?*

Gabby's thoughts were interrupted by nearly getting creamed by a football. She heard someone yell, "Watch out!" But it was too late. The ball landed right in front of her chair, covering her with sand.

Luke came running over.

"I'm so sorry. Are you okay?" Luke asked.

"I'm fine, just a little sand," she assured him, wiping the sand off her.

"Sorry about that." Luke handed her and his sister water bottles. Then he scooped the ball up and tossed it to Jase. "I'll be back in a bit," he said as he trotted back to the game. Gabby smiled as she watched him dart away.

"My brother really likes you," Sophie said.

"Really?" Gabby asked, feeling her heart beat a little faster.

"He does, I can tell. And I've been praying for you to come into his life."

Gabby laughed. "You just met me six days ago."

"That's true, but I knew you were out there," Sophie said wistfully.

"What do you mean?" Gabby was confused. How could she have prayed for her before they met?

"I prayed he would meet a woman who was strong but kind, confident but humble, and who has a strong faith. You are all of those things."

"Thank you, I'm flattered. I can't believe that someone hasn't scooped him up yet," Gabby admitted.

"They've tried. He was even engaged, but she wasn't right for him. Luckily, he figured it out before the wedding."

"What?" It wasn't that Gabby hadn't assumed that Luke had had girlfriends, but she hadn't known there had been one that was serious.

"Maybe I shouldn't have mentioned that," Sophie admitted, but then she continued. Her name was Priscilla. They had been high school sweethearts. He broke up with her when he joined the

Army because he didn't want her waiting. From what I've heard, she didn't anyway. When Luke got home, Priscilla tried to make it work with him again. She liked the idea of having an Army hero as a husband. But the reality was different than she expected, I think. Then, when he became more involved with the church, she wasn't on board. She liked being seen at church with him, but she wasn't really there if you know what I mean."

"I do," Gabby said.

"Priscilla thought it would fix things if they got married. She didn't really want a marriage. She wanted a ring and a wedding. Once again, the reality of everything was not in her plans, at least not with him."

"What happened?" Gabby asked expectantly.

"The week before the wedding, Luke called it off. Priscilla was upset; so was he. He felt bad he let it go that far, knowing they weren't right for each other. She quickly found the comfort of a local firefighter, though. Apparently that worked out for her, since they are about to get married."

"Wow," was all Gabby could manage.

"Don't worry. He's completely different with you. He's himself, which is pretty great," Sophie said with a smile.

"He is pretty great." Gabby smiled, watching Luke play with the other guys. "Oh, and thank you for setting things up last night."

"He wasn't supposed to tell you that was me," Sophie exclaimed.

"I was very impressed either way," Gabby said. "It was a really great night."

"I'm so glad," Sophie said.

"How was your night? Did you all have fun?"

"Jase didn't tell you about last night?" Sophie asked, sounding surprised.

Panic flooded Gabby's heart. "No. Did something happen?"

Sophie hesitated and then smiled. "The comedy club was great. He had a great time there, and so did we."

"But...?" Gabby pried.

"I think Jase is struggling," Sophie said quietly, leaning toward Gabby.

"I think so too. I just don't know what to do for him," Gabby confided

"Maybe it's not so much what you can do for him, but with him," Sophie offered.

"What do you mean?" Gabby asked. There had to be something she could do to help her brother move forward in life.

"Just let him in. Let him know how you are feeling about things. Just talk to him, you know?" she said with an encouraging nod.

"Just talk to him," Gabby said, nodding her head. "I can do that." She wondered what her brother had said to make Sophie think they needed to talk. Gabby knew they did, but she wondered what specifically Jase was thinking.

They went back to watching the guys play. Jase overthrew the ball to Seth, who went chasing after it. Gabby's eyes followed past Seth and noticed something else down the beach. Was that a snowman?

"Sophie, am I seeing things, or is that a snowman down there?" She asked, sure she was seeing things.

Sophie peered down the beach. "It is! There are a bunch of them," she said excitedly, her face lighting up. "It must be the sandman contest."

"We should...no, never mind." Gabby stopped herself as she remembered that the Jacksons were festive-free. She felt bad seeing the disappointment on Sophie's face. Gabby had to admit, she really wanted to do it too.

"Let's go play with the guys," Sophie suggested. "Dad," she called out, "come help us beat the boys."

Ben must have been waiting for the invitation. He dropped his book and jumped up, shouting, "I'm coming!"

They ran over to join them and started a new game of guys against girls, plus Ben.

CHAPTER 38: JASE

J ase had worried today might be awkward after his temper tan-
trum last night, but it seemed that all was forgiven. He just
hoped Sophie hadn't told Gabby about his outburst. She would
probably scold him for it. Today, he felt great. As he and the guys
tried the skimboards and then played football, Jase even forgot
for a bit that the whole world seemed wrong right now. It was a
welcome relief.

Playing football made him realize that he missed being part
of a team. He was pleasantly surprised that his knee hadn't bothered him once. He figured after slacking off on his workouts that
it would be hurting. He wasn't sure his coach would be happy to
hear he was skimboarding and playing football on a beach, but his
knee felt good.

Jase, Luke, and Seth huddled up and made a plan to get past
the girls and Ben.

"Jase, you get past Dad and into the endzone," Luke said.
"Seth, you're going to distract the girls."

"Sounds good," Jase and Seth said in unison.

Both teams lined up, and Seth hiked the ball to his brother.

Jase ran deep while Seth tried to guard the girls.

Jase kept glancing back over his shoulder as he ran until he saw Luke ready to throw the ball to him.

Ben tripped over Seth and knocked Gabby over with them. *Not shocking,* Jase thought with a laugh. Gabby never had been able to stand on her own two feet.

Jase watched the ball sail through the air and caught it. He was ready to make the turn and run it between the makeshift flags, but he was knocked down with shocking force.

Jase groaned as he rolled over in the sand, still holding the ball. Even more shocking was Sophie standing over him smiling.

"You okay there, champ?" she asked, smirking down at him.

"Yeah," he grunted. He slowly rose to his feet. "I'm good."

Everyone joined them laughing.

"Dude, our sister took you out," Seth said.

"She sure did," Jase said, still confused about how that had happened and amazed at how strong Sophie was.

"We forgot to warn you about her. She's a tall, skinny beast," Luke said.

"No kidding," Jase said, rubbing his side.

"I grew up with brothers. I had to learn to hit," Sophie said proudly.

"You've accomplished it," Jase said, handing over the ball.

They were all laughing, including Gabby, who seemed equally stunned by Sophie's strength.

"Are you okay?" Gabby asked Jase, still giggling. "Is your knee good?"

"The knee is fine," Jase told her. "The ego took a bit of a hit, though."

Gabby laughed. "I'm sure it did. I really wasn't expecting that."

"Me neither, but wow! I think I might ask her to marry me." He said, only partially kidding.

This made Gabby laugh even harder. "You'd have to give up your most eligible bachelor title."

"That's fine with me," Jase said, running his hand through his hair.

"Maybe you have a concussion," Gabby said, pretending to check his head.

"Maybe I do." Jase rubbed his head. Sophie had hit him good.

Olivia, who had been taking photos of everyone, suggested a quick water break. Jase thought it was a great idea. Grabbing two bottles, he scanned the beach for his sister. She was watching the people build sandmen. Gabby had that wistful gaze on her face. Jase knew she wanted to be over there too. She would be all over it if they hadn't agreed to be holiday holdouts. He didn't want to hold her back. He didn't want to build sandmen, but he knew she would love it.

"Hey, everyone," Jase shouted. "Gather round. Olivia, you too, please."

Olivia put her camera down and joined the rest of her family and Gabby to gather around Jase.

"You know what I think we all need?" Jase looked at the group seriously with his hand on his hips.

Everyone glanced curiously around at each other.

"We need to build a sandman," Jase said with all the enthusiasm he could muster as he pointed to the sandman building contest.

Gabby seemed more shocked and excited than anyone. "What?"

"We've all proven to be a pretty competitive bunch, and I could use a little non-contact event," Jase said, rubbing his side that Sophie had hit.

Everyone had a good laugh over that.

"So let's go win the sandman competition," Jase said and put a fist up in the air.

Jase had to smile and knew he'd made a good decision when a round of cheers went up and planning for the perfect sandman started.

CHAPTER 39: GABBY

Gabby felt equal parts shocked and elated that Jase suggested the sandman building contest. She wondered what had caused his change of heart. Maybe he was finally coming out from under the dark cloud he had been living under for the past six months. She hoped so. Either way, she was grateful for this time and playful attitude. Gabby could see the childlike excitement in everyone's faces as they made plans for the sandmen they would build.

They decided to create a life-sized scene of sandmen on holiday, with one sandman burying another sandman in the sand. They all worked together to make these vacationing sandmen come to life.

Gabby, Sophie, and Olivia worked on the sandman that was doing the burying while the men worked on the buried friend.

They'd been working for about thirty minutes when Luke asked Gabby to help him get water for everyone. Gabby dusted herself off and joined him. The cloudless sky let the sun bear down on them, but there was a lovely breeze coming off the ocean that kept it very comfortable. The sand was hot beneath her feet as they walked back over to where their chairs and cooler were.

"It looks like you're having a good time," Luke said.

"You know, I really am." She smiled.

"I'm not going to lie, I was a little shocked that Jase wanted to do this. I mean, you both said you didn't want to do any of the holiday stuff," Luke said.

"I was more than a little shocked," Gabby said. "I don't know what changed his mind, but I'm glad he did. This is a lot of fun. And I think our tourist sandmen have a great chance of winning."

"Me too! They're great. Did you see some of the competition?"

"I know," Gabby smiled as she observed that most of the other sandmen were very tiny or just not well-formed. "I have to admit, there are a few good sandman sculptures, but I still think ours is the best. "And ours are almost life-sized."

Luke nodded in agreement as he reached into the cooler, picking up some water bottles.

"You know, Gabby, I had a really great time last night. I hope we can do that again." Luke said with a smile.

Gabby couldn't stop herself from smiling back, "I did too."

"And I don't just mean here," Luke continued. "I think we have something special happening, and I'd like to see where it goes."

"Really?" Gabby teased, "I was thinking just a nice vacation fling was enough."

"Oh," Luke said, and his smile dropped.

"I'm kidding, Luke," Gabby laughed and reached for his arm. "I'd really like to see where this could go too."

"Oh, thank God. I really thought I'd just made a huge fool out of myself. I haven't dated in a really long time." Luke admitted.

"Since Priscilla?" Gabby asked.

"Yes, since Prisc..." Luke stopped. Confused, he asked, "Wait. How did you know about Priscilla?"

"Sophie." Gabby scrunched her face, hoping he wouldn't be mad at Sophie for telling her.

"Of course, from Sophie." Luke rolled his eyes. "I was going to tell you about her. We just haven't had enough time to tell all the stories yet."

"It's okay, I get it. We don't know every story yet, but that will come," Gabby assured him.

"I haven't dated in a long time. I've been waiting for something that I couldn't even explain, just a feeling that it's right, you know?" He cocked his head to the side.

"I get it," Gabby answered, knowing exactly what he was talking about. She also wanted something that was more than just an attraction.

They were interrupted by Seth yelling, "Bro, water! We're dying over here."

"We'd better go and hydrate our team before they all turn to dust," Luke joked.

"Good idea," Gabby agreed, grabbing more water bottles. Then they walked back to continue building their sandman friends.

When they were finished, they had one sandman who was leaning next to his friend, whom he had buried up to his neck. The other sandwoman was covered with a mountain of sand shaped to look like a mermaid. Sophie had found shiny black stones for the eyes and mouths, and they used two cone-shaped shells for the noses.

"I think they are great," Olivia exclaimed.

"I think it's missing something," Seth said, examining their creation. "I got it!"

He ran to the water's edge and started searching. A few moments later, he came back with two abandoned shells and made a bikini top for the buried sandwoman.

"Now it's perfect," Seth said, stepping back to admire his handiwork.

Gabby stood with the Andersons and her brother near their sandmen. She watched anxiously as the three judges walked around scrutinizing all the sand sculptures. The two men in khaki shorts and white linen shirts with Hideaway Cay imprinted on them made comments as the shorter woman in a khaki skort with the same shirt scribbled notes onto her clipboard. Gabby was trying to decipher their expressions as they made comments.

When the judges completed their rounds, one of the men used a horn to bring everyone's attention to them to announce the winners.

"Atención por favor!" The lady judge shouted with a Mexican accent. "Gracias to all our guests who participated in the Hideaway Cay Resort's holiday sandman building contest! There were many beautiful sand sculptures today. Mucho bueno! We had to make hard choices. Without further ado, in third place, we have the Rogers Family from Texas with the Rogers Sandmen Family."

There was a round of applause from the crowd. Gabby saw that the family had made a sandperson for each member of their family. They had even dressed the sand people in some of their clothes.

"Those are cute," Gabby said.

"Ours are way better," Seth said.

The judge continued, " In second place... Our newlyweds, Mr. and Mrs. Williams from California."

Everyone clapped again. Gabby liked their impressive bride and groom sandmen couple, complete with bridal veil and bowtie. The bride even had a large piece of sea glass for a wedding ring.

"Finally, in first place, is the Anderson and Jackson Families from Michigan with their snowmen tourists!"

They all jumped up and down celebrating and hugging.

"This is amazing," Gabby exclaimed

"I knew we'd win," Seth declared.

"I knew we had the team to win with," said Jase.

They all gathered for a picture. They received a cute little snowman trophy as well as a gift certificate to the steakhouse for dinner, for a private dining experience.

"Is anyone opposed to celebrating our championship at the steakhouse rather than the cantina?" Ben asked.

"Heck no," Jase said. "Steak and lobster for everyone!"

Gabby felt overjoyed that today was going so great. She had finally seen a real glimpse of the old Jase. She hoped he was here to stay.

CHAPTER 40: JASE

After dinner, Jase said good night to his sister. He walked into his room, closed the door, and sat on the bed. *Today had been a good day*, he thought. He ran a hand down the soft curtains. He'd never reopened them after closing them that first day. He felt like it was time to come out of this darkness. He opened the blinds and let the moonlight fill the dark room. Then he opened the windows. Jase took a deep breath as the breeze flowed in.

He felt different somehow, and it wasn't just being full from the amazing celebration dinner. His heart felt lighter. Maybe it was from the sun and sand today. Or maybe it was from actually doing something just for fun, not because it was his job or because he felt he had to. He had played today because he wanted to. Even though it was just the guys today, having that team mentality again felt good.

Jase lay back in the king-size bed, leaving his legs to dangle over the side. He didn't even feel like turning on his video game.

Then he heard a little chime. *What was that?* Scanning the room for the source, he saw his phone blinking. He was surprised the battery hadn't died. He hadn't touched that thing in days.

Jase checked his phone and found a message from Sam, his agent; several messages actually. They all begged Jase to call. Sam was concerned that Jase fell off the face of the earth. Jase wasn't sure how much longer he could avoid the inevitable. He was sure the Defenders would be releasing him. He had given his whole adult life to them. Now they were just going to let him go, or worse, trade him for someone younger.

Jase could feel himself getting worked up over the thoughts swirling in his head. *How could they do this?* He wasn't even sure he wanted to go back and play, but he wanted it to be his choice, not theirs. He would be the one to say when he was done, not them.

The phone started to ring in his hand. He practically growled at it before tossing it on the bed. Not today. He was going to keep this peace a little while longer. Returning calls was yet another thing he could deal with when they had to go back to reality.

The phone had stopped ringing. He watched, waiting for a voicemail or text to come through next. Instead it started ringing again. *Ugh*, Jase groaned. *Okay Sam, you win.* Jase let the phone ring a few times before deciding he might as well face the music. He hadn't wanted to ruin such a great day, but he knew it wouldn't last forever.

"Sam, what's up?" Jase answered with no emotion.

"What's up?" Sam yelled. "I've been trying for almost a month to get a hold of you. Where have you been?"

"Around," Jase replied.

"Around?" Sam barked.

"Yeah, around," Jase said casually.

"Where are you now?" Sam demanded.

"Cozumel," Jase said.

"Fantastic, I hope you're having a great time," The agent said sarcastically.

"It's been good," Jase said flatly.

"How's the knee feeling?" Sam said, sounding like he was genuinely asking.

"It's fine," Jase was getting irritated. *Just give me the bad news already,* he thought.

"That's what the physical therapist said, too," Sam informed him.

"Is that what you called to tell me? Cause I know that already," Jase said impatiently.

"No, but since you are being so nice, I'm going to give you an early Christmas present," Sam scoffed.

"What's that?" Jase asked, thinking it was probably an early retirement.

"The Defenders want you to retire with them," Sam said.

Jase felt his stomach drop. He'd known this was coming, but it was another thing to have it confirmed. The Defenders wanted him to retire. They were throwing him away. Then he felt anger boil in his heart.

"They want me to retire? Who says I'm ready to retire, Sam? Maybe I'm not ready, maybe I have more years left in me!" he shouted into the phone. He was about to hang up when he heard Sam again.

"Jase, Jase, buddy, did you hear what I said?" Sam laughed, trying to calm him down.

Jase scoffed, "Yeah."

"I don't think you did," Sam said eagerly. "Jase, they want you to retire *with* them. That means they want to offer you a five-year contract to finish your career with them."

"They what?" Jase couldn't believe what he was hearing. His arms dropped to his sides in disbelief. His head felt like it was swimming. The anger was quickly dissipated, replaced by sheer shock. *They still want me.*

"Jase, you there?" he could hear Sam saying through the phone.

Lifting the phone back to his ear, "Yeah, man, I'm here."

"So, when you coming home? Let's get this thing signed," Sam sounded like he was bouncing around.

"I'll be home the day after Christmas," Jase told him.

"That's five days away," Sam said anxiously. "Want me to over-night it to you?"

"Sam, they've waited this long. They can wait a few more days," Jase said.

"Jase, buddy, come on. This is what we've been waiting for," Sam pleaded with him.

"I'll be home, and we can meet then," Jase said. He felt a little guilty as he hung up the phone. Sam was right. This is the news he had wanted to hear. Now that the choice was his, he wanted the night to think about if going back to baseball is what he still wants.

CHAPTER 41: GABBY

The next morning, Gabby sat with her feet soaking in the pool off their patio while she did her morning devotionals. She loved being here. She felt relaxed and rejuvenated. This trip was exactly what she had needed. She hoped their trip was having the same effect on Jase. If his actions and attitude yesterday were any indication, it seemed to be.

No official plans had been made with the Andersons for today, so Gabby decided to go to the pool with her book. She dressed quickly and left a note for Jase, then she gently closed the door behind her and headed for the pool.

She quickly selected a place where she would get the best sunlight. She wasn't surprised to see Sophie already sitting in that area.

Sophie glanced up from under her wide-brimmed hat and waved Gabby over as if she'd been expecting her.

"Hey there," Sophie greeted Gabby. "I saved a seat for you. We'll have the best sunlight here for the most amount of time."

It was like Sophie had read her mind.

"How did you know I'd be coming down?" Gabby asked as she spread her towel over the lounge chair.

"We had no plans. It just made sense that you'd be here too." Sophie said, smiling.

Gabby laughed and settled into the chair Sophie had reserved for her. She pulled her book out and noticed Sophie had gone back to reading hers.

"Yesterday was a lot of fun," Sophie said suddenly.

Gabby put her book down and turned to her friend. "It really was, wasn't it?"

"You know," Sophie leaned in closer to Gabby and whispered, "They have other activities you might be interested in here."

Gabby couldn't help but smile. The way Sophie said that seemed so devious. "Do they?"

"They do," Sophie said, continuing in a whispered voice. "They have a cookie decorating station, ornament making, paint your own tropical holiday, and I'm sure other fun Christmas activities."

All of that sounded fantastic to Gabby. Then she thought of Jase.

"I'm not sure Jase will be up for any of that," Gabby said regretfully.

Sophie pouted. "He had so much fun yesterday. We could at least ask him."

"That's true," Gabby said slowly. "He did seem to have a lot of fun building the sandmen."

"I'm just throwing it out there," Sophie said. "I'm also content to lay right here all day." She raised her face to the sun and stretched her long legs out on the lounge chair.

"I'll see what Jase wants to do if and when he wakes up. I don't want to hold you guys back from anything, though. You should go if you want to." Gabby said, feeling guilty that she was keeping Sophie from doing things she really wanted to do.

"We'll see. Really though, I'm quite happy here." Sophie assured her.

"I am too. This whole trip has been exactly what I needed." Gabby said, breathing in the salty air and feeling the sun cover her.

"I didn't even know how badly I needed this," Sophie agreed.

"It's always good to get away and break your routine a little."

"It sure is. I love my job and everything, but I pour so much of myself into it. Between the kids at school and teaching Sunday school, I'm constantly planning and doing."

"I get it. It's like I forget to do things for myself," Gabby sympathized.

"Exactly!" Sophie sat up in her chair so quickly that Gabby jumped, thinking something was wrong.

"What's wrong?" Gabby gasped.

"Nothing. I just had a great idea!" Sophie was so enthusiastic, Gabby could feel the excitement radiating from her.

Gabby relaxed and breathed a sigh of relief. "What is it?"

"When we get home, we should have a monthly play-hooky day," Sophie said practically jumping out of her chair.

"What?" Gabby laughed.

"Once a month, we should do something just for us,"Sophie said.

That did sound pretty good to Gabby, but she wasn't sure how she could manage it. "I'm not sure how we can make that happen, but it does sound great," she admitted.

"We can even have a few other women who never take time for themselves join in."

Immediately, Gabby thought about Holly. She needed to do things for herself, too. Letting the idea sink in further, Gabby decided this was a fantastic idea. "What would we do?"

"It doesn't matter. Anything we want," Sophie said.

Anything we wanted, Gabby thought. They could take day trips, spa days, painting classes, heck... just a long, leisurely lunch would be nice.

"Okay, let's do it," Gabby said with a nod and a smile.

Chapter 42: Jase

J ase stood at his bedroom window admiring the view. The palm trees swayed gently with the wind, and he couldn't get over how blue the ocean was. He thought he could even see some dolphins jumping in the waves. He smiled and ran his hand through his hair. He still couldn't believe what Sam had told him last night. The Defenders wanted him back. Maybe he could get his old life back. He could be the superstar everyone wanted him to be and live in the spotlight again. But is that what he really wanted?

He needed to go work out, that always helped him think things through. Entering the living room, he announced that he was heading to the gym. When no response came, he searched the patio, then Gabby's room. He figured she must have gone out. Heading for the door he saw the note. She was at the pool.

As Jase stepped out the door, he noticed he felt different. Something was missing, but he wasn't sure what. Then the realization hit him. The anxiety he usually experienced when he didn't know where his sister was, was absent. Instead, he just assumed that she was out. He hadn't immediately thought she was out getting hurt or worse. He thought she was just out, probably enjoying herself. That was a good feeling.

Jase walked into the gym and was greeted by two familiar voices

"Hey, Jase, what are you doing here?" Seth asked while spotting for his older brother.

"Hey, I should ask you guys the same thing."

Luke rested the bar back onto its stand and sat up, rubbing his stomach. "After a week of all this amazing food, I figured we should hit the gym before we grew Santa bellies."

"Same here," Jase agreed, starting to stretch.

"Plus, you'll need to get back into shape for spring training." Seth grinned until his brother gave him a sharp poke in his ribs, knocking him off balance. "Dude, what?"

"Actually, funny you should say that..." Jase hesitated. Did he want to put this out there? Is this what he wanted? Both Seth and Luke were staring at him in anticipation.

"My agent called last night," Jase started.

"And..." Seth said anxiously.

"The Defenders are offering me a five-year contract," Jase said.

Seth let out a whoop and ran over to him. "That is sweet."

"That's awesome, dude," Luke said, coming over and giving him a high-five. "Congrats, man."

"So you want to go celebrate tonight? I'm sure Gabby is thrilled," Luke said.

Jase felt a pang of guilt. This was the biggest news he'd had in a while, and he hadn't shared it with his sister. The one person who, next to Mom and Dad, had always supported him.

"I haven't exactly told her yet," Jase confessed.

"Why not?" Luke asked

"I'm still not sure what I want to do."

"What's holding you back?" Seth asked.

Jase shifted his feet uncomfortably.

"Jase, listen," Luke looked him in the eyes. "I know life doesn't seem fair right now. You and your sister have gone through something most people will never have to experience. But God has given you a gift. You can go be a great athlete and be a role model for kids all over the country."

Jase hung his head a little. "I don't feel like a role model."

"You can be. You can show kids, and adults for that matter, that life can kick you down, but you can get back up and keep swinging for the fences. You can inspire people with your story and your actions. There aren't many people that have that opportunity." Luke said.

"To what, exploit my parents' death?" Jase grumbled.

"Exploit? No. Honor them. Honor what they sacrificed for you. Honor the love they gave to you. Honor the commitment they made to you," Luke urged.

Jase had never thought of it that way. He had been so deep in his own misery, he couldn't think about anything except what he had lost. He hadn't wanted to go on living, but he was being given a chance to have a new life and to be a better person.

"You're right," Jase said. "I can do this and do it better than the first time."

"So, can we celebrate now?" Seth asked excitedly.

Jase ran his hand through his hair. Was he really doing this? Was he really going to go back to playing ball?

"Yes," Jase announced. "Yes, we can celebrate now."

Luke and Seth each gave him a fist bump, congratulating him on deciding.

"But I want to be the one to tell Gabby," Jase said. "So don't go off telling anyone until I tell her." Jase and Luke both glanced at Seth.

Seth put his hands up in defense, "I won't say anything to anyone."

"You'd better not," Luke told him in that big brother tone. He then turned to Jase. "And you."

"What'd I do?" Jase asked, confused.

"You better start getting into shape so you can kill it this season," Luke said with a big smile.

"Yes, coach!" Jase laughed and headed to the treadmill. "Let's go, guys. I need a team to work out with."

Jase was on the treadmill between the two brothers, each of them trying to go faster than the other. Right then, Jase knew he'd made the right decision. He loved the feeling of competing to win, even if there was no prize besides bragging rights.

Chapter 43: Gabby

Gabby and Sophie were joined at the pool by Olivia and Ben after they played nine holes of golf. Around 11:00 am, Gabby noticed the three guys walking toward them. They all appeared to be limping in pain and sweating profusely. Something seemed wrong. Gabby jumped to her feet.

"What's wrong?" Gabby gasped as she rushed to meet them. She scanned the guys for injuries, trying to figure out what might have happened.

"Well," Luke started, "there may have been a race."

"A race?" Gabby asked, feeling confused. "Like a 5k?"

"Not an organized one," Jase answered.

Seth lifted his arms over his head, stating proudly, "I won!"

"How do you think you won?" Luke asked.

"I went the fastest," Seth said.

"For how long?" Jase asked with a mocking tone.

Olivia came from behind Gabby and asked, "So you three were racing where exactly?"

"In the fitness center," they all answered at the same time.

"I'm not sure that any of you won," Sophie shook her head.

Gabby chuckled as the guys bickered back and forth about who actually won. Suddenly, Seth pushed Luke into the pool. The giant splash made everyone laugh. Seth was laughing so hard that he didn't notice Jase come up behind him and shove him in too. Gabby knew what was coming when Jase let out a cry, "King of the hill!" He raised his arms in triumph over his head. The words were barely out of his mouth before Gabby saw him flying into the pool too. Sophie stood with her hand on her hip and a wide grin on her face.

"Queen of the hill," she said, smiling broadly.

Sophie walked over to Gabby and put her arm around Gabby's shoulder. They both laughed at the guys, who were all treading water in the deep end of the pool.

Suddenly, Gabby felt Sophie's arm tighten around her shoulder, and they tumbled into the pool as well. When Gabby came up for air, Ben was bent over with laughter. Before Gabby could do anything, she saw Olivia bump her husband with her hip, and he landed in the pool with the rest of them.

"Go, Mom!" Luke shouted.

"Way to go, Mom," Seth said.

Olivia took a bow.

"Long live the queen!" Sophie cheered.

Gabby climbed onto Luke's shoulders and Sophie onto Jase's. They started a game of Marco Polo. Olivia even jumped in to join in the fun.

After a few rounds of Marco Polo, they climbed out, dried off, and ordered a poolside lunch. Gabby couldn't remember the last time she and Jase had let themselves have fun like they had the past few days. She could tell Jase was enjoying it, and the black cloud that had been surrounding him was lifting. His laugh was genuine and he was smiling more. Gabby prayed to God that the black cloud was gone for good. She prayed this was the start of a new chapter for them.

After lunch, Gabby felt ready to do something and was curious about the activities that Sophie had mentioned earlier. Sophie must have had the same thoughts.

"So, what's the plan for today?" Sophie asked.

"I'm good with anything," Gabby said.

"Want to just walk around and see what activities we might come across?" Sophie asked.

Gabby looked at Jase. He shrugged and agreed.

"Great, we'll just do whatever comes our way," Sophie cheered.

CHAPTER 44: JASE

Do whatever comes our way? Jase thought. He knew that would probably mean more Christmas activities. As they strolled through the resort, that was all that was in sight. More Christmas activities wasn't exactly what Jase wanted to do, but he also didn't want to be the Danny Downer of the group. Everyone else obviously wanted to participate in the activities. So, when they came across the ornament making tent, Jase went inside with a forced smile.

It was mostly families with little kids. There were only a few tables of four open. Jase suppressed a groan when he saw the assortment of glass bulbs and ceramic tiles available to paint and decorate. A seemingly never-ending supply of paint, glue, seashells, and other nautical trimmings covered the tables. He almost turned to walk out when he saw all the glitter remaining from previous guests. Everything from the tables and chairs seemed to be covered in it. *That stuff will stick on him forever.* He decided to stick it out and selected some items. He searched for Gabby.

He found that she, Sophie, and Olivia were still trying to select between the glass bulb or ceramic plate. Figuring they were going to be there for a while, he decided to join Luke, who had already sat at a table.

Sitting next to Luke with his glass ornament, he noticed the table was sparkling.

"I didn't see the glitter when I sat down, and now I'll never be rid of it," Luke said to Jase as he tried to wipe glitter off his board shorts.

"No kidding," Jase agreed. He chuckled seeing Luke had glitter all over his forearms from leaning on the tables.

"Have you told Gabby yet?" Luke asked.

"No, I haven't had a chance," Jase said quietly, looking to see where his sister was.

"You've seen her all day," Luke said.

"I know. I don't know why I'm hesitating telling her," he said, keeping an eye on Gabby to make sure she couldn't hear him.

"She's going to be so excited for you," Luke said quietly too.

"Maybe that's why," Jase sighed. "Maybe she's going to think that life will be magically better for me once I'm back on the team and around my teammates."

"Maybe it will help," Luke offered.

"Maybe," Jase said.

"Well, can it make things worse?" Luke said.

Jase thought about that. Could it make things worse? "Probably not."

Seth sat down on the other side of Jase with his hands full of shells and a ceramic plate.

"What are you guys talking about?" Seth asked as he unloaded an armful of ornament making things onto the table.

Luke hushed him.

"When I should tell Gabby about the Defenders," Jase told him quietly. Looking around to make sure Gabby hadn't snuck up behind him.

"Maybe you can tell her over dinner tonight," Luke said. "Unless you wanted to tell her alone?"

"No, telling her over dinner would be good." Jase still felt nervous about telling Gabby. She'd always loved and supported him. But this wouldn't be a magic fix or make everything that happened go away. Mom and Dad would still not be here. Losing them was something he had never imagined before. It had never crossed his mind. He had to admit, baseball was probably a better distraction than playing video games all night in his room. Thinking about his room made him wonder where he would live now. How could he leave Gabby alone in that house? The thoughts were making him tense.

"Jase!" Seth exclaimed. Grabbing Jase's wrist, Seth removed the shattered pieces of glass, examining Jase's hand carefully.

Jase glanced down to see that the glass bulb he had been holding had shattered. Apparently, his thoughts were making him more tense than he realized.

Gabby was at his side in an instant, asking if he was okay.

"You're good," Seth announced and released his wrist. "You got lucky, nothing pierced you."

Jase examined his hand and held it up for Gabby to see. "No blood," he said, forcing a smile.

"Well thank God for that! Are you sure you're ok?" Gabby asked again.

"Yeah, I was just lost in thought," Jase explained.

"Apparently," she said.

Gabby helped him clean up the pieces of the shattered bulb.

Seth came over with another ornament and handed it to him. "Want to try again He-man?"

Jase couldn't help but laugh. "Sure," he said, taking the glass bulb.

Luke leaned over. "I didn't mean to stress you out."

"No. It's fine. It's just stuff I've got to deal with."

"I'm here for you if you need anything," Luke said.

"Thanks, man."

Jase was grateful everyone went back to decorating their ornaments and the attention was off of him. He decided to make one with a dolphin for his sister and give it to her for Christmas. Even though they weren't going to give each other gifts this year, he thought she'd like it anyway. Besides, they'd already strayed from a festive-free holiday.

CHAPTER 45: GABBY

Gabby went back to her table but continued to watch her brother carefully. *Something has him wound tight*, she thought. She couldn't believe he had broken the glass ornament. She thanked God again that he hadn't been hurt.

Gabby finished her ornament and decided to give it to Olivia and Ben as a thank-you for making her and Jase's vacation extra special. She wasn't sure what this vacation would have been like for her and Jase without the Anderson family. Gabby thanked God for putting such a wonderful family in their path. Hopefully she and Jase would see the Andersons when they all returned to Michigan. She hoped to see a lot more of Luke when they got home too.

Gabby was startled when Luke walked up behind her.

"That's nice," he said.

She held the ornament up to inspect her work. "Thanks." She smiled and then whispered to him, "It's for your parents."

"You're good at this. They'll love it," he said. Gabby held back a giggle when she saw the glitter sheen on Luke's arms when he took the ornament from her and examined the artwork.

"Thanks. My mom was crafty and had me do projects with her. I complained about it a lot, but as I got older, I appreciated the time with her. Looking back, though, I realize it was a lot of fun." She said, taking the ornament back.

"Do you still do crafty things?" Luke asked.

"I haven't in a while. Mom was the one with the ideas, so..." Gabby trailed off.

"My mom and sister do crafty things, too," Luke said. "You should join them when you get back."

"That would be nice," Gabby agreed.

"Join who for what?" Sophie asked as she sat back down with more shells for her ornament.

"I was just telling Gabby that you and Mom do this sort of stuff at home, and Gabby should join you," Luke explained.

"Yes," Sophie said excitedly. "We'd love it if you joined us for craft days."

Gabby smiled, and Sophie continued, "Actually, we'd love it if you joined us for all sorts of things, wouldn't we, Luke?"

Gabby caught the meaning in Sophie's question and glanced at Luke.

Luke appeared to have been caught off guard with the comment, but then answered, "Yes, we would." Then he went back to the table he, Jase, and Seth were sitting at.

Sophie turned to Gabby and whispered, "He's so into you, and I love embarrassing him."

"Sophie!" was all Gabby could manage.

Sophie just giggled, then asked, "After this, there is cookie decorating or one of those instructor-led canvas painting classes. There is an adorable snowman on a beach scene that is one of the painting options. I'm not sure I can go home without it. What do you say?"

Gabby looked over to see how Jase was doing. He seemed better than he had a bit ago. He was staring intently at whatever it was he was painting on his new bulb.

"As long as Jase is good with it, I'm game," Gabby said.

"Fantastic, Jase will love it," Sophie said, putting her ornament down to stand.

Gabby was about to object to the "Jase loving it" part, but she didn't want to dampen Sophie's jovial mood.

Gabby watched as Sophie sauntered over to Jase. He seemed genuinely intrigued by her. *Maybe God is at work in more than one way here*, Gabby thought.

She watched as Sophie squealed with delight and threw her arms around Jase. He clearly didn't know how to react and stiffened with her embrace.

Sophie called out, "He said we could do the cookies and the painting!"

Gabby smiled at Sophie, clapping quietly.

Jase added, "The cookies better be delicious."

"I'm sure they will be," Gabby called back. Every meal they'd had so far had been amazing. She hoped the cookies would be too.

Three hours later, Gabby was starving. They had decorated cookies, which they hadn't allowed themselves to eat yet. Then they did the beach sandman painting activity, which was fun. Her painting turned out adorable, and Gabby was excited to have it as a keepsake. Now she was ready for that steak dinner.

Gabby was not alone in experiencing hunger pains and was glad when they decided to meet at the restaurant in a half hour after a quick change.

They were seated quickly at a round table. After they had all ordered, Gabby noticed that the three guys were all restless, silently communicating with nods and expressions that Gabby couldn't decipher.

Finally, Gabby asked, "Is something up with you guys?"

Jase, Luke, and Seth exchanged glances, making Gabby's stomach tighten. She couldn't tell by their expressions if something was wrong.

Jase finally spoke up. "I have some news."

Everyone went silent and waited for Jase to continue. Gabby wasn't sure if this was good or bad. Where was Jase going with this? What news could he possibly have?

"My agent called last night," Jase paused, "and the Defenders want to sign me to a five-year contract."

Gabby gasped, and her hands flew to her mouth. All the nerves and tension she had felt a moment ago drifted away, replaced by heart-thumping excitement. Jumping from her seat, she quickly went to her brother and wrapped him in a hug. *Thank you, Jesus. This is what I've been praying for.*

"Congratulations! I knew they weren't done with you," she cried, wrapping him in a tighter hug.

When Gabby stepped back, she watched her brother, who appeared to be relaxed. He happily accepted congratulations from everyone at the table.

"Is this why you've been stressed all day?" Gabby asked him.

"I wasn't sure how I felt about it," he admitted. "But I think it's a good thing to go back."

"I think you're right!" She beamed at him.

Everything is finally falling back into place, Gabby thought. God is good. Yet even while she watched everyone celebrate Jase's news, she couldn't kick the lingering feeling that something was still not right with him. Of course, she didn't think this would suddenly make everything better, but she hoped it was a good start. She prayed that this decision would start Jase on a path of healing. She prayed it would help them both move on to the next step.

CHAPTER 46: JASE

*O*kay, my decision is out there now, and I have to follow through
with it, Jase thought. He knew the news elated his sister.
He could see the hope in her eyes that this was going to
make him feel better. He hoped it would too, but only time would
tell. Jase felt good about this decision, though. He would just enjoy
this moment.

However, as dinner progressed, the conversation moved to
what activities the following days could include. Christmas Eve
and Christmas Day were coming. With the reminder that those
days were approaching, Jase felt a little darkness slipping back into
his heart. He tried with everything he had to stay light and posi-
tive. Even a thousand miles away, in a tropical paradise, there was
really no escape from Christmas.

Jase tried to focus on what everyone was saying without suc-
cess. He nodded and agreed when the others at the table would.
Agreeing to activities that he hadn't really heard what he had

agreed to. Ben said something about a walking Nativity the following night in a town close to the resort.

Watching Gabby get all excited about the activities both delighted Jase and frustrated him. She was the type of person who got easily excited about things, and that excitement was easy to get swept up in. At the same time, did she not realize that their parents were gone? This was going to be the hardest Christmas ever, and she was acting like it was just another day. She seemed happy with this substitute family, or whatever they were. How could she replace and forget their parents so quickly?

Jase took some deep breaths. He needed to stop this.

Jase heard them talking about matching Christmas pajamas and decided he needed to join the conversation. The Andersons were trying to make this holiday a good experience for Jase and Gabby, or at least a better one.

"What about pajamas?" Jase asked.

"I was just saying that after Christmas Eve Mass, we would let the kids open one gift each," Olivia said.

"And the gift was always pajamas," Seth said, rolling his eyes.

"Our parents did that too," Gabby chimed in.

"Your mom probably wanted nice pajamas for Christmas morning pictures, too," Olivia said.

"Yes, that's what she said," Gabby said. "Jase was the one who figured it out."

"I did," he said, thinking back on the memory of that year. "I was probably ten or eleven. We had just gotten home from church and asked if we could open a gift. Of course, Mom said yes and handed us a package."

"But then Jase looked at Mom," Gabby continued the story, "and he said, 'I'd like to open one that isn't pajamas this time.'" Gabby laughed.

"Mom was so shocked. She asked, 'How do you know it's pajamas?'" Jase continued, "And I said, 'Because it's always pajamas.'"

"Mom was so surprised that he figured it out that they let us open two presents that Christmas Eve," Gabby said. "And I probably still wouldn't have figured it out until this day."

"She's got all the book smarts and sometimes lacks common sense," Jase said, touseling his sister's hair and laughing.

"Hey now!" Gabby laughed as she swatted her brother's hand away and fixed her hair. "He's right, though. I always joked that they saved all the good genes for him."

"They did give me some good stuff," Jase said, not even trying to be modest as he flexed a muscle. "But they gave you the good stuff that counts."

He saw Gabby smile. He continued, "And what did Dad always tell you?"

"That the best things come in small packages." Gabby smiled.

"That's right," Jase said as he patted his sister's shoulder. If he didn't know any better, he'd think she had tears in her eyes. *We can do this,* Jase thought. *We will make it through this first Christmas.*

CHAPTER 47: LUKE

Sitting at the table, Luke observed Gabby and Jase. Gabby was talking to Sophie, and the two of them laughed. Luke couldn't agree more that Gabby's parents had given her some great gifts. She was loyal, kind, smart, not to mention easy to look at. Most of all, her parents gave her a gift of a strong faith. His gaze moved to Jase. He could see him still wrestling with demons inside him. Jase was laughing and smiling at the appropriate times, but he could tell they were mostly forced emotions. Luke spent years battling his own demons and recognized when someone was just going through the motions. Trying to make those around them think they were fine. Luke wondered how the faith that Gabby held hadn't passed to Jase as well. Luke wanted to help Jase and bring him closer to God. He didn't know how to bring people to God like his dad could. Maybe he and his dad could talk about how to best help Jase together.

In the meantime, Luke wasn't ready to say goodbye to this place in just a few short days. Tomorrow should be fun. His mom had heard about the walking Nativity. It sounded exceptional, and hopefully, everyone would have an amazing time.

Jase and Gabby had also agreed to join Luke's family for Christmas brunch at their villa. Luke wanted their last few days to be memorable ones, not just for Jase and Gabby but for his family too. He didn't know how many more Christmases they would all have together. Both his parents were healthy, but the Jacksons were proof that you could be called to heaven at any time. There would also be weddings and kids, and who knew where life would lead all of them?

After they cleared the plates, Luke's dad stood and held out his hand to Luke's mom.

"How about a romantic stroll on the beach, my dear?" his dad asked.

"I'd be delighted," she smiled, taking his hand and grabbing her wrap. Waving over her shoulder she said, "See you later, kids!"

"Don't stay out too late, you two," Seth called after his parents. Then he turned to the rest of the group with a mischievous grin. "So, what are we going to do?"

"Since we didn't do dessert, we could go get some," Sophie suggested.

On the other side of the resort, there was a place called the Sweet Spot. Gabby slipped her arm into Luke's as they walked there. Arriving at the Sweet Spot, Luke gazed at the extremely colorful displays. Candy, cakes, cupcakes, cotton candy, and other sugary foods were everywhere he looked.

Luke couldn't help but laugh at Seth and Jase. They were acting like kids in a candy store. They grabbed bags of candy until their arms were so full they had to take their treats to the counter.

Luke noticed that Sophie and Gabby were more selective, each choosing a local pastry to try. Luke stuck to his tried-and-true favorite of mint chocolate chip ice cream in a waffle cone.

Jase insisted on paying for everyone's and, after some debate, Luke finally gave in and let him. They walked back outside where Seth led them over to the sea wall to sit on. Luke helped Gabby up and then took a seat next to her. It was nice sitting there in silence, listening to the waves.

"I can't believe we have to pack up and leave in a few days," Seth said, breaking the silence.

"This has been fun. I'm going to be sad to leave, I think," Jase added to Luke's surprise. Gabby seemed even more surprised by Jase's statement. She beamed at her brother.

"It's been an amazing trip," Luke agreed. He felt for Gabby's hand next to him and gently took it in his, making her smile.

"It really has been," Gabby agreed. "It's been filled with wonderful and unexpected surprises." She smiled at Luke.

"I know," Sophie added. "As much as I fussed about coming here rather than the ski resort, I've really liked it. We should all come back here every year."

Luke smiled knowing that Sophie meant it. He couldn't help but wonder where they would all be in a year. It was easy to agree right now to do this every year; that's what people did on vacation, after all. They made plans and dreamed of the future. Luke knew that the future can't always be planned and that sometimes things happen that shake up those plans. Then there were times, like now, when plans turned out even better than you originally envisioned.

Luke remembered one of his dad's favorite sayings. "If you want to hear God laugh, tell him your plans." There was so much truth to that. Luke had a completely different plan for how this past year and this vacation would go. God had other plans. So far, Luke had to agree that God's plans were better than Luke's had been.

CHAPTER 48: GABBY

At dinner the night before, Gabby had managed to talk everyone into a quick snorkel trip in the morning. She was so pleased that even Jase woke up in time for the trip. It had been an amazing snorkeling tour. There had been even more fish than the first trip she'd gone on. Even a few sea turtles and stingrays, but thankfully, no sharks. She took hundreds of pictures of everyone, wanting to capture all these special moments. When she had woken up that morning, she couldn't help being sad, thinking about what she would have been doing today if her parents hadn't died. Looking around at the Andersons and her brother, she was so thankful that they had been here together. The Anderson family had been such a blessing. She wasn't sure what today would have felt like without them.

After snorkeling, they went to the pool and had another poolside lunch. She had watched Jase carefully throughout the day, and he seemed content. He had seemed to enjoy the snorkeling and carried on happy conversations at lunch. He even seemed content as they wrapped up the afternoon with shuffleboard, table tennis, and some games around the resort. Gabby couldn't believe how quickly the day went by. She wished time would slow down so this trip could last longer. But time doesn't work that way, and before she knew it, it was time to get ready to go into town for the walking Nativity.

Gabby wore a long skirt and light sweater with her comfortable walking sandals, wanting to be both cute and comfortable. She met her brother in the living room. He had on jeans and a blue polo.

"Hey, ready to go?" she asked.

"Yeah, I'm ready," he replied flatly.

"You good?" she asked, concerned that his mood seemed down compared to earlier.

"I'm fine," he grunted.

"If you don't want to go, we can stay here," she said gently.

"No, I'm fine. I'm ready," he replied as he checked the mirror.

Gabby wasn't sure what mood he was in, but they had to meet the Andersons in the lobby in just a few minutes.

"I'm ready too," she said, picking up her purse. She opened the door, and Jase followed her. They walked in an uncomfortable silence to the lobby. Gabby replayed the day in her mind. She couldn't pinpoint anything that would have caused Jase to suddenly spiral down. They'd had a good day. But maybe the realization of Christmas looming around the corner was setting in for him.

Gabby's thoughts were interrupted when she saw Luke standing in the lobby and smiling at her. She couldn't stop the butterflies in her stomach from seeing him. Even though they had only parted an hour ago, she nearly skipped over to him.

Their small group loaded into the shuttle that would take them to the downtown area. Once they were there, Gabby couldn't help but think how this had to be something out of a movie. The palm trees were strung with Christmas lights. Local people dressed in colorful traditional Mexican clothing. Tourists were shopping, eating, taking photos, and enjoying themselves. With every step, there was a different smell to take in, from spices to traditional Mexican dishes to sugary sweets being sold by street vendors. It was a feast for the senses. Gabby loved it! The very air felt alive.

Olivia gathered everyone to give some instructions. *Such a typical mom move*, Gabby thought.

"Okay everyone, we need to meet over by the big Christmas tree in about an hour. Mary and Joseph will be starting their walk from there, and we can follow them down the road to the manger," Olivia explained. "So you have an hour to go shopping, grab some food, or whatever you'd like."

Gabby watched Olivia and Ben walk off, holding hands. After 35 years of marriage, it made Gabby smile that they were still so in love. Gabby waved goodbye to them and joined Luke, Jase, Sophie, and Seth in exploring the adorable little shops.

Gabby kept track of where each of her group was in each of the stores. She didn't want to lose sight of them or have them leave the store without her. She worried she might never find them again. As she browsed through the tourist shops, looking for gifts for each of the Andersons. Since she and Jase would be joining them for Christmas brunch, she didn't want to show up empty-handed. She selected a pair of delicate gold earrings for each of the ladies. Next, she found woven leather bracelets for the men. Lastly, she bought two handmade Nativity scene ornaments, one for the Anderson family and one for her and Jase to remember their trip. Even though they had agreed to no presents, Gabby picked a hat for Jase that she thought he'd like. She also bought a hand-woven blanket for Tucker, who loved his blankets.

Right before the hour was up, Gabby found the perfect necklace and matching earrings for Holly. Since they were so cute, she got a matching set for herself too. She noticed Jase making a purchase as well. She wondered what he was buying. If she had to guess, it was probably more candy. Jase loved his candy.

Pushing their way through the bustling crowds in the plaza, they arrived at the meeting spot just as Ben and Olivia appeared as well.

"Oh good, you all made it back on time!" Olivia waved them closer..

"They are going to start in a few minutes. We want to be on the opposite side of the big tree," Ben explained. "We were told that the show will start from the white tent over there."

Gabby followed Ben's extended arm. In the middle of the plaza, there was a wide tree with a ten-foot by ten-foot fully enclosed white tent in front of it. It reminded her of a smaller version of the party tents they'd had for outdoor summer parties.

With Ben leading the group, followed closely by Olivia, they all moved together in a tightly formed chain. Jase grabbed her by the arm while Luke took her opposite hand. Gabby felt a little anxious being in such a large crowd as they shuffled their way slowly to the other side of the giant tree. She wasn't sure what to expect when they arrived at the spot Ben selected. They all just waited silently, scanning the crowds around them, filled with tourists and locals alike.

Suddenly, the street lights all went out, and a hush fell over the crowd. Gabby was amazed that with all the people crowded in, you could have heard a pin drop.

Then, the sides of the tent dropped, and a bright star appeared over it, illuminating the scene. Standing where the tent had been was a pregnant Mary sitting on a donkey that was being led by Joseph. Oohh's and ahh's rippled through the crowd. Those who had been standing in the brick-paved streets gently parted as men dressed in all black carried ropes to help move the people out of the way of the expectant holy parents. As Mary and Joseph walked, the star floated ahead of them, guiding their path. The crowds filed in behind the procession.

Gabby followed along with everyone in awed silence.

"This is so beautiful," Gabby whispered to Luke, taking his hand. Then she turned to her brother, taking his arm with her free hand and smiling at him. Jase seemed genuinely moved by the walking Nativity, and he gave Gabby a genuine smile. Gabby noticed Luke had put his other arm around his sister, who had linked arms with Seth, forming a chain. Ben and Olivia followed hand in hand, right behind their little flock.

They followed the star leading Mary and Joseph for about fifteen minutes. Gabby wasn't sure how long the path was, but it seemed like they had walked half a mile.

As they approached what appeared to be the end of the road, Mary, Joseph and the donkey strayed from their path and started knocking on doors. Each door was opened, and while no words were spoken, Gabby could tell Joseph was silently pleading with the people at each door to give them a place to stay. He pointed at his wife's belly while each person shook their heads and closed the door on the couple.

Finally, they came to the last house. Joseph knocked, and a man opened the door. Joseph dropped to his knees with a silent plea to give them a room. The man stepped out and walked Mary and Joseph to the side of the house. The crowd followed and pushed in tighter to see. Gabby stood on her toes to see the wooden structure. It looked like the barn of the Nativity scene they had at their house. Three walls and a pitched roof, all made out of wood. There was a dirt floor with some bales of hay stacked around the manger. Joseph helped Mary off of the donkey, bringing her into the barn.

The star they had been following came to rest over the barn. The star shone even brighter for a moment, and then it faded a little to reveal Mary holding up a crying baby Jesus. The crowd erupted in cheers. Gabby felt goosebumps on her arms, and a tear slid down her cheek. She noticed she wasn't the only one moved by this experience. Everyone in their party, including Jase, had the sheen of tears in their eyes.

Gabby snapped some photos of the scene, reviewing each photo and deleting it. She took a few more before she realized that the photos would never do justice to the experience.

"The kids' pageant at church is always cute, but this was just..." Gabby couldn't find words to finish.

"I've never seen anything so moving," Sophie agreed, still wiping away a tear.

"Their struggle was real," Jase added. "Seeing Joseph plead with people and being turned away...I just wanted to be like, dude let him in!"

"That's what God wants from all of us," Ben said. "To just let him in."

They all soaked in Ben's words of wisdom - just let him in.

Gabby noticed the crowd starting to disperse and head back to the main part of the plaza. Their group followed the rest of the crowd. They walked in silence for a moment, then Seth piped up with, "Where do you think that baby was the whole time?"

Leave it to Seth to break a beautiful moment of silence with his humor. Luke draped an arm over Seth's shoulder and asked, "Didn't Mom and Dad have the talk with you about where babies come from?"

This caused another round of laughter. For the first time since Gabby had known the Andersons, she saw Seth's face flush red.

Seth pushed his brother's arm off. "I mean that baby, she didn't give birth there," Seth said.

Jase came to his defense. "That's actually a legit question. Was the lady caring for him that whole time? Or did they stash the baby in the barn?"

"Exactly," Seth said, pointing to Jase.

"I'm not sure either," Ben said. "But that was one of the best experiences of my life, and I'm glad we could all share it together."

Gabby couldn't agree more. That was one of those life-changing experiences that would not be forgotten.

CHAPTER 49: JASE

J ase hadn't been sure about coming to the Nativity, but he had to admit, it was one of the best things he'd ever seen in his life. It was more moving than he had thought it would be. He was glad that he had shared it with his sister and the Andersons. Jase missed doing things as a family.

Jase thought more about what Ben had said about letting God in as they walked back to the center of town. The picture of Joseph knocking on all those doors replayed in his mind. He wondered if God had been left out in the cold knocking, and Jase wasn't even getting up to answer the door. He had been so angry at God that the thought of letting him in just brought on more anger.

Even though he had dreaded Christmas Eve, he felt at peace after seeing that Nativity. He had even enjoyed the shopping and picked up a few things. He found a little something that he knew Gabby would love, so he bought it to go with the ornament he had made her. He had a feeling that she was going to sneak gifts in for him too.

Jase noticed his sister and Sophie wandering off to do some more shopping as Luke approached him.

"Hey, did you like the show?" Luke asked.

"That was pretty amazing," Jase admitted

"It was. I don't want to lose my man card here, but I almost cried," Luke confessed.

"If you don't tell anyone, I'll admit I almost did, too," Jase confided in Luke.

"I guess crying over Jesus isn't the worst thing to cry about," Luke said happily.

Jase shook his head, "I guess not."

"So, when do you leave for spring training?" Luke asked as he sat on a bench outside the store their sisters had just gone into.

"I'll probably head down pretty soon after the New Year. I'll want to get settled in, and get in better shape, and start working with the trainer and hitting coach again. Plus, catchers and pitchers report earlier than the rest of the team to start practicing." Jase replied and sat next to him.

"Are you excited to get back?" Luke asked.

"I guess so," Jase replied, his heel bouncing on the ground.

"You guess?" Luke seemed confused. He sat up to look closer at Jase.

"I'm just not sure how I'll feel leaving Gabby by herself. I know she won't come with me because she has a business to run," Jase explained.

"I'll keep an eye on her," Luke assured him.

Jase laughed. "I'm sure you will."

"I'm serious. I really like your sister, and I'd like to date her when we get back," Luke stated.

"Are you asking if you can date my sister?"

Luke grinned at him. "I guess I am."

Jase stopped and turned to Luke. "Gabby is her own person and makes up her own mind about things. And she's been through a lot. She's the greatest person I know, and she deserves someone just as great."

Luke nodded.

Jase finally continued, "You make her happier than I've seen her in a long time. I know you're a good man, and you'll treat her the way she deserves to be treated."

Luke smiled. "I will."

"You're good in my books," Jase said, extending his hand for Luke to shake. Then he laughed and shook his head. "But my sister still has a mind of her own and has to make that choice for herself. I wish you luck, man."

Luke gave a laugh. "Thanks."

CHAPTER 50: LUKE

This night has been incredible, Luke thought. The walking Nativity was the best reenactment he'd ever witnessed. He had held Gabby's hand the whole time. And to top it off, Jase seemed cool with him dating his sister. Luke also thought he had seen a glimmer of hope that Jase was coming closer to God. Luke wasn't sure this night could get any better.

It was probably too early to be thinking about this, but Gabby fit in so well with Luke's family. He could picture her being a part of it someday. *First things first,* Luke reminded himself. He had to see what would happen when they got home. He hoped they could make something work.

Jase had wandered off with Seth to enjoy more street food. Gabby and Sophie were strolling back from some shopping. Luke's mom and dad were sitting by a fountain, talking and laughing.

"Hey there, what did you ladies get into?" Luke asked Gabby and his sister, noticing they had more bags than before.

"Just some stuff I went back for that I saw earlier," Gabby said with a smile.

"Same here," Sophie said. "Gabby is just as big of a souvenir junkie as I am."

"Guilty," Gabby said. "I've never met a gift shop that I couldn't go crazy in."

"I have to go show Mom something," Sophie said, leaving Luke and Gabby standing there alone.

"What do you do with it all?" Luke asked as he observed the bags.

"Some are gifts. Some things I keep in a box with a plan to hang them up in my office to remind me of my travels."

"But for now, they sit in a box?" Luke asked.

"Sadly, yes. I really need to get around to hanging them," Gabby said, shaking her head. "I'll get around to hanging them someday."

"I was wondering if you had plans later?" Luke asked Gabby.

"Later tonight?" Gabby asked with a laugh.

"I know it's late, but we're only here a few more days, and I'd like to see you more."

"We just spent all day together," she said seriously.

"That's true..." Luke didn't know what else to say.

"Luke, I'm kidding!" Gabby laughed. "I'd love to do something with you tonight."

Luke laughed. "I thought maybe you were tired of me already."

"Not yet." She winked at him. "I'm not sure I'll be tired of you anytime soon."

He smiled and replied, "Me neither."

Something behind him must have caught Gabby's eye as she looked past him and waved. "Your mom's waving me over; I should go see what she wants."

"Okay," he replied. He watched her join his mom, who started digging through bags. Sophie walked up to him and nudged his shoulder with hers.

"You are smiling like an idiot," Sophie said.

Luke was in such a good mood he wasn't even going to argue with his sister. "Yup, I am."

CHAPTER 51: GABBY

Even though Gabby was sitting in a shuttle next to Sophie, she felt like she was floating. How could all of these wonderful things be happening at the end of the worst year of her life? She believed that everything happened for a reason. If her parents hadn't died, she wouldn't be here. She wouldn't have met Luke and his family. She still felt the sadness that her parents weren't here with them. She didn't want to get into that tailspin of emotions, though, so she pushed them down to deal with later. For now, she was going to enjoy the last few days here and every minute she could with Luke. She wondered what he wanted to do tonight.

After they all unloaded from the shuttle, Gabby said goodnight to everyone and they all went their separate ways. Sophie and her parents went back to the villa while Jase and Seth were going to hit up a bar.

Luke asked Gabby if he could stop by their villa to grab a few things. Gabby waited outside. He came back quickly carrying a beach bag. She could see a blanket poking out of it.

"Did you already have that packed?" Gabby asked.

"No, but it was all sitting right by the door," Luke told her.

"Impressive. So where are we going?" Gabby asked, following Luke on the walkway.

"I figured we could find a quiet spot near the water," Luke said. They walked past a few other tourists and until they found a good spot on the beach. Luke laid the blanket on the ground. Then he handed her a bottle of water.

The lights from the resort gave the water a blue-tinted glow. Gabby watched the waves crash gently to the shore.

"I can't believe that in two days we'll be heading back to a foot of snow," Gabby said.

"I know," Luke agreed. "It doesn't seem possible that this is on the same planet as home."

"I know. This feels worlds away," she agreed.

"So, have you figured life out while you were here?" Luke asked with a chuckle.

"Life?" Gabby laughed. "No, but I think I have some clarity on things."

"Like what?" he asked.

"Your sister asked me what I might have done if I hadn't gone to work with my dad. I had never really given it a thought. It was just always expected, or at least I felt like it was what was expected. It's funny she asked because before we came here, I had told my best friend I was thinking of selling the business."

"What would you do if you sold it?" Luke asked, leaning back on an elbow.

"I don't know. I've always loved photography. I even have some prints for sale in some local shops, so I could do that full-time." Gabby said, twisting her mom's ring.

"Would that take the fun out of it?" Luke asked.

"I can't imagine anything taking the fun out of it," Gabby said with a small laugh.

"Well, if you were relying on photography to be your main source of income, it would be a job," Luke said.

Gabby hadn't thought of it that way. She would have to worry about selling enough prints or booking enough assignments to make a living. Sure, she had enough money right now with her savings and life insurance from her parents. But if she never sold a photograph, how long would that all last? Then she'd have to start over doing something else.

"You have a good point," she conceded.

"What are your other options?" Luke asked, sitting up facing her full-on.

"Move here and open a scuba shop?" She laughed.

"It is nice here," Luke agreed.

"I don't think I want to sell the business, but I do need to hire someone who can help me with it. I have to stop living to work and get more balance in life. Besides the occasional dinner with friends, I don't do anything for myself."

"Since Jase is going back to baseball, what does that open up for you?" Luke asked.

"I can stop worrying about him rotting away in his room playing video games," she said, then continued with a sigh. "And worry more about him being on the road where I can't see him and know he's okay."

"Did you worry about him, like you do now, before the accident with your parents?" Luke asked, leaning back again.

"Well, no," she said thoughtfully. "Actually, I don't think I ever worried about him."

"So why now?" He asked, looking into her eyes.

Gabby shrugged. "He's all I have left."

Luke gently took her hand. "I get what you mean, but he's not all you have left."

Gabby could feel the heat from the touch of his hand creep up her arm and reach her face.

"He'll be okay," Luke said. "You both will."

Gabby smiled and looked out to the water. She believed him. She knew, eventually, she and Jase would both be more at peace with their parents being gone. She just wanted that peace to come sooner.

"So when you get home, you're going to hire someone to help at the office. You're going to make time for yourself. What are you going to do with that time?" Luke asked, bringing her attention back to him.

"I'm not sure," she said.

"You can start with turning the office into your own and hanging the photos you like," he suggested.

"That would be a good start," Gabby agreed. Maybe that was another reason she hadn't really ever thought of it as hers. Everything from the chair in the office to the photos that hung on the wall were still her dad's.

"Second," Luke said, leaning toward her. "I hope you can make some time to see me." He smiled.

Gabby smiled back. "I would like that."

"Me too." He took her hand and kissed it. "I'm so lucky to have met you. I was thinking, if you don't have plans for New Years, would you like to come to my parents' New Year's Eve party as my date?"

"I feel blessed to have met you, too," Gabby said softly. "And I'll have to check my schedule, but I'm nearly certain New Year's is completely open. I'd love to come."

"Fantastic!" Luke's smile lit up his whole face, making her smile too.

"I'm really grateful to have met your whole family," Gabby added.

"They are pretty great, I have to admit." He nodded.

"Honestly, I don't know how this vacation would have gone if we hadn't met you all."

"I'm sure it would have still been a nice vacation."

"I don't know," she said seriously. "I feel awful saying this, but you and your family were like a buffer for Jase and me."

"A buffer? You guys are so close you don't need a buffer." Luke shook his head in disbelief.

"But we did. We have avoided talking about anything important ever since our parents died. I feel like we've even avoided being together this entire trip. We haven't done a single thing with just the two of us."

Luke was quiet, so Gabby continued, "I'm afraid to talk to him."

"Afraid?" he asked, concern flooding his voice. Gabby could see him tense up.

"Not like he's going to hurt me," Gabby assured him, placing a hand on his leg. "He would never physically hurt me. He has a quick temper and gets loud, which makes me nervous. But then he'll get real quiet, which also makes me nervous. I guess I don't know how to approach him. Especially when neither of us wanted to say out loud that they were really gone."

"So, you back away when things might get hard," Luke said, relaxing a little.

"Exactly. He's been so emotional these past six months, and understandably so," she was quick to add. "But I'm not good at standing up to him, so I avoid it."

"You can't avoid things forever," Luke said, gently stroking her hand.

"I know. I've been praying for strength, but it's hard. I don't want to end up like those families who never speak to each other because they let a death in the family separate them."

"You know, hard conversations don't have to be mean conversations," he said.

Gabby let that sink in and nodded.

"From what I can tell, you are a caring and reasonable person, Gabby. I know you'll find the right words to say to Jase," Luke assured her.

"I hope so," she said. "I feel like this trip and being here has really been helpful. It's like Jase and I took a step forward into living again. I don't want to ruin that or take a step backward from that. I will talk to him when we get back home. It's a little easier now that he'll be leaving for spring training soon."

"Do it when it feels right," Luke encouraged. "It doesn't matter where or when, just as long as it happens."

Gabby nodded in agreement. Then she heard some laughing in the distance. The moon was almost full and illuminated the beach area. She noticed other couples had lined up blankets to watch the water too. She wondered what they were talking about as she heard more laughter.

"I'm sorry," she said. "I didn't mean to turn a nice evening into a sob story."

"You didn't," he assured her. "I'm glad you feel comfortable enough to share all this with me."

"I know this sounds strange, but I feel like I've known you forever."

"It's not strange," Luke said and wrapped an arm around her. "I feel the same."

Gabby leaned into him, resting her head on his shoulder.

It seemed like God put Gabby and Luke at the same place at the same time so they could meet.

"So, how about you?" she asked.

"What about me?" he responded.

"Has this trip changed your life?" Gabby wondered.

CHAPTER 52: LUKE

"Has this trip changed my life?" Luke chuckled. Letting her go so he could look at her.

"Why is that funny?" Gabby asked.

"Just because it has, in more ways than one," he said.

"How so?" she asked.

"I appreciate what I have and my life more. I told you that I gave my life over to God after the Army. I think that was step one. I live each day in service to him, or at least I try to. But mostly, I realized that I'm not living the life I've been coaching the high school kids and the guys in my veteran group to live."

"So it's like you're playing it safe?" Gabby concluded.

"Kind of," Luke said, trying to find the right way to explain it. "I spend time teaching, planning for teaching, coaching, and planning for coaching. But I don't put myself out there and let people in. I don't live the way I coach people to live."

"And now?" Gabby asked curiously.

"Now I think I'm ready to let people in." Luke grinned and took her hand. "Or at least let someone in more."

"That's good to know." Gabby offered him a sweet smile. "Anything else?"

"That wasn't a good enough answer?" He laughed.

"I just wondered if there was anything else you learned on this trip?" she said.

"I did." He gave her a sly grin. "Snorkeling isn't so bad."

They both laughed.

"I'm glad I could help you expand your horizons." She smiled at him.

"You have definitely done that, Gabby Jackson," he said.

Luke liked that he could be open with Gabby. They talked for the next hour about books, movies, T.V. shows. He thought it was awesome that she was a huge fan of all the Avengers movies. She also liked the Histories Mysteries TV series he enjoyed and sometimes got lesson ideas from.

Some other tourists walked by, making Luke check his watch. He was surprised to see it was just at 11:00 pm.

"I should probably walk you back," Luke said.

"I didn't realize it had gotten so late. I hope Jase isn't worried," she said, jumping up. She started to quickly gather the water bottles and tugged on the blanket he was still on.

"He knows you're with me," Luke said as he stood up.

Gabby gave a little laugh and started folding the blanket. "I'll be surprised if Jase isn't worried about that too."

"He's fine," he told her and took the blanket to put it back in the bag. Then he took Gabby's hand and started walking back to her room.

Luke guided them the long way around the resort just to spend a little more time holding Gabby's hand. He felt disappointed when they arrived at her door.

The entire night had gone so well. He had felt so comfortable until this moment. He felt like he was taking his first date home, afraid her dad, or brother in this case, was watching out the window for them to come back.

"Here we are," Gabby said, turning to look at him.

"You guys will be over in the morning?" Luke asked.

"Yes, we will be there." She smiled at him.

"Good. I'm looking forward to seeing you," Luke said, not sure what to say or do. He watched as she fidgeted with her ring again.

Gabby brought her gaze up to meet his eyes, and Luke felt even more nervous. He wanted to kiss her. This was the moment he had been waiting for. He was about to lean in, but then he paused. *Maybe I'm not ready for this.* He took a deep breath and straightened up.

She gave a little sigh and said, "Well, good night then."

"Good night," he replied.

She turned to let herself in, and he let go of her hand. He started to walk away.

Why am I walking away? he thought. This had been the perfect night, and it was the perfect time to kiss her. How many times had he told her that he wanted to see her when they got back home? What would she think he meant? Professionally? As a buddy?

No. He stopped walking about halfway down the hall. He had said that he wanted to start living the bold life he was telling others to live. That meant taking chances and putting himself out there. Gabby was the woman he'd been waiting his whole life for. He wanted to show her that he cared. He spun around. She was still standing in front of her room.

"Gabby," he called out.

Her head snapped his way. He walked right up to her and gently cradled her head in his hands. He noticed her eyes flash with shock and delight, and then a smile danced across her mouth. He bent his head down and gently kissed her. Her lips were soft and tasted like the salt from the sea air. He could stand here all night holding her in his arms, kissing her sweet lips. Reluctantly, he stepped back, opening his eyes.

Gabby's eyes were still closed. Slowly, she opened them. She took a step back as well. Luke tried to read her expression. Maybe he had moved too fast for her.

"I'm sorry, I just..." he mumbled.

A smile spread across her face. She took his face in her hands, stood up on her tiptoes, and quickly kissed him again.

"Don't be," she said as she put her heels back down to the ground.

He rested his forehead against hers. "I'm really glad that wasn't a mistake."

"I'm really glad you came back," she whispered.

Luke was finally able to breathe again. "I'll let you get some sleep now."

"Okay, I'll see you in the morning." She smiled. "Have a good night."

"You too," he said, giving her another quick kiss. "Sweet dreams."

Luke practically jogged back to his villa. This was the start to living that life that he talked about.

When he walked into the living room, he was shocked to find his siblings sitting on the couch.

"Hey, what are you guys still doing up?" he asked, trying to stop smiling.

"Maybe we should ask you the same," his sister said, exchanging a glance with Seth.

"I just walked Gabby back to her room. They'll be here in the morning," he rambled.

"I'm sure that's all you were doing." Seth grinned.

"Shut up," Luke said, still not able to stop smiling.

"Whatever. Don't take your shoes off. Mom and Dad gave us a mission to complete," Seth said.

"A mission?" he asked.

His sister stood, giving him a wide smile, and held up two neatly wrapped packages.

CHAPTER 53: GABBY

Gabby slipped into her hotel room and leaned back against the door. She smiled and put her fingers to her lips. She could still feel Luke's lips on hers. She had been kissed before, but not like that. *That was definitely the best kiss of my life,* she thought.

When she came out of her haze, she noticed Jase's feet propped up on the table in the living area.

"Hey," she greeted him, trying to sound casual, but the words squeaked out like a chipmunk.

"Hey to you." He peeled his eyes off the TV and scanned her face. "Have a good time?" he asked, raising an eyebrow.

She knew there was no reason to deny it. She had no poker face, and the dreamy smile that wouldn't go away told Jase the truth.

"The best time," she said as she sat next to her brother on the sofa.

"Good," he said, sounding genuinely happy that she had a good time.

They both sat there while the TV filled in the silence.

Gabby rose to her feet and announced she was heading to bed. "Are you sure you're still up for brunch tomorrow?"

Jase didn't acknowledge her, but then he grunted, "Yeah."

She wasn't sure that he meant it, but she decided to roll with it. "Okay then," she replied.

She walked into her room and opened the drawers to pull out her pajamas. She saw the little wrapped packages next to her clothes. She was debating whether to give them to Jase tonight when she heard a knock at the door.

She walked back into the living room, where Jase was already on his feet, heading to answer it.

She peered from behind him as he cracked the door open and scanned the hall.

"Who's there?" she whispered, unsure why she was whispering.

"No one," he said. Then he bent over to pick something up.

When he turned around, he had two beautifully wrapped packages, one red and one blue with gold curling ribbon and bows. There was an envelope with their names on each one. He handed her the one marked for "Gabby," and they both went to sit on the couch.

"Are we supposed to open these now?" Gabby asked him.

"I'm not sure," he said, examining the package. "It doesn't say not to."

Gabby opened the envelope. A lump formed in her throat as she read, "Some traditions should be kept alive. Love, the Anderson Family."

She glanced over and noticed the same message on Jase's note.

Jase tore off the wrapping paper while Gabby delicately tried to open the package without ripping the lovely red paper. When they opened the boxes, she saw a white shirt trimmed in green. Pulling it out further, she saw a cartoon head of the Grinch who was smiling and wearing a Santa hat.

Jase pulled a matching shirt from his box, making them both chuckle. Still in their boxes were red, green, and white-striped pajama bottoms. There was also a note for them to wear pajamas to brunch the following day.

"Is this supposed to be a self-portrait?" Gabby asked, holding up the shirt.

"No," Jase replied. "The Grinch has less hair."

"Hey," she exclaimed and hit him with the shirt in her hand.

Gabby watched as Jase held up his new pajamas. He seemed conflicted, a little sad, but amused.

She felt the sudden need to hug him, so she leaned over and wrapped her arms around his neck. He patted her arm in return.

"I had a good time this trip," he said. "Thanks for getting me out of the house."

"I did too," she agreed.

"Even the Andersons turned out to be a good thing," Jase said.

"They were an extra blessing," she said. She expected an eye roll, but it never came. Jase just nodded. Gabby wanted to add that she was excited about him getting re-signed. Maybe that would open the conversation about other things, but she stopped herself. It was a nice moment; she wouldn't ruin it. Then Jase started talking again.

"It was nice to get away from things. Not that it stopped the feelings and missing Mom and Dad, but it was still nice to get away." Jase said, leaning back on the couch.

"It was. I think we both needed this." Leaned to the back of the couch, still looking at Jase.

"We did." He wrapped his arm around her shoulders. "Plus, you will be leaving with a boyfriend as a souvenir."

She gave him a little nudge. "Stop it!" Then she couldn't go on. Was she leaving with a boyfriend? Or someone who could be a boyfriend? Maybe that wouldn't be such a bad thing either.

They sat silently again. Gabby could feel the emotions of the week and the past six months slowly start to boil in her heart. She didn't want to upset her brother or have him see her cry. She decided it was time to get some sleep. Thankfully, Jase agreed. They said good night and walked to their rooms. Just as she was about to close the door, she heard Jase call from his door.

"Hey Gabs," he said softly.

"Yeah?"

"I love you," he said with a small grin.

His words warmed her heart. She replied, "Love you, too" before watching him close the door. She crawled onto the pillow-topped bed and let herself cry. She cried for herself and for her brother. She cried because she missed her parents and wanted them here.

Gabby curled into a ball, hugged a pillow to her chest, and just lay there crying and praying for God to take the pain away. She prayed for life to be easy again for both her and Jase. She prayed that something good would come out of this sadness. She knew God had a plan for everything, and she begged him to reveal that purpose to her, to help her understand. She prayed until she ran out of words, and all she could do was let the tears speak for her.

CHAPTER 54: JASE

Jase closed the door and looked at the pajamas in his hands. The picture of the Grinch made him smile. It was so fitting for this Christmas. He was sure the Anderson family thought he and his sister were a pair of grinches when they first met. Who didn't want to celebrate Christmas?

Jase pulled off the shirt he was wearing and changed into the Grinch pajama set.

He admired the outfit in the mirror and was impressed Olivia had picked the right size for him. He assumed it was Olivia at least; this was a mom move.

He thought about all the pajamas his own mom had chosen for him over the years. He-Man, G.I. Joe, baseball-themed. She had chosen Defenders pajamas when he was ten or so. He had proudly worn them and announced that he would play for that team someday. His mom had taken him in her arms and told him she believed he would.

The memory hit him hard. A tear rolled down his scruffy cheek, and he quickly wiped it away. But that tear was followed by more. He threw himself onto his bed, burying his face in his pillow to muffle his crying.

Jase mentally cursed himself for being weak. He was a big, strong man. Men didn't act like this. He had only seen his dad cry twice in his life. Jase was sure that his dad would be disappointed in his son for being so emotional. He had always wanted to live up to his dad, the strongest and best man he knew. Jase felt like he was constantly failing him.

His thoughts turned to his mom. When he was little, she would lay his head on her lap and run her fingers gently over his head, comforting him and telling him to let out the sadness. He wished she was here to comfort him now. He hadn't needed comforting since he was young, and he hadn't appreciated his mom like he should have. The guilt of that washed over him and another flood of tears came.

"Why, God? I still don't understand. I'm trying to let you in. But I just don't understand," he cried out through his sobs.

His tears eventually stopped as his emotions fluctuated from anger to guilt to sadness. The painful emotions rolling through him felt like a hurricane ripping his chest apart. He stood up and punched the bed over and over again until he finally collapsed to his knees. He buried his face in his hands, genuinely pleading, "God, please help, I can't do this."

He crumpled all the way to the floor and just lay there, too weary to move.

CHAPTER 55: GABBY

Before dawn on Christmas morning, Gabby made some tea and sat on the patio for her morning devotional. When she flipped to her bookmarked page, it read "Christmas Day." This was the day they had been dreading. Yet, as she sipped her tea, a beautiful sunrise was spreading across the sky. A light breeze touched her skin, and a strange calm settled within her. She wasn't sure what she had been expecting today to be like, especially after she broke down last night. Was it the tropical surroundings that made it feel less like Christmas? Maybe she just needed to release all of the emotions she'd been holding deep inside, and that's why she felt at peace. At the moment, she didn't care. She was just content that the world had kept turning. She realized that she and Jase would keep going too.

Gabby thanked God for the years they had with their parents and the blessings her mom and dad had left. Her parents had always focused on family first. She and Jase were not like other families who had fought and broken apart after their parents passed on.

While they still needed to figure out how to divide up the material things and what to do with the house, Gabby knew there was not a single possession they would fight over. The only thing they might get heated over was who would get custody of their furry sibling, Tucker. Even that, they would manage peacefully.

For a day she and Jase had been working so hard to escape, it was starting off okay. Gabby prayed it would continue that way.

CHAPTER 56: JASE

J ase picked himself up off the carpet while making a mental note that he was too old to spend the night on the floor anymore. He groaned at the ache in his muscles, and he tried to stretch them out.

He looked out the window. The sun was just rising over the ocean, and it was a beautiful sunrise. The emotions of last night had settled, and he felt the promise of a new day. He was aware of what day it was, and he wasn't sure how to approach it yet. He hoped his sister wasn't out there trying to throw a last-minute Christmas decorating party to surprise him. He promised himself he wouldn't explode on her if she was. He would just try to roll with it.

To his pleasant surprise, when he entered the living room, it was the same as it had been the whole week, blissfully Christmas-free. His sister was sitting on the patio with her Bible. He wasn't sure he should interrupt. She heard him and gestured for him to come over.

"Good morning," he greeted her.

"Good morning." She smiled. "How did you sleep?"

"Okay, I guess. You?" Jase said. He decided not to mention that he had had a breakdown and spent the night on the floor.

"Pretty good," she said, but something in her voice made him question if that was true.

"What are you doing?" he asked.

She held up her Bible. "Devotional," she said.

"I can leave you to it," he said, about to turn away. He didn't want to get roped into that, even if it was Christmas.

"No, you have good timing. I was just finishing," she said in a calm, happy voice, gesturing for him to sit down.

"So...," he said. Sitting down, he wondered which of them was going to acknowledge the day first.

His sister nodded her head knowingly. "So."

They sat there, neither knowing what to say. Gabby popped up out of her chair and hurried to her room. Jase wondered if this was the moment she was finally going to break down. He felt guilty, as part of him hoped it was. *Just sit and be miserable with me, Gabs*, he thought.

Instead, she returned with a couple of packages. He tried his best not to groan, but a small moan escaped. He quickly covered it with a cough.

"I know, I know," she said, putting the packages on the table. "We said no gifts. In fairness, there is one present from Holly for each of us, and the other two I just thought you might like."

Jase stood and walked off to his room, leaving Gabby there looking confused or hurt or both. He opened his drawer and pulled out the package. It was still in the paper bag they had sold it to him in. He also picked up the ornament he'd made and went back out to the patio. Gabby's face brightened as he returned.

"I wasn't sure you were coming back," Gabby said, sounding relieved.

"No, I broke the rule too," he said with a grin, revealing the package he had for her. "I saw something that I thought you would like too."

For a moment, he thought his sister might cry. Then she took a deep breath and handed him the package from Holly labeled 'Jase.' Gabby had another one that was about the same size addressed to her. They opened them together. The gifts were identical. A weathered wood frame with two cardinals carved into the top corners held a photo of their family.

There we are, the complete Jackson family, laughing and smiling together, Jase thought. No one was facing the camera. Instead, they were looking at each other. They were all laughing hysterically, like someone had just told a joke. Jase and Gabby both stared at the photo until Gabby finally said, "I don't even remember taking this picture."

Jase had to choke back his emotions. He couldn't place it either.

Suddenly, Jase recognized it and gasped.

"What?" Gabby nearly jumped.

"It's the last time we all had dinner together," he said, stunned.

"What?" Gabby scanned the photo again.

"We had gone to Kennedy's Pub for dinner right before my surgery because Mom didn't want to cook. Remember, Holly and her family met us there. Mom spilled her drink on me, and look, there's the stain." He pointed at the red stain on his shirt.

"Oh yeah! It must have been just after that happened. Holly must have snapped the photo and saved it."

"It's a good photo," Jase said.

"It is." Gabby reached over and squeezed his hand.

Jase had to look away, but he decided it was a good time to hand Gabby the ornament he'd made and the paper bag.

"Is this the ornament you made?" she asked as she held the glass bulb up to the light. She spun it around to see the kind of globby dolphins jumping in the water.

"I know it's not great, but I wanted you to have it," Jase said sheepishly. "We didn't get our annual ornaments this year from Mom, and Olivia is right. There are some traditions that should be kept alive."

Gabby did tear up at that. Their mom had painstakingly selected an ornament for each of them every year to celebrate something they had accomplished that year. They had each received one every year, starting with their first Christmas.

"Thank you, I love it." She sniffed. "It's also perfect timing to open this one."

Gabby handed him a small box. He removed the lid. Inside was a Cozumel ornament. He held it in his hand before he glanced at his sister. She smiled and shrugged. "Traditions," was all she said.

Jase carefully put the ornament back in its box and handed his sister the brown paper bag.

"Sorry it's not wrapped up fancy," he said.

"You know we don't need fancy wrapping." She smiled at him, then took the bag and opened it.

She pulled out a little black box and eyed her brother suspiciously. When she opened the velvety box, inside was a thin necklace with a gold cross that had a small star engraved in the center.

"Jase," Gabby gasped. "This is so beautiful."

Jase smiled at his sister's reaction. It made him feel good that she liked it so much.

"I saw the cross and thought it was pretty and small, like you. Then I noticed the little star in the middle, and it reminded me of the Nativity and the star that we all followed to the manger."

She removed the necklace from the box and placed it around her neck.

She reached over and hugged him. "I love it so much!"

When she released him, she handed him the last box on the table. It was a little bigger than a shoebox. He tore off the paper and lifted the lid.

He pulled a woven straw hat out of the box. With a smile, he put it on, showing it off to his sister.

"This is great. I saw these in that one shop, and I almost bought one," he said.

"I saw that, and I was glad you didn't so I could get it for you," she said with a big smile.

Then Gabby's eyes guestured back to the box. She wiggled with excitement in her chair. He leaned it toward him and saw a smaller box inside. He removed the small cardboard box and eyed his sister suspiciously. He wasn't sure what was inside, but he knew if he didn't open it, she might burst.

He popped the lid off and could only stare at what was inside. Taking the silver metal chain between his fingers, he lifted it out of the box until a round medallion appeared as well.

He stared from his sister back to the chain.

"Is this...?" he couldn't believe what he was seeing.

"Yeah," she nodded, and tears came to her eyes.

Jase stared again at the chain and pendant. It was the five-way cross medallion that their dad had worn every day for as long as they could remember. His dad had given it to Jase when he went to college. After the accident, it was nowhere to be found. They had both assumed it was lost forever.

"But how? I thought it was lost in the accident," Jase stuttered.

"I thought so too. Apparently, Dad had taken it to the jewelers to be cleaned and the clasp replaced. When Holly and I went shopping after Thanksgiving, we stopped at the jewelry store. They told me they still had it and apologized they hadn't called us sooner. It had fallen behind a desk, and they just found it the day before Thanksgiving."

"Wow, that's crazy," he said, grasping onto the metal.

"I know. It was meant to come home to us. I was going to give it to you then, but I decided I'd save it for today."

Jase had a hard time choking back tears. This was a piece of his dad that could be with him forever now. He put it on and held it to his chest.

He sat silently, feeling like he was holding his parents with him. He was so grateful that Gabby had given it to him. He knew it meant a lot to her too.

"Gabby, thank you. This is..." he didn't know what to say. "This is amazing, thank you."

Gabby wasn't the only one wiping away a few tears, but Jase didn't care. He hugged her again. Then he took a few deep breaths and looked out at the ocean view. They would be leaving tomorrow, but for now, he would simply enjoy being with his sister for a bit.

"I see you like the pajamas," Jase said.

"I see you do, too," she teased. "I'm not going to lie. I was shocked to see you in them this morning."

"Me too, but man, they're really soft," he said, rubbing his hands over the pajamas.

"They really are," Gabby agreed, running her hands over the soft sleeves. "Are you sure you want to go to brunch at the Andersons' today?"

"I wasn't sure, but they've been really nice to us on this trip. It would be rude of us not to show up now."

"I know, but I think they'd understand," she said gently.

"I'm sure they would, but it's close to when we're supposed to be there. And I'm hungry."

Gabby laughed at her brother. "Let the stomach be the guide."

"I need to enjoy all this indulgence before real training begins, and all this has to go," he said as he leaned back rubbing his belly.

Truthfully, Jase wasn't sure he wanted to go over to the Andersons', but it was one more day to endure.

Chapter 57: Luke

L uke groaned when Seth jumped on his bed to wake him up. It was only 7:00 am, and Seth woke everyone up like a ten-year-old wanting to open presents. Luke's parents made coffee, tea, and hot cocoa with mini marshmallows, even though it was already over 70 degrees outside.

Luke wasn't sure where his parents had found lights to decorate the two-foot potted tree. But there was a hotel tree decorated with Christmas lights and presents underneath for all of them. There were even a few gifts for Jase and Gabby. They decided to open one present each and wait for Jase and Gabby to get there for the rest. No one expected Gabby and Jase to bring presents, but Luke's family didn't want their new friends to feel awkward opening theirs when no one else had anything to open.

After they each had opened a present, Olivia announced that the Jacksons would be there soon.

Ben said, "Everyone, come here." He gestured for them to hold hands before he began to pray.

"Heavenly Father, today we celebrate the birth of your son, Jesus Christ. We thank you for sending him to wash away our sins so we can spend eternal life with you in Heaven. We thank you for this time we were able to spend together as a family. And thank you for putting us here, where we were able to cross paths with the Jackson kids. I pray that we have been as beneficial to them as they have been to us. They have shown us to love and appreciate family, to always be by each other's side, no matter the circumstances, and to appreciate what we have while we have it. We know our time on earth is temporary, and someday we'll be called home to you. Let us celebrate each other and love each other like you love us. Amen."

They all repeated, "Amen."

"That was beautiful, my love," Olivia said to her husband, kissing him on the cheek. "I just knew we were all meant to be here."

Luke was anxious to see Gabby again, especially after their kiss last night. When there was a knock at the door, he jumped to get it, but his mom beat him there.

Olivia squealed with delight when she saw Jase and Gabby wearing their matching pajamas.

The Andersons all had on their matching Grinch pajamas. Luke had been a little concerned that trying to carry on their family tradition would be too emotional for the Jackson siblings. They both seemed in good spirits, though. He wasn't sure how to greet Gabby. He decided on a hug and a kiss on the cheek, which made her cheeks glow rosy. The pajamas were cute on her.

"Merry Christmas," she said to Luke.

"Merry Christmas to you, too," he replied.

"Oh Gabby, these pajamas are adorable on you," Olivia greeted her with a big hug.

"Thank you so much for the pajamas. That was really thoughtful of you," Gabby said graciously.

"It was my pleasure," Olivia said.

"Where should I put these?" Gabby held up decorative bags, each labeled with a name.

"You didn't have to do this," Olivia said.

"We wanted to. You all have been so wonderful! We don't know what this vacation would have been like without all of you."

Olivia beamed and took the bags, placing them by the tree.

Luke was amazed at how thoughtful Gabby was to get each of his family members a gift. She really was something special. He took her hand, leading her to the living room. They sat down on the sofa near the tree.

Sophie sat on the floor across from them, giving Luke a wink when she saw he had Gabby's hand in his. He just hoped Seth didn't say something stupid to embarrass Gabby. Thankfully, Seth just smiled and gave him a thumbs up.

His mom had ordered brunch to the room, and when the food arrived, everyone pounced on the table as if they hadn't been eating like kings and queens all week. After they stuffed themselves and cleaned up, they decided to open gifts.

"I have to say, even though we have a tree and our Christmas PJs, this beautiful weather is making it hard to believe it's Christmas," Sophie said.

"I know. It's so hard to think about leaving tomorrow to go home to all that snow," Gabby added.

"It's hard to imagine leaving here at all," Seth said. "Maybe I'll stay for a few more weeks or months."

"You would," Sophie teased her brother. Luke knew Seth was kidding, at least mostly, but it did seem plausible that his brother would do something like that.

Seth handed out presents to everyone. Everyone started tearing off wrapping paper, and pretty soon, there was a huge pile on the floor.

Sophie and Olivia gushed over the beautiful earrings that Gabby had given them. Luke laughed when he opened his gift to find a woven bracelet. As he snapped it on his wrist, he saw that his dad and Seth had received the same thing.

"What's so funny?" Gabby asked, her smile fading. "You don't like it?"

"I love it," Luke assured her. "It's just great minds, I guess." Then he picked up a gift bag and handed it to her.

Luke watched as Gabby carefully untied the ribbon securing the bag and pulled out the little box. Her eyes went wide, along with her smile when she pulled out the gold bracelet with the cross on it.

"Luke, this is too much," she said, but she was already putting it on.

"I knew you'd like it." Luke smiled. He was so glad he had picked out something that she actually liked.

Gabby leaned over and gave him a quick kiss on his cheek.

While Luke had a hard time taking his eyes off Gabby, he kept one eye on Jase. He had gotten more and more quiet throughout the day. Luke was concerned that Jase was getting overwhelmed but wasn't really sure what to do to help him. Maybe after the presents were opened, he'd suggest changing and going for a run. A good run had always helped him clear his head; maybe that's what Jase needed, too.

Chapter 58: Jase

J ase watched as everyone opened their gifts. He had felt emotionally strong when he started the day. He had still been okay after the sentimental moment with his sister and their private gift exchange this morning. He was fine with the pajamas; they were just pajamas. He didn't mind going to brunch at the Andersons, although he never understood why people got excited about brunch or why it was even a thing. They'd had several meals together this whole trip, so what was one more?

Jase was happy to see his sister finally loosening up and having a good time. He didn't know what happened with her and Luke last night. But he could see the start of something there. He hoped it continued to grow.

As Jase watched Seth tell a story, he hoped they really did stay in touch so he could see what Seth would do with life. Seth's family might think he was floundering, but the kid had a lot going for him. When Seth figured out his path, he would set the world on fire.

Then there was Sophie. Jase knew he wasn't in a place to start anything with a woman. But man, she was incredible. It wouldn't be fair to her to try dating him right now, so he didn't even want to risk trying. Maybe someday he would try, if she was still available, which seemed unlikely. Jase hoped he would find someone like her someday.

And Ben and Olivia were so much like his own parents that sometimes it hurt to be around them. Other times, Jase wanted to hug them like they were substitute parents.

Jase had thanked them graciously as he opened the unexpected gifts. Seth and Luke had given him a local Mexican team's baseball jersey, which he had to admit was pretty cool. Sophie, with her awesome sense of humor, had given him kids' swim floaties for the next time she pushed him into the pool. That had everyone rolling with laughter.

Jase felt shocked when he realized how much he'd come to care about all of them. He really enjoyed their company.

But being here now, on Christmas, a family holiday, was getting harder by the moment. Jase's body tensed as he sat watching everyone in their matching pajamas, laughing, and exchanging gifts and love.

He was trying his hardest just to breathe and hold it together. He prayed–yes, he Jase– found himself praying to make it through this day with no embarrassing outbursts.

Then Ben came over to him and handed him a package.

"This is from Olivia and myself," he said. "We just want you to know that we both have come to care a lot about you, and we would be honored to be your friends. We hope you don't forget about us when you go home and become famous again."

Jase laughed. "I don't think I will ever forget any of you. What you all gave up for my sister and me..." he paused before quietly adding, "I don't think we'll ever be able to thank you enough."

Jase looked at his sister, who smiled at him like she was proud of him.

He was hesitant to open the package in front of everyone. He was barely hanging on by a thread as it was. Their eyes were on him expectantly, so he opened the box. A small leather-bound Bible had his name engraved on it.

Jase stared at his lap. He could feel the emotions boiling to the surface. He was inexplicably angry like he had been the night before. He was angry at God for taking everything from him. He was angry at the Andersons, who obviously didn't understand. Nothing bad had ever happened to them, so they still believed that God was so good and could solve anything. And Jase felt infuriated with his sister, who couldn't even be bothered to miss his parents.

It was a beautiful Bible. In spite of his anger, he wanted to be gracious and just say thank you. But that wasn't what came out of his mouth.

He stood abruptly, causing the box to fall to the floor.

"What do I need this for?" he shouted, causing everyone to jump. "What has God done for me lately? Does he even care about what he took from me?"

Ben calmly met his eyes. "Son, God has done so much for you. You just need to open your eyes and see it."

"Oh yeah, so much!" Jase said bitterly. "I got injured, lost half a season of my career, and lost my team the playoffs."

"And what did that time off give you?" Ben asked earnestly.

"What do you mean? It gave me a month of rehab and living with my parents."

"Yes," Ben replied softly. "You got to spend that time, time that you wouldn't have had with the people who loved you most."

"Yeah, that was great till he took them away from me, too," he said through gritted teeth.

"And I'm sorry for that," Ben said sorrowfully. "Sadly, death is a part of life. Whether it's today or in 80 years, that day comes when the good Lord calls."

"I wasn't ready," Jase yelled.

"We are never ready. I lost my dad when he was 85 and had been sick for over a year. We knew it was coming, and I still wasn't ready," Ben exclaimed.

"I don't care that you lost your dad at 85," Jase snapped. "He had a good, long life. My parents had their lives robbed from them."

"I know it feels that way, Jase, and I'm sorry for that," Ben said softly.

By now, Jase had tears streaming down his face, but he didn't care. He continued, "He's taken everything from me."

"It might feel that way, but look at all the good that has happened even this week. You have your career back. You have people who truly care about you. You were able to laugh and have fun, relax, and enjoy life again." Ben said, motioning around to the rest of his family and to Gabby.

"And I felt guilty for that every moment I was here," he said. He felt defeated.

"You don't need to feel guilty about living life. That's what God wants you to do. The mere fact that you woke up this morning tells me that God is not done with you," Ben said.

"Well, maybe I'm done with him," Jase growled.

"Life is better with him, son." Ben picked up the Bible to hand it back to him.

Jase growled in a low voice, "I'm not your son, and I don't need your Bible or your God."

Ben's face fell, but he said quietly, "He still loves you."

Jase's jaw clenched, and he scoffed at Ben's words, folding his arms tightly across his chest.

Then Ben continued, "God also gave you a sister to grieve with you. She loves you deeply."

Jase whipped his head towards Gabby. Her expression said she was horrified. "Yeah, a sister who can't be bothered to grieve for our parents. She just traded them in for the first family that came along. I'm not even sure she misses them."

Jase watched as Gabby's mouth dropped open and a tear rolled down her face. Luke stood up and started to say something, but Gabby placed her hand on his arm, stopping him.

Jase snapped, "She knows I'm right."

He needed to get out of there. He turned and stormed out the door, slamming it behind him.

CHAPTER 59: GABBY

Gabby could feel herself shaking. She started apologizing the moment the door slammed. She couldn't believe what she had just witnessed. What awful words her brother spewed at these lovely people! How could he think that she didn't miss her parents?

"I'm so sorry," she said again. "I knew today would be hard for him, but I had no idea he was this upset."

"Honey, don't be sorry." Olivia came to her side to comfort her. "It's not your fault."

"I'm not so sure about that," Gabby said.

"Gabby, we all deal with things in our own ways," Ben said. "Maybe I pushed too hard. He seemed receptive all week, and I thought he was ready for a bigger push."

"I appreciate that, Ben, and this isn't your fault either," Gabby tried to assure him. "I should have been expecting an eruption of emotions from him. You were right about everything you said. He just isn't listening." She shook her head, disappointed in herself for not being more attentive to Jase. "I need to go after him. I am so sorry again. You all have been so wonderful, and I'm sorry we ruined your Christmas."

She hurried out of the villa and stopped at the path, trying to decide which way to go. *Jase couldn't have gotten far*, she thought.

Gabby decided to check their room first. She took one step that way when she heard Luke calling after her, "Gabby, wait."

He jogged up to her and took her hand. "Just wait a minute, Gabby."

"Luke, I have to find him and make sure he's okay," she said, trying to hurry.

"He just needs a little time and space," Luke said gently.

"Time and space?" she barked. "All I have given him is time and space. This is my fault! I didn't give him the attention that he obviously needs right now. He thinks I haven't done a good enough job watching after him and being there for him."

"Gabs, how much more could you be there for him?" Luke said earnestly.

"What's that supposed to mean?" She asked defensively.

"You've given up your whole life to be there with him. You've put your own grief on hold to try to help him. You walk on eggshells every day to make sure days like this don't happen."

Gabby couldn't listen anymore and snapped at him, "What do you know about it? There's no book on how to properly grieve. At least, I haven't found one."

"You're right, but you need to look after yourself, too," Luke said, still holding her hand.

"I'll tell you what, Luke," she said brazenly, yanking her hand away from him and placing them on her hips, "After both of your parents are suddenly killed in an accident and you are left responsible for everything, then let me know what you do and how you feel. Until then, just enjoy your family and don't tell me what I need to do for what's left of mine."

Luke's face fell, but Gabby whipped around and went to search for her brother.

As she walked, she felt awful. Luke hadn't deserved her anger. None of them did. They were all just trying to help. And God was not smiling at Gabby's reaction right now. She could feel the devil laughing over her shoulder that she had given into anger so quickly. But where did Luke get off telling her how she should take care of her brother or herself?

Deep down, she knew Luke was right, but that didn't matter right now. She had to make things right with her brother before it was too late, and they became one of those families that didn't speak anymore.

Though she was still in her Grinch pajamas, Gabby searched all over the resort. She checked their room first to make sure Jase hadn't just packed and left. Then she went to the lobby and the pool. She searched high and low with no sign of him. She kept praying he hadn't done something irreversibly stupid. She had never seen him like this, and she was becoming more worried with each moment she couldn't find him.

Gabby was about to give up when she heard children laughing. She wandered over to a garden area and saw a sign that said, "Story Time with Santa." Peeking into the garden further, she saw a jolly Santa with a big white beard, but he was wearing a red, white, and green poncho and matching sombrero. He was reading "The Night Before Christmas," and the children surrounding him were hanging on his every word. The sight made her smile in spite of her turmoil. She was about to turn the other direction when she saw a figure hunched over with his head in his hands, sitting on the bench in the back of the story area. It was Jase.

Gabby rushed over, but then she hesitantly approached, unsure of what to say. He seemed calmer, but she knew that could change in an instant. Slowly, she lowered herself to sit next to him.

"Hi," she said. "I've searched for you everywhere."

"Well, you found me," he said without lifting his head.

"I did," she said softly.

With his head still hanging down and his shoulders hunched, he asked, "Remember when Mom used to read us that story?"

"I do." Gabby smiled at the memory. "Every Christmas Eve."

"Yeah, me too. I miss that," he said sadly.

"I do, too," she said softly.

She wasn't sure what to say or do next, so she folded her hands in her lap and just sat there.

Finally, Jase turned his head slightly toward her. Bitterness filled his voice when he said, "Did you come here to scold me for ruining your perfect holiday with your perfect new family?"

"What? No," she defended.

He narrowed his eyes to look directly at her now. "Then what do you want?"

"I wanted to make sure you were okay." She reached a hand out to touch him but put it back in her own lap instead.

He gave a joyless laugh. "Oh yeah, Gabs, obviously I'm great. Life is wonderful. I'm sitting in stupid pajamas outside a kids' story time crying my eyes out. I'm just fine."

She sat silently, still not knowing what to say.

"You've seen me. I'm fine, so go back to them," Jase said, waving a hand at her dismissively.

"You're not fine, and I want to be here with you," Gabby said, crossing her arms over her chest.

"Oh, so now you want to be here with me?" he scoffed.

"What's that supposed to mean?" Gabby's brow furrowed.

"It means you've spent the whole trip avoiding being alone with me and now you want to be here?"

"That's not fair. I have asked you every single time if you wanted us to go, and you always agreed." Gabby could feel herself getting more upset.

"What was I supposed to do? You obviously wanted to do things with them. I was supposed to take your fun away, too?"

"You could have said no, and I would have done anything you wanted."

"Whatever, Saint Gabby," Jase said in a mocking tone.

"Excuse me?" Gabby said, feeling herself get angry.

"The perfect child, always so selfless and doing things for others."

"What are you talking about? You were the golden boy that could do no wrong," she snapped back at him.

"Mom and Dad worshiped the ground you walked on and bragged to everyone about how smart and talented you are. Dad chose you to run his business."

"Like you were going to stop playing baseball to run it?"

"Well, no, but..."

"Exactly, Mom and Dad wanted you to lead the life you wanted. We have followed you all over the country since you were ten to watch you achieve your dreams."

"Is that why you don't miss them, you think they didn't do anything for you?" Jase was angry again, nearly shouting at her.

"Don't miss them? Are you insane?" she was yelling back now.

"You don't cry. You smile and thank people for their thoughts and prayers. You get up every day and go to work in the same office that Dad sat in, and you don't bat an eye. You are functioning like a normal human, like our world wasn't destroyed. And I..." he stopped to catch his breath, tears streaking his face. "And I can barely get out of bed. I can't even imagine what a season back with the Defenders will be like. I can go knock a few balls out of the park and be everyone's hero for a couple of hours. I can sign some autographs and smile for some photos. Then go home to my empty loft and not want to live."

Gabby took Jase's shoulders and turned him to face her. "Jase, I miss them with every breath. Maybe I'm just better at compartmentalizing than you are. What was I supposed to do, crawl into a hole with you and live in the dark? Life was happening, things had to get done, so I did them."

"You make it look easy," he growled. "And yes, I just want you to sit in the dark and be miserable with me."

"I assure you that I have wanted to." Gabby put her hand on his arm. "I've tried to be the good Christian girl who says I know they're in a better place and watching over us. Still, I feel angry and sad and scared. I feel all of that every day."

"Every day?" He asked with a hint of doubt in his voice.

"Every day," she assured him.

"How do you get through it and not let it show?"

"A little bit of fake it till you make it, sometimes crying alone in the car, and a whole lot of faith." Gabby knew she was treading on thin ice, but she continued. "Jase, I know you are struggling with your faith, but Ben was right. God is watching over us. You just need to open your eyes and see it."

"What exactly am I supposed to see?" he asked sincerely.

"Ben was right. You got to spend more time with Mom and Dad this year than you had been able to in a long time."

"We did become closer," he admitted. "They were like my best friends."

"If you hadn't gotten injured, you wouldn't have had that time with them." Gabby watched Jase's face as he absorbed that.

"Then I moved in, and we've gotten to be together through it all," she added. "We still needed to sort things out, but we were never alone. I was able to get through most nights because I knew you were right in the next room."

"I didn't realize that," Jase said.

"I probably need to do a better job of letting people in and showing my grief, especially you. I didn't know you thought I didn't miss Mom and Dad."

"That was pretty selfish of me," Jase hung his head.

"How were you supposed to know?" Gabby said softly.

"I just should have," Jase shrugged.

"And look at what God has done for us here," Gabby said. "He put a family in our path who got us out of our comfort zones and helped us start to live life again. They got us talking about real things again, not just the weather or food."

Jase laughed. "We have talked a lot about the weather and food these last few months."

"We have," Gabby agreed with a small laugh. "I'm surprised we don't both weigh 500 pounds."

"My trainer is going to be so mad come spring training," he said, shaking his head.

"And that too," Gabby exclaimed, throwing her hands up. "The Defenders want you back so much they are willing to sign you until you retire."

"Yeah, I guess you're right." Jase shrugged.

"God has been good to us, but we have to be willing to see the good."

Jase stared at the ocean, and Gabby hoped he was finally considering these truths. She draped an arm over his broad shoulders.

"We're going to make it through this," she said to him.

To her shock, Jase wrapped his arms around her waist and cried. She ran her fingers through his hair, just like her mom used to do to her when they were younger.

"I'm sorry, Gabby. I'm so sorry," he said, holding her tighter.

"It's okay." Gabby let her silent tears fall.

"It's not, it's not okay. You deserved better. I was living in a dark, miserable world, and you tried to pull me out. But I wanted to drag you into the darkness with me."

"Jase, it's okay. It's all going to be okay."

"I don't know what to do," he choked out.

"We're going to go home. Then we are going to sort through the paperwork that's piled up and decide how we are going to continue on."

Jase straightened up. "Should we go and apologize to the Andersons?"

Gabby cringed, thinking about her last words to Luke. "Um, I may have blown that. After you left, I may have said some unkind words to Luke."

"What? Gabby, I'm sorry. I didn't mean to ruin anything. I owe them an apology too."

"You didn't. Maybe I'm just not ready for anything like that. I have more work to do on myself first," she nodded, not sure if she was trying to convince him or herself.

Jase peered at her skeptically. "You don't even want to say goodbye?"

"Let's just go home. I'm sure we can find some flights for tonight," she replied, avoiding the actual question. She was too emotionally drained and embarrassed to see them right now. "By the time we get home, Christmas will be over, and we can start fresh."

"Okay," Jase said skeptically as he stood. Then he helped Gabby to her feet and wrapped her in a hug, picking her up off her feet. "I do love you, Gabby."

"I love you, too." she said, hugging him tightly.

CHAPTER 60: LUKE

Luke had helped his parents clean up the living room. None of them knew what to say. He knew his dad felt bad. Luke didn't know what he could say that would help his dad feel better. Seth knew enough to just stay quiet. His mom and sister kept busy straightening the villa up, then went to the patio to read. Jase and Gabby had left about an hour earlier. Luke now lay on his bed, replaying the scene from earlier. He should have known this thing with Gabby was too good to be true. What had he been thinking? Did he really think that he would meet the girl of his dreams while on vacation with his family?

His sister knocked, then came in and sat on the bed next to him. "What are you doing in here?"

"Just thinking," Luke replied, staring at the ceiling.

"About Gabby?" his sister asked.

"No," Luke stated. "I was just thinking about the Roman Empire."

"Really?" she asked, sounding shocked.

"No, not really." He sat up to look at her.

"I didn't think so, but you never know," Sophie shrugged.

"I can't believe I messed it up with her that bad," Luke said, throwing his hands up.

"It's not over. It's just a fight, and your first one."

"And probably the last. I doubt she'll ever speak to me again," Luke stated.

"She will," Sophie encouraged him.

"How do you know?" He looked at her doubtfully. His sister hadn't seen the anger in Gabby's eyes just before she stormed off.

"Because I know," Sophie said, rolling her eyes at him. "It's just a gut feeling."

"I shouldn't have stopped her. I mean, she knows her brother better than I do. Just because I like space when I'm upset doesn't mean everyone else does."

"True. And there's a time when you need someone there. Gabby's right. She gave Jase months of space. But right then, he needed someone," she said.

"The worst part is, I could see Jase getting agitated," he admitted.

"You could?" Sophie asked, tucking her legs under her.

"I recognized the signs. I've seen men tested to their limits in training. I should have gotten him out of there. This could have been avoided." Luke was angry at himself.

"Luke, this isn't training or war. It's Christmas. And maybe he needed that release. Maybe he and Gabby both needed it."

"They needed an argument?" he asked.

"They needed to finally talk about their parents and be honest about their feelings with each other. I'm sure they've mentioned they've not been talking much about the important things. Maybe this opens that conversation." Sophie smiled and put a hand on his shoulder. "Everything will work out."

She was right, as usual. Luke was so worried about Gabby being upset, first by her brother's words and then by his. He hadn't thought this might be what they each needed. He wasn't sure how he was so good at giving advice to his students, players, and fellow vets, but so bad at following it himself.

"What can I do? How can I fix this?" Luke asked as he stood up.

"Well, the first thing you can do is take their gift over to them," Sophie said.

Luke nodded. "I can do that."

"Then when you get there, you put on your best groveling smile and tell Gabby you are sorry, and she was right."

"What if she slams the door in my face?" He was concerned that was a real possibility.

"Trust me, she will be feeling bad too," Sophie assured him. "Then you can invite them both back over for dessert."

"It'll be that easy, huh?" Luke gave a hopeful grin

"Maybe," his sister smiled at him. "Hopefully."

"What about Jase? What if he hasn't calmed down yet?" Luke wasn't sure how to handle that.

"You'll figure it out. The right words will come." Sophie sounded confident. More confident than he felt.

"I'm going to go so you can get changed and go over there," Sophie said as she walked towards the door.

"Changed?" Luke asked.

"Well, you really can't go over there in pajamas," Sophie said, closing the door behind her as she left.

Luke agreed he would make a better impression if he put some real clothes on.

After he changed, he grabbed the bag that his mom had put together with Jase and Gabby's presents and headed to their room. He practiced what he would say on his way, making a checklist in his head.

He was sorry. He didn't want to leave things like this. He would check on Jase and make sure he was okay. Then, he would invite them back over for dessert.

He felt nervous as he arrived at their room. He took a deep breath and knocked. There was no answer. He knocked again and waited.

"Excuse me, ma'am, have you seen the couple who is staying in this room?"

"Si, señor. They left."

"Did you see where they went?" Luke asked and looked down the hall like he might see them.

"I do not know, maybe aeropuerto?" the maid replied.

"The airport? Are you sure?" Luke asked. *This can't be right.* They weren't leaving till tomorrow.

"They have the suitcases and ask el botones if the shuttle was here," the maid explained in her thick Mexican accent.

"Are you sure that was the people in this room?" he asked, pointing at their door.

"Si, señor," she said.

"They can't be gone," he insisted. "They were here less than two hours ago."

The maid went back to work, and Luke turned to leave.

Slowly, Luke walked back to the villa. *I can't believe they left without saying goodbye.*

His family was waiting anxiously to hear what happened when he walked in.

"Well?" his mom asked hopefully.

"They're gone," he said glumly.

He was peppered with questions from his family. "What? How? Why? When? What do you mean gone?"

"When I got there, the housekeeper said they left in a hurry with all their bags," he explained, slumping onto the couch. "They didn't even say goodbye. I guess it really is over."

Sophie rolled her eyes. "You're not giving up yet. We live twenty minutes from them."

"Yeah, I guess," he said, still stunned. "I just can't believe they wouldn't say goodbye."

"The brother I know wouldn't be scared to chase down something he truly cares about," Sophie said.

His sister was right. Luke wasn't a quitter. He would go see her when they got back. He'd bring flowers and apologize. He knew she had to feel what he was feeling. He'd prove that he could be counted on to show up. That he would be there for her no matter what.

CHAPTER 61: JASE

After finding flights and several hours of travel, Jase and Gabby made it home at just after 2:00 am the morning after Christmas. Jase was exhausted. He gladly dropped his suitcase and flopped onto his own bed, getting a big whiff of home. He made a mental note to wash his bedding tomorrow. He had let laundry go for far too long. He'd let a lot of things go for too long. His sister was right. Since he was 21 and was called up to the big leagues, he had people doing everything for him, and it was about time to start doing things for himself.

He'd put off talking for too long. The past six months, he had hidden in this cave, playing video games and drowning in his own grief. He'd felt bitter that he was alone, yet he had blocked anyone from coming in, especially God.

Jase and Gabby had talked for hours on the flights back, like they hadn't talked in years. They had talked about Jase going back to play. He decided to buy a loft downtown, close to the ballpark. It was 45 minutes away from Gabby, close enough to get together with her often. And Jase was actually excited to be with his team again. One thing he had realized on their trip was that he had enjoyed trying to mentor Seth. He might like to get into coaching or managing when he was done playing. He was going to set up an appointment with the owner of the Defenders to see what opportunities he might have there.

Jase hadn't realized that Gabby had thought of selling the business. He was relieved when she told him on the flight that she wasn't planning to sell anymore. That would have been a big change, too, and one he wasn't sure he was ready for.

As exhausted as Jase was, he was still tossing around in his bed. He still felt bad the way they'd left things with the Andersons. Even though she didn't say it, he knew Gabby felt bad. Before he left for spring training, he'd go see Ben and apologize. Maybe Jase would even take Ben up on his offer to come to his men's group at church. There were a lot of changes on the horizon for him and his sister, but he would think about those tomorrow. Right now, he just needed some sleep.

Before he closed his eyes, he took a deep breath and prayed. "God, I know I've been a disappointment to those I care about and to you. Help me do better. And I'm sorry I'm mad at you. I know I have no right to be, but I'm working on it. Thank you, for everything. Amen."

With that, he closed his eyes and succumbed to much-needed sleep.

CHAPTER 62: GABBY

They'd been home for two days now. The first day was spent sleeping, but today, Gabby needed to go to the office. Holly had said she would bring Tucker there, and Gabby couldn't wait to see him.

She walked into her dad's office and glanced around at his sports photos and memorabilia. She decided it was time for change. She was going to take everything down, repaint, and hang up new photos. She would even pull out the different items from her travels and hang those. She had only been in the office for a few minutes when she heard the bells hanging on the front chime. Then she heard, "Gabby?"

She recognized Holly's voice and the clinking of Tucker's dog tags.

"Back here," she called.

Tucker trotted over to her, his whole body wiggling with excitement. He circled her legs before twisting himself to the ground and rolling over for belly rubs. Gabby happily complied.

"Hey there Tuck, did you miss me? I missed you! Yes I did," Gabby cooed to him while scratching his belly.

"Did you miss me too?" Holly asked with her arms outstretched for a hug.

Gabby stood and embraced her friend. "You know I did! You and I should take a trip back to Cozumel sometime."

"I'm game for that, maybe next week? Escape this snow?" Holly suggested playfully.

"I wish," Gabby said to her friend. "I have too much to do here."

Holly rolled her eyes and plopped herself down on the couch in Gabby's office. "I see that the taking time off and enjoying life part is over."

"No, actually, I'm taking your advice." Gabby smiled. "I'm keeping the business."

"Really?" Holly asked, nearly jumping with joy.

Gabby sat down next to her friend.

"All this time, I kept saying this is just what was expected of me. I realized that my parents would have loved me no matter what I chose to do. I chose this because I wanted to make Dad proud. But while Jase and I talked on the flight home, I realized that I love this, too. I love when clients come in and tell me all their stories about what's happening in their lives. I love that when bad things happen, like accidents, fires, and even..." she took a deep breath, "deaths, I'm one of the first people they have to talk to. And I can try to help make their situation just a little easier by listening, caring, and helping them get their claims in."

"Those are the reasons my parents always said your dad was so successful," Holly said with a smile. "He cared for his clients. They weren't just a number like most places."

This made Gabby smile. "But I decided that I need to hire a couple people as soon as possible."

"Good for you," her friend said, nodding her head in approval.

"Oh, I'm going to need your help this weekend," Gabby added. "I'm taking everything down and painting in here."

"It's about time for an office makeover!" Her friend cheered. "You're finally going to make it your own."

Gabby scanned the office, thinking about her dad, knowing he'd want her to make it her own. Smiling, she said, "It's time."

"It is," Holly said. "So it sounds like things went well for you and Jase. You talked a lot and sorted things out?"

"Jase and I talked, like for-real talked. And it was good," Gabby said.

"That's fantastic!" Her friend's face lit up.

"Oh, and I forgot to tell you, Jase was given a new contract with the Defenders," Gabby exclaimed.

"Yay!" Holly clapped. "That's amazing! I know he was worried they didn't want him. Plus, I guess he'll have to leave the house now."

"He will." Gabby laughed. "He's even going to move back downtown."

"Whoa, another big step."

"It is," Gabby agreed, feeling slightly apprehensive about it.

"What are you doing with the house?"

"I'm going to stay there for now and go through everything. Then, when the season is over, we'll decide if we want to sell it or if one of us wants to buy the other half from each other. I think that'll be the hardest part to decide. Everything else is just paperwork."

"I'm so happy for you. I can see the relief on your face. You seem like a whole new person."

Gabby blushed at the compliment, but she thanked her friend.

"So spill!" Holly leaned closer to her friend.

"I thought I just did," Gabby said, knowing what her friend wanted and avoiding the topic.

"You know what I mean." Holly narrowed her eyes. "I want to hear all about Luke."

"There's nothing to tell," Gabby said nonchalantly.

"What do you mean?" Holly asked disappointedly.

"I mean, there's nothing. That's over, if it ever even really started."

"Oh, come on. Every time I talked to you, you were practically falling over yourself."

"We are just in different places right now," Gabby said. Then sheepishly, she added, "And we kind of got into a fight before we left."

"Kind of got into a fight?" she asked tentatively.

Gabby recapped Christmas day for her friend. She told her about Jase's explosion, followed by hers toward Luke. She shared about how she and Jase fought and made up. When Gabby was done, she shrugged and said, "So it's over."

"Gabby," her friend said in a scolding tone. "Go apologize."

"What?"

"Go. Now. Apologize." her friend stood and pointed at the door.

"It's too late."

"It's not too late. Don't let this be the thing you regret."

Gabby knew her friend was right. She felt terrible about how she left things. Not only with Luke but with his whole family.

"Hol, I'm so embarrassed by the way I acted. I wouldn't blame any of them for not wanting to see me again."

"From all you've told me, they seem like the most understanding people on the face of the earth. I'm sure they will forgive you."

Gabby wasn't sure. Her friend hadn't witnessed her outburst. She couldn't stop the memory of Luke kissing her. Even now it sent sparks flying through her. She touched the bracelet on her wrist, the one he had given her. Maybe she should go find him and see if he would be willing to forgive her.

"I have to get back to the shop," Holly interrupted her thoughts. "In other good news, we have been so busy. It turns out you were right; the Loco seems to be a no-go." Holly snickered at her own joke. She gave Tucker's ears another scratch. "Bye, Tuck. I'll miss you," she cooed at him.

"I'm sure he'll miss you too. Thanks again for watching him." She waved goodbye to her friend.

"I'll watch my furry buddy anytime you need."

The bells chimed again as Holly left the office. Tucker lifted his head up from his office bed and, for a moment, Gabby thought he was going to follow after her friend. She offered him a treat, and he settled content in his bed again.

Gabby shuffled through the notes from Sue. She wasn't sure how she would ever find a replacement for her. She opened a document and started creating a job posting description when she heard the bell at the door ring again.

"Holly? Is that you bringing me back coffee? Because that makes you the best friend ever," she called out.

She nearly jumped out of her seat when she heard a man's voice from the doorway.

"It's not Holly," he said.

"Luke?" Gabby's stomach flipped at the sight of him. "What are you doing here?"

Tucker got up from his bed to greet Luke.

"Hey there, you must be Tucker." Luke leaned over and scratched Tucker's ears.

"I hope you don't mind me dropping in like this," Luke said.

"No," Gabby replied too forcefully. She took a deep breath and went on, "I'm just surprised to see you."

"I wasn't sure you wanted to," he said.

"Luke, I..." Gabby started, but he interrupted her.

"Wait, Gabby," he put a hand up, stopping her from continuing. "I want to say I'm sorry. You were right. I shouldn't have tried to stop you from going after Jase. He's your brother, and he needed you. You knew that, and you didn't need me telling you what to do. I'm really sorry."

Gabby was stunned. He was apologizing to her? After the way she acted, she deserved to be read the riot act, not receive an apology.

"Luke, please don't apologize," she said, shaking her head. "I had no right to say the things I did. Especially when I know all you've been through, and I know you were trying to help."

She stepped out from behind her desk and took his hands in hers. "I am truly sorry. And I feel terrible about the way I left without saying goodbye to you and your family."

"We get it," he said softly. "No one was mad. We were all just really worried about both of you."

"Really?" She asked quietly.

"Really." He smiled at her and gave her hands a light squeeze.

Gabby sighed with relief. *Could these people really be this amazing?*

"As a matter of fact," he said, letting go of her hands and leaning over and scooping a bag up off the floor. "I was sent here to deliver this to you and your brother."

He handed her the bag, and she peeked inside. It was all of the gifts Gabby and Jase had left behind.

"Thank you. This is so sweet," Gabby said, feeling humbled. She took the bag and placed it on her desk.

Luke scanned the office. "So this is the big office. It's nice."

"It is." She smiled, "But there are some big changes coming to it in the next couple of weeks. It's time for new paint, carpet, and decorations."

"Are you finally going to hang the treasures from your adventures?" Luke asked, taking slow steps towards her.

"You remembered that?" Gabby couldn't believe he remembered that she mentioned that.

"Of course," he said, standing in front of her now. Taking her hand and making butterflies soar through Gabby's stomach. Then he went on. "I also remember you mentioning that you would check your calendar and get back to me about being my New Year's Eve date to my parents' party."

Gabby smiled. "You're right, I did."

He moved his hands around her waist, bringing her closer to him. "And?" he said as he leaned in closer. "Are you free?"

"Totally free," she whispered as he leaned in and kissed her.

CHAPTER 63: JASE

Man, what a trip we had, Jase thought. *And what a difference it made.*

He and Gabby had only been home for a few days, but they had managed to get a lot done. Jase was grateful that Gabby had taken care of the insurance paperwork and the things that had needed immediate attention after their parent's death. Everything that hadn't had to be dealt with landed in a box that remained closed until now. It had been like ripping off a Bandaid when they opened the box containing their parents' legal papers. They had talked a lot and settled most of their parents' estate that needed attention. They organized it all, made the required calls, and signed the appropriate papers. Overall, it had been a fairly painless process. They were both grateful that their parents had been efficient at planning for the unthinkable. It made the process a little easier on Jase and Gabby.

They had also started going through the house and boxing items up to donate. There had been some tears when they found the stack of letters and cards their mom had saved from them over the years. She had saved all their letters to Santa along with a photo of them opening presents each year. Gabby had found their baby calendars. Their parents had written something every day for the first year of their lives. Gabby teased him that according to their calendars, she started sleeping through the night after a week, but Jase had kept them awake for a year. There were so many memories to go through and cherish.

While Jase and Gabby were packing up the past, they had looked into the future. Jase had reached out to a few of his teammates. They told him about an old building that had just been converted to luxury lofts close to the field. Some of his teammates had bought a few and wanted him to come check them out. Jase knew it was perfect as soon as he walked in. It was a large open space with wide windows that had views of the river and the field. Gabby, of course, went right into how they could decorate it, while he was just happy there were lots of restaurants and so close to "work" that he could sleep in longer.

The one thing Jase still hadn't done was apologize to the Andersons. He thought about them every day and couldn't stop feeling guilty about his actions on Christmas. He didn't want to ring in the New Year with that looming over his head and decided he needed to see them in person. He wanted to start fresh and be better. He knew that not all days were going to be great. It was still a struggle every day not to crawl back into the comfort of the darkness. But he wanted to do better. He owed his sister that. He owed himself that. And he owed his parents that.

Jase was hesitant to stop by the Andersons' without calling first. He was afraid they might say no if he called first, though. On his drive over there he figured if nothing else, he could get out an "I'm sorry" before they slammed the door in his face. He hoped 9:00 am wasn't too early, but he remembered them saying they were "up at the crack of dawn" every day. He stepped out of his car and hesitated. But determined to make things right, he walked to the door.

Jase knocked and then stood tall, bracing himself for whatever reaction he received from them. Hearing steps approaching the door made his stomach turn. *Maybe this wasn't such a great idea. Maybe I could make it back to my car without them recognizing me.* He was about to turn away when he heard the door open, and Olivia's friendly face peeked around the corner. Jase quickly removed his hat and stood up straighter.

"Jase," she said, obviously shocked at his presence.

"Hi Olivia," he said, still waiting for the door to slam on him.

But the slam didn't come. There was no yelling, no harsh words at all. Olivia stepped onto the porch in her slippers and embraced him in a warm hug. That's all it took for the tears to start.

"I'm so sorry," he cried onto the top of her head, and she squeezed him tighter. "I'm so sorry."

She finally let go and grabbed his hand instead. "Come on in. I was just making Ben and myself breakfast."

"Oh no, I don't want to intrude," Jase said. "I just wanted to say I was so sorry."

"Great!" Olivia smiled. "You can say it over breakfast."

Jase debated for a moment and decided he could eat. He followed her inside to the kitchen where Ben was sitting at the table, reading. He looked up from his book and seemed shocked to find Jase standing there.

"Jase," he exclaimed. Then he stood up and wrapped Jase in a hug.

Jase was speechless. How could these two people, whom he had been horrible to, welcome him, literally with open arms? He had said mean things and ruined their Christmas. He probably ruined their entire family's vacation. Yet they wanted to hug him and feed him breakfast.

"What brings you by?" Ben asked, settling back down at the table. He waved a hand at the chair next to him, offering it to Jase.

Jase slowly sat down next to Ben.

"I wanted to say how sorry I was," Jase started. "My behavior was unacceptable, and I'm so embarrassed. That's not who I am."

"Who are you, Jase?" Ben asked.

Jase laughed, but then he saw Ben was serious. Jase wasn't sure what to say. "What do you mean?" he asked.

"You say you aren't that person, and I believe that," Ben said with his hand open.. "But who is Jase Jackson, then?"

"I don't really know," Jase admitted, shaking his head. He wasn't sure who he was anymore.

"Who do you want to be?" Ben asked gently.

"I want to be like my dad and like you," Jase said without even having to think about it.

"I'm honored by that, Jase, truly I am," Ben said. "You're closer than you think to being the man you want to be. I saw it in you from the way you were with Seth, taking him under your wing all week. I saw the way you did things that you didn't want to do just because you knew Gabby really wanted to."

"Building a sandman doesn't make me a great man," Jase laughed.

"It says more about you than you realize," Ben said.

Olivia came over to the table with plates heaping with eggs, bacon, and toast. She set a plate in front of each of them.

"Wow, this looks delicious," Jase said, picking up a fork. He set it back down when he saw Ben folding his hands. Olivia joined them with her plate and folded her hands. Jase didn't even roll his eyes; he just folded his hands and bowed his head.

"Thank you, Lord, for this breakfast we are about to eat. Thank you, especially for bringing our new friend back to us. Help guide him along his path to becoming the man he wants to be. Lead him where he can serve you best. Be with him and comfort him. Amen."

Jase was left speechless again. While a lot of people had said they were praying for him, he had never actually heard someone do it. He felt honored and humbled.

"Thank you, Ben. I appreciate that, truly," Jase said. "I know things are starting to get better. I guess I just need a nudge."

"Whatever I can do to help you, you just let me know," Ben said.

"Let any of us know," Olivia said, smiling at him.

Jase knew they meant it. He also knew that he would need them to help keep him on a good path. Maybe Gabby was right. God was good to them. Even when everything was falling apart, He had given them a glimmer of hope and helped them by sending them the Andersons.

CHAPTER 64: GABBY

abby and Holly sang along with all the songs on the radio on their drive to South Bay for the Andersons' party. Gabby still couldn't believe it was New Year's Eve already. So much had happened since Thanksgiving. This year had changed her and Jase's lives forever. Now, it was time for them to let go of the grief and jump back into life. She was never going to stop missing her parents, but it was time to rejoin the living and stop hiding in the darkness.

Gabby had seen Luke a couple of times since he came to see her at the office. He even met Holly when he brought Gabby lunch one day. Holly was her normal self, asking him a non-stop barrage of questions. Luke had patiently answered each one and even invited Holly to come to their New Year's Eve party. She had happily accepted, of course.

Holly seemed just as excited as she was to be going to this party. Gabby laughed as her friend danced in her passenger seat to the music. They hadn't gone out for New Year's Eve since college.

Both preferred to stay home in their pajamas and watch the ball drop from the comforts of Gabby's couch. But this year, they were all dressed up and ready to party.

Things were going well with Jase, too. She was still concerned about him, but she had seen some promising changes in him over the past week. She prayed he would continue to make progress. Since Christmas, they had each made a point to have a daily feelings inventory with each other. It helped to check to see where they were and what they were feeling. It was a way to keep them honest with each other and themselves. To be honest, this exercise was uncomfortable. Gabby was so used to keeping things bottled up inside. It was getting easier day by day, though.

Turning onto the street the Andersons lived on, she got even more excited.

"I am so excited to meet the rest of the Anderson family," Holly said as Gabby searched for parking.

"You're going to love them," Gabby assured her.

"If they are like Luke, I'm sure I will," Holly said. "Are they all as attractive as he is?"

"Oh yeah, you'll see." Gabby laughed. "I'm sure with the 20s-themed party, you'll see them completely decked out and wonder if there's a Great Gatsby photo shoot happening."

"Really?" Holly asked.

"I'm not kidding," Gabby said with a laugh. "You seriously want to hate them, because they are so good-looking. Then you meet them, and it's impossible not to love them."

"Are we dressed okay?" Holly asked, running her gloved hands over her dress.. They had both splurged and bought elegant, black, silky 1920s-style dresses. They had added feather boas, headbands, long black gloves, and long strands of pearls.

"You look incredible, my friend," Gabby assured her as they walked up to the door and knocked. "I wonder if Jase is here already?"

"I'm not sure," Holly said as the door swung open.

"Gabby," Sophie squealed in excitement and threw her arms around Gabby.

"Hi, Sophie," Gabby said. Sophie, of course, was stunning with her black flapper dress trimmed in gold. Gabby wondered if Sophie had her hair professionally styled. The pin curls were perfect. "This is my friend..." Gabby started.

"Holly," Sophie exclaimed, as if they were long-lost friends. Sophie wrapped Holly in a hug as well. "I feel like I know you already."

"Me too," Holly smiled.

"Come in, come in," Sophie said, leading them through the doors.

Holly mouthed, "I love her."

Gabby smiled and mouthed back, "I know."

As they walked into the living room, it was like being transported back in time. Everything was decorated in black and trimmed with silver and gold. Every person had honored the themed attire request. All the women wore flapper dresses with fishnet stockings and long gloves. The ladies were wrapped in feather boas and adorned with pearls and gemstones. The men all wore crisp black tuxedos. The tables were covered with black silk and pearls draped around black and gold vases, which were bursting with large white feather plumes.

There were people drinking champagne and munching on hors d'oeuvres in the kitchen area. Others were dancing in the living room, where the furniture had been pushed back to make room for a dance floor. Roaring Twenties music played throughout the entire house.

Gabby was caught off guard when Luke swooped in behind her and swung her around. He gave her a quick kiss.

"Well, hello there." Gabby beamed at him. He was a spectacular sight in his tuxedo.

"You ladies look gorgeous," Luke said to her and Holly.

They both giggled like schoolgirls in return.

Seth came bounding up just then. He was dashing in his tuxedo and tophat. "Gabby," he shouted over the music, giving her a hug.

"Hi Seth." She smiled, "This is my friend Holly."

"Hi friend Holly. It's a pleasure to meet you." Seth said, shaking her hand and giving a little bow, making Holly laugh.

"Nice to meet you, too," Holly said.

"Where's Jase?" Seth asked, looking behind them.

"I'm sure he'll be here soon," Gabby assured him.

"In the meantime, may I have this dance, Miss Jackson?" Luke asked, extending his hand.

"Well of course, Mr. Anderson," she replied in her most polite voice.

Luke took her hand and led her to the dance floor. As they twirled around the dance floor, Gabby was impressed at the rhythm Luke had. Gabby noticed that Seth was taking Holly for a spin as well.

Gabby was having such a great time, she hadn't even noticed Jase and Sophie join them on the dance floor. Jase was dressed in a tux with tails. Gabby couldn't help but laugh.

Jase asked Luke if he could cut in. Luke handed Gabby over to her brother and started dancing with Sophie.

"Well, well. Look at you, Mr. Gatsby," Gabby laughed.

"I feel ridiculous," Jase said, tugging at his jacket.

"Well, you're not. You look great," Gabby assured her brother and straightened his bowtie.

"Did you think we would end the year like this?" he asked.

"At a 20s themed New Year's Eve party?" Gabby shook her head. "I would never have guessed this in a million years."

"No," Jase said. "Like this, having fun and being around people. You know? After what this past year has been like."

Gabby smiled. "If I'm being honest, no. I figured we would be at home in pajamas. You would be playing video games, and I'd be asleep on the couch by eleven."

"I'm glad that's not what we're doing," Jase said. "This is the start to a new year, a better year, and we need to be better."

"We will," Gabby assured him.

"I know I was a pain this year and made it worse for you," Jase said. "I want you to know I'm sorry, and I'll work hard every day not to go back where I was."

"And I'll work at being open and honest, no matter how hard it is," Gabby said.

"I wouldn't have made it through this year without you," Jase said seriously.

"Me neither," she said, hugging her brother. "I love you."

"I love you too," Jase hugged her tight.

Then the music picked up, causing couples to break from their slow dancing and change to Charleston dance moves. Jase gave it a go for a minute, then he went back to just bopping along with the beat.

Sophie came to his rescue and twirled him away, while Seth and Holly were laughing hard as they tried out some 1920s dance moves. Gabby noticed Olivia had been swept away by her husband to join the others on the dance floor. Olivia smiled at Jase and Sophie and sent a wink Gabby's way. Ben twirled his wife around the floor. Luke rejoined Gabby and spun her into a low dip, then swept her back up to keep dancing.

Gabby's heart felt full as she scanned the room. Her brother was happy and having fun. The strangers who had become like family and been such a blessing to her were all enjoying themselves. Gabby's best friend, who was always by her side, was having a wonderful time. Then there was Luke. He was the unexpected love she had sworn she didn't have time for and never believed she would find. Yet here he was.

Oh yes, God does work in mysterious ways, Gabby thought.

All of them had booked a trip thinking they could escape Christmas. Instead, they had found each other, found themselves, found peace, found forgiveness, and found love.

Printed in the USA
CPSIA information can be obtained
at www.ICGtesting.com
LVHW042027291024
795143LV00005B/90

 9 798891 852037